THE HORUS KILLINGS

THE HORUS KILLINGS

Paul Doherty

HEADLINE

First published in 1999 by
HEADLINE BOOK PUBLISHING

10 9 8 7 6 5 4 3 2 1

British Library Cataloguing in Publication Data

Doherty, Paul
  The horus killings
  1. Egypt – History – Fiction 2. Detective and mystery stories
  I. Title
  823.9'14 [F]

Hardback ISBN 0 7472 2241 X
Softback ISBN 0 7472 7528 9

Typeset by Palimpsest Book Production Limited,
Polmont, Stirlingshire
Printed and bound in Great Britain by
Clays Ltd, St Ives plc

HEADLINE BOOK PUBLISHING
A division of Hodder Headline PLC
338 Euston Road
London NW1 3BH

My thanks to Gracc (GIG).

List of Characters

THE HOUSE OF PHARAOH (main characters)

Menes: First Pharaoh of a united Egypt. Founder of the Scorpion dynasty, he and his son ruled *c.*3310–2890 New Kingdom 1550–1457 BC (Dynasty XVIII) Tuthmosis II, 1492–1479

Hatusu: his half-sister and stepmother of the young Tuthmosis III

The Royal Circle

Rahimere: disgraced former Grand Vizier of Egypt

Senenmut: Rahimere's successor. Lover of Hatusu, First Minister in her government

Valu: royal prosecutor, the eyes and ears of Pharaoh

Omendap: commander-in-chief of the Egyptian forces

Peshedu: royal treasurer

The High Priests of Egypt (called after their gods)

Hani: high priest of Horus
Vechlis: his wife

Amun, Hathor, Isis, Osiris and Anubis

The Hall of Two Truths (principal court of Egypt) Thebes and Lord President of the courts of Egypt

Amerotke:	Chief Judge of Egypt
Prenhoe:	Amerotke's kinsman, a scribe in the Hall of Two Truths
Asural:	captain of the temple guard of the Temple of Ma'at in which the Hall of Two Truths stands
Shufoy:	a dwarf, Amerotke's manservant and confidant
Norfret:	Amerotke's wife

Servants of the Temple of Horus

Neria:	chief librarian and archivist
Sengi:	chief scribe
Divine Father Prem:	scholar and astronomer
Sato:	his servant

HISTORICAL NOTE

The first dynasty of ancient Egypt was established about 3100 BC. Between that date and the rise of the New Kingdom (1550 BC) Egypt went through a number of radical transformations which witnessed the building of the pyramids, the creation of cities along the Nile, the union of Upper and Lower Egypt and the development of their religion around Ra, the Sun God, and the cult of Osiris and Isis. Egypt had to resist foreign invasion, particularly the Hyksos, Asiatic raiders, who cruelly devastated the kingdom. By 1479–1478 BC, when this novel begins, Egypt, pacified and united under Pharaoh Tuthmosis II, was on the verge of a new and glorious ascendancy. The Pharaohs had moved their capital to Thebes; burial in the pyramids was replaced by the development of the Necropolis on the west bank of the Nile as well as the exploitation of the Valley of the Kings as a royal mausoleum.

I have, to clarify matters, used Greek names for cities, etc., e.g. Thebes and Memphis, rather than their archaic Egyptian names. The place name, Sakkara, has been used to describe the entire pyramid complex around Memphis

ix

and Giza. I have also employed the shorter version for the Queen-Pharaoh: i.e. Hatusu rather than Hatshepsut. Tuthmosis II died in 1479 BC and, after a period of confusion, Hatusu held power for the next twenty-two years. During this period Egypt became an imperial power and the richest state in the world.

Egyptian religion was also being developed, principally the cult of Osiris, killed by his brother Seth, but resurrected by his loving wife Isis who gave birth to their son Horus. These rites must be placed against the background of Egyptian worship of the Sun God and their desire to create a unity in their religious practices. The Egyptians had a deep sense of awe for all living things: animals and plants, streams and rivers were all regarded as holy while Pharaoh, their ruler, was worshipped as the incarnation of the divine will.

By 1479 BC the Egyptian civilisation expressed its richness in religion, ritual, architecture, dress, education and the pursuit of the good life. Soldiers, priests and scribes dominated this civilisation and their sophistication is expressed in the terms they used to describe both themselves and their culture. For example, Pharaoh was the 'Golden Hawk'; the treasury was the 'House of Silver'; a time of war was the 'Season of the Hyena'; a royal palace was the 'House of a Million Years'. Despite its breathtaking, dazzling civilisation, however, Egyptian politics, both at home and abroad, could be violent and bloody. The royal throne was always the centre of intrigue, jealousy and bitter rivalry. It was on to his political platform, in 1479 BC, that the young Hatusu emerged.

By 1478 BC Hatusu had confounded her critics and opponents both at home and abroad. She had won a great victory in the north against the Mitanni and purged the royal circle of any opposition led by the Grand Vizier Rahimere. A remarkable young woman, Hatusu was supported by her wily and cunning lover Senenmut, also her First Minister.

Hatusu was determined that all sections of Egyptian society accept her as Pharaoh-Queen of Egypt. Like all revolutions in ancient Egypt, the favour and support of the priests were vital.

Paul Doherty

EGYPT c. 1479 B.C.

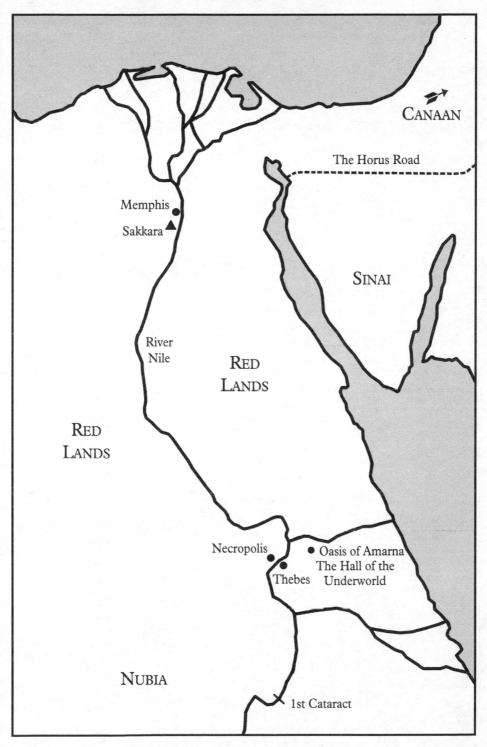

CANAAN

The Horus Road

Memphis
Sakkara

SINAI

River
Nile

RED
LANDS

RED
LANDS

Necropolis

Oasis of Amarna
The Hall of the
Thebes   Underworld

NUBIA

1st Cataract

Eater of Hearts: a demon
in the Egyptian Hall of
Judgement.

PROLOGUE

The sand-wanderer climbed down from his dromedary; its yellow and red saddle and harness were covered in fine dust, rather tattered and battered since the sand-wanderer had taken it from the corpse of a royal messenger who had lost both his way and his life in the arid Red Lands to the east of the city of Thebes. The sand-wanderer, a scout sent forward by his tribe, plucked a small horn bow from his back and made sure the quiver of arrows was close at hand. He was dressed from head to toe in dirty, ragged, grey cloths. Only his eyes peered out across the strange purple-blue dusk of the desert.

He had reached the oasis of Amarna but had been attracted by the sound of chariot wheels and voices on the desert air. He had to be careful. The scrublands were never as empty as they looked. Chariot squadrons and scouts from Thebes often came here, not to mention the hunting parties. All these had to be avoided. They were usually well-armed and well-provisioned. Moreover, Theban nobles always made their anger felt so the sand-wanderers only attacked if they were sure of an easy victory. The desert contained other dangers. Chatter and gossip passed from mouth to mouth among the tribes. How, in the oasis of Amarna, a huge, golden-maned lion had appeared, a man-eater that preyed on the desert people, often attacking campers at night.

The sand-wanderer notched an arrow to his bow and crept forward. The chariot stood by itself, its T-shaped bar resting on the ground. But where were the riders? The horses? He peered through the gathering darkness and noticed the marks of another chariot, the one he had heard so recently, galloping back towards the city. The sand-wanderer pulled down the cloth covering his mouth and nose. He smelt a fragrant perfume and savoured it. It reminded him of the day his tribe had camped outside Thebes and he had gone into a pleasure house. He would always remember that sinuous dancing girl with her oiled wig, dangling earrings and copper-skinned, perfume-drenched body. He had paid well for the use of it, an experience which, even now, made him swallow as his mouth watered.

The sand-wanderer edged forward. He caught the fragrance of cooking smells. He saw the remains of a fire, a broken cup and a wineskin. More confident, he approached the chariot. The leopardskin sheath which housed the throwing spears was empty. The bow and quiver of arrows, which usually hung on a hook on the bronze rail, had also been taken. But where was the owner? The sand-wanderer studied the chariot carefully. The wickerwork was dyed blue, embossed with silver stars; the four small wheels were red, the axle a smart black – not a war chariot but the plaything of some Theban nobleman. Behind the sand-wanderer, the usually docile dromedary snorted with fear. Its long neck was shaking, head going up. The sand-wanderer was torn between fear and greed. The chariot was worth something and Theban noblemen in their cups could be easy prey; their armour, clothes and jewellery would command a good price in the many markets along the Nile. Yet he had to be careful.

Suddenly on the night air, faint but clear, came the words of a song:

When I clasp my dear one near,

> I am like a man who has sailed to Punt,
> The whole world's a flower,
> Burst in a shower of roses!

The sand-wanderer recognised the words: a favourite love song often sung by the troops. He had once served as a scout in the Horus regiment when it had marched north, only a short time ago, to crush the Mitanni.

The dromedary was now kicking at the cord which hobbled its front legs. The sand-wanderer moved forward, crouching down. He stared across the desert and faintly made out where the singer must be. The sand-wanderer's tribe always stayed away from there, a man-made maze in the desert, called the Hall of the Underworld. The Ancient Ones claimed that the cruel Hyksos, who had ravaged Egypt and occupied its cities, had built a huge fortress to command the oasis. After an earthquake, the Hyksos had pulled down the granite blocks of the fortress and formed this tortuous labyrinth. The grey slabs, some eight to ten feet high, had been laid out to form a maze which stretched at least a mile across. Few people dared go in yet the sand-wanderer knew, from camp fire gossip, that Theban noblemen would often try to thread their way through as a feat of courage. Were the owners of the chariot there? How soon would they return? He stared up at the sky which seemed so close, the stars brilliant against the purple-tinged darkness. He ran his hand along the bronze rail. He couldn't leave it here. He turned. The dromedary was now kicking up, screaming in fright. But what was the source? He heard a low growl, a dark shape moved through the night. The sand-wanderer muttered a prayer:

> I have sat among the fiery gates.
> I have passed by the House of the Night Barque.
> Almighty God protect me now from the Eater of Flesh,
> The Crusher of Bones!

These were the names given to the man-eating lion. The sand-wanderer sniffed the night air. He caught the smell of carrion just as the great lion bounded out of the night towards him.

The Divine House of Horus, the huge temple, built on a more ancient site, lay on the banks of the Nile to the south-east of Thebes, that garden city, the home of the gods, with its golden gates. The Temple of Horus was regarded by all as a holy place. Its complex of sprawling buildings was protected and ringed by a high wall with guard towers over the gates facing out. At the centre was the broad sanctuary containing the Temple of the Barque, the Naos, or tabernacle, housing the statue of the god Horus. Around this, stretching like spokes of a wheel, were the side chapels. The sanctuary itself could only be entered through the Hypostyle, its Hall of Columns fashioned out of faded red granite. Outside this lay the other principal buildings: the House of Silver, its treasury; the House of Devouring where beasts were slaughtered both for food and sacrifice; the House of Life, the academy for scholars. Each was ringed by beautiful paradises, man-made gardens, shaded by palm trees, sycamores and acacias, where exotic plants and flowers thrived in the rich, black soil brought specially from Mesopotamia.

The temple boasted vineyards and orchards, all irrigated by cunningly devised canals which brought in water from the Nile. A rich, powerful place, its House of Stores contained jewellery, precious stones, stands of flowers, incense, casks of wine, sacks of grain, grapes, beans, figs and dates, and huge wickerwork baskets full of the choicest vegetables, cucumbers, leeks and herbs to make more delicious the meals served to the temple priests.

Now, however, the Horus gardens and houses were empty. The priests, the hesets, or dancing girls, its choirs and guards had all thronged down to the main entrance. Hatusu, Pharaoh Queen of Egypt, escorted by her Grand Vizier

Senenmut, was about to arrive to sacrifice to the gods as well as to gain the approbation of the priests. Hatusu had been driven to the temple in a chariot of blue electrum pulled by two milk-white Syrian mares. Behind her, in a gorgeous river of colour, streamed her nobles, advisers, the commanders of the regiments.

Hatusu was the Pharaoh Imperial, King and Queen of the Two Lands, possessor of the Land of the Nine Bows. She had destroyed all enemies both within and without but, so the gossips prattled in the marketplaces, she was still a woman. Could there be a Pharaoh Queen in Egypt? The signs and portents had been good. The Nile flowed free and heavy. The crops looked thick and rich. Trade routes had been re-opened and strengthened. The garrisons from the Nile Delta to the south, beyond the First Cataract, had all felt her power and determination to rule. Chariot squadrons patrolled the desert to the east and west of Thebes. Tribute flowed in from the Libyans, the nobles of Punt, the leopard-skinned warriors of Nubia. Even the Mitanni, who lay across the great Sinai desert, had bowed their necks in submission. All of Thebes had accepted her glory. Temples and palaces, the Houses of Adoration, were being refurbished and developed. Lapis lazuli, amethysts, gold and silver flowed from the mines of Sinai and the air was rich with the fragrance of incense sent as peace offerings from the Land of Punt. Yet was it only a passing phase?

Hatusu had destroyed all opposition. Nevertheless, shouldn't the crown be worn by Hatusu's six-year-old stepson? The gossips whispered that the true ruler must be the male heir of Hatusu's husband, Pharaoh Tuthmosis, whose mummified corpse now lay in its specially built House of Eternity in the City of the Dead across the Nile.

If such doubts disturbed her, Hatusu showed none of it. She stepped down from the chariot dressed like a goddess. The oiled wig on her head was bound by a gold band decorated with precious rosettes. At the front of it reared the

Uraeus, the spitting cobra of Egypt, wrought from costly turquoise, its fiery eyes the brightest rubies. Heavy rings like sun discs hung from her ears and the tresses of her wig were gathered in jewelled silver sheaths. She was dressed from head to toe in the costliest gauffered white linen. A gold and silver pectoral decorated with carnelian, turquoise and lapis lazuli hung round her neck. Its blue, inlaid medallion depicted the goddess Ma'at, ostrich plumes in her hair, worshipping before her father, the Sun God Ra.

A handmaid knelt down to ensure the gold sandals were properly bound then Hatusu, holding the crook and flail, climbed the long range of steps to the altar decorated with masses of hyacinth, lotuses and acacia leaves. Alabaster jars full of the costliest fragrances perfumed the air. Priests and priestesses clashed cymbals and shook the sistra, the sacred rattles, while a choir of blind singers intoned a divine hymn:

> To Horus, Golden Hawk,
> Giver of breath to the right,
> Taker of breath to the left.
> You who dwell in the fields of the eternal West
> Glory of the heavens!

Hatusu allowed herself a brief smile as she reached the top of the steps. Were they singing about Horus? Or really about her? She stared up at the soaring white figure of the hawk-headed Horus, which stood behind the altar. Not yet past her twentieth year, Hatusu kept her thoughts to herself. She did not truly believe in the gods of Egypt. True power lay in her chariot squadrons and massed ranks of foot soldiers, in the Red House and the White House, the treasuries of Upper and Lower Egypt, and in the man standing next to her, so silent yet so close. People called him her shadow, the manifestation of her Ka, or soul. Hatusu's sloe eyes crinkled in amusement.

'We offer incense, Senenmut,' she whispered. 'I who am a god pray to a god!'

Senenmut bowed, his harsh-lined face impassive but his eyes full of adoration for this young woman who was both his Pharaoh and his lover.

'You must do it according to the rite,' he hissed. 'We have everything but the priests. We need their favour.'

Hatusu's lips puckered in disdain. In a few hours the high priests from all the great temples of Thebes would gather, ostensibly to discuss the change in government, in fact to debate whether a queen could wear the double crown of Pharaoh, as well as the vulture coronet of the Queens of Egypt.

Senenmut gazed back down the steps to where Hani, High Priest of the Temple of Horus, stood waiting. A bald-headed, middle-aged man, Hani's narrow, shaven head, close face and light-blue eyes concealed a brain as sharp as a razor. He and his wife Vechlis had remained silently supportive during Hatusu's rise to power. Now Senenmut was determined that his Pharaoh should receive the public acclaim she was due from the priests.

He stepped closer to Hatusu. 'Your love,' he whispered, 'holds me captive and my heart sings with yours.'

'I think only of your love. Your heart is bound to my heart,' Hatusu whispered back as she bowed towards the statue.

A collective sigh rose up from the priests below. The choir of blind singers began to hum as Hani climbed up the steps, a bowl of incense in his hand. Hatusu, at Senenmut's quiet instruction, went down the steps and, as a courtesy, escorted him up. A murmur of approval rose from the priests gathered below and cymbals clashed noisily. Before the altar, Hatusu allowed herself to be incensed, a sign that she was purified. Then, with Hani on her right and Senenmut on her left, she made offerings to the gods.

A few hours later the Temple of Horus lay silent, its pure white halls, painted pavements, its walls covered in glazed tiles and beautiful hieroglyphics filled with nothing but shadows. Beneath the temple, however, in the ancient underground passageways and galleries, Neria, librarian and archivist in the House of Life, the school attached to the Temple of Horus, threaded his way towards the Hall of Eternity. Every so often he stopped to light one of the passageway oil lamps from the lamp he carried. The flames danced and grew, throwing his shadow larger, more menacing. Neria smiled. Only the chief priests were allowed down here. Now it was deserted. But why shouldn't others come? These caverns and passageways had once been the hiding place of Egypt, during the Season of the Hyena, when the cruel Hyksos invaders had swarmed across the Nile and devastated the city with fire and sword. This was a holy place and, at its centre, lay the Hall of Eternity.

Neria hastened on until he reached the hallowed centre, the narrow doorway of this underground temple guarded by statues of the gods Apis and Horus. Here he fired a pitch torch and entered the cavernous chamber.

The floor was tiled with fire-glazed slabs. Every inch of the surrounding walls was covered by a frieze or detailed picture depicting the history of Egypt. The mummified corpse of Egypt's first Pharaoh, Menes, founder of the Scorpion dynasty, lay in its huge black marble sarcophagus in the centre of the room. It was a tomb of striking beauty, at least eight feet high and three yards across. Gold cornices decorated each corner; the walls of the sarcophagus were covered with magical symbols in electrum and silver. On one side a door had been painted, surmounted by two red, staring eyes so that the dead Pharaoh could, when he wished, stare out into the land of the living. On the top of the sarcophagus rose a marble vulture with outstretched wings. At one end was the god Osiris, at the other his wife Isis.

Neria stopped to marvel. This was indeed a holy place! He bowed towards the sarcophagus then hastened over to study the frieze in a corner of the chamber. He sat and crouched for a while, holding the torch up so he could make out every detail. Yes, he was sure, what the frieze depicted was what he had seen in the library. What if this became known? Neria smiled to himself. He could just imagine the plaudits of the court, the patronage of the new Pharaoh. Neria touched the tattoo on his thigh for good luck, bowed once more to the source of his undoubted future prosperity and hastened out of the Hall of Eternity, back along the passageways. He reached the foot of the stone staircase and began to climb, his steps echoing. He remembered the oil lamps he should have extinguished and turned. The door at the top was abruptly flung open. Neria started in astonishment. A shadow stood against the light, a leather bucket in its hand.

'What . . . ?'

The figure, a mask of a dog over its face, brought up the bucket and, before Neria could step back, drenched him with oil. Neria slipped on the steps. He looked up. A burning rag was falling towards him. Neria fell down the steps, scoring his ankles and wrists. The flaming rag caught the oil and within a few heartbeats the figure of Neria was turned into a living torch.

In the council chamber of the Temple of Horus the high priests of Thebes took their seats for the first session of their important conclave. They were powerful men, dressed in the pure linen robes and leopard skins of their office. Gold gorgets and bracelets decorated their throats and wrists; their shaven heads and thin, narrow faces gleamed with precious oils. They were the holy ones, those who went into the sanctuary of the gods and offered sacrifice before the sacred Naos, or tabernacle, containing Horus's likeness. They were men of power who ruled their temples with a rod of iron.

They sat on gold-fringed cushions before small tables of acacia bearing manuscripts, rolls of papyrus and writing pallets. They openly preened themselves; not only was all of Thebes watching them but the divine Hatusu, the new

Pharaoh, had asked for their advice. Had any woman ever sat on Pharaoh's throne, worn the double crown and held the crook, the flail and the rod? Hatusu had swept to power by her own cunning as well as her great victory in the north. Now she sought their approbation. It was well known in the city that this approbation would be grudgingly given, if at all. Here, in this chamber, its walls decorated with scenes from the life of Horus, the golden, hawk-headed god, they would debate the matter. Their words would run like fire through the stubble along the broad highways and narrow streets of the city.

At the top of the chamber sat Lord Hani, High Priest of the Temple of Horus; next to him was Lady Vechlis his wife, much younger than he. A tall, imperious woman, Vechlis' shaven pate was covered by the most gorgeous wig, her athlete's body draped in the softest linen. A woman of power, chief concubine to the God Horus, Vechlis now sat tapping her purple-painted nails, half smiling to herself. These two were regarded as Hatusu's only real supporters. The rest of the high priests, known by the gods they served, waited to begin: Amun, Hathor, Isis, Anubis and Osiris. Grouped around each of them were scribes and clerks, experts in theology, temple worship and the history of Egypt. Hani clapped his hands and, bowing his head, intoned a prayer.

'Shall we begin?' He looked to his left where his chief scribe Sengi sat, stylus poised, ready to transcribe the proceedings.

'We know why we are here,' High Priest Amun spoke up. He glared round the assembled company. 'Let us start with the question from which all else will follow.' He paused for effect. 'Has there ever, in the history of the people of the Nine Bows, been a woman ruler on Pharaoh's throne? Can anyone provide proof of this?' He smiled in triumph at the deep silence which greeted his question.

Ma'at: Egyptian Goddess of Truth, often depicted
as a young woman kneeling in prayer.

CHAPTER 1

In the Hall of Two Truths, in the Divine House of the goddess Ma'at, Pharaoh's justice was about to be pronounced. Amerotke, Chief Judge of Thebes and Lord President of the courts of Egypt, friend of Pharaoh and a sworn member of the royal circle, sat erect in his judgement chair, a tall, severe-looking man with deep-set eyes and a sharp nose, his generous lips pulled into a tight line. Amerotke was dressed in a white-fringed robe and sandals of the same colour to symbolise purity. Around his neck hung a gold and turquoise pectoral depicting Ma'at the Goddess of Truth kneeling before her father Ra.

The court was silent. All eyes were on the judge's solemn face and stern mouth. Now and again Amerotke would touch the lock of black hair which hung down against his right cheek. He would play with the gold bracelet on his left wrist or stare at the judge's ring on the little finger of his right hand. He breathed in. Always an early riser, he had not eaten except some dates and honey cake. Instead he had wandered the markets, his diminutive manservant, the cheeky-eyed, disfigured Shufoy, hopping beside him. Shufoy carried his master's parasol, ever ready to protect Amerotke against the early-morning sun or proclaim, for all to hear, that Amerotke, Chief Judge of the Hall of Two Truths, was approaching. Amerotke usually told him to shut up but Shufoy was irrepressible. He always liked to see the stir his master created, whether it be checking the scales, weights and measures of the marketeers or visiting the lesser courts which were held in the antechambers of the temple: the Kenbet, Saru and Zazat.

Amerotke was always on time for his own court. The sun had barely touched the gold-tipped obelisks and the temple choirs were still singing their morning hymn to the rising sun when Amerotke took his seat to dispense the justice of Pharaoh.

Amerotke licked his lips. This was a solemn moment. He just hoped his stomach wouldn't rumble or some messenger, a Rabizu, hot and dusty, arrive from the House of a Million Years. Amerotke had received secret information that Pharaoh Hatusu and her Grand Vizier Senenmut wished to have words with him. Amerotke was angry. The case he had just listened to had filled him with rage and disgust; nevertheless, he remembered the teaching of the priests: 'Fly into a rage only when a rage is necessary.'

He lifted his head and stared at the prisoner, scrawny-faced, cruel-eyed and mealy-mouthed, his lithe, tanned body covered by a dirty robe, sandals of woven reed on his calloused feet. Amerotke believed in demons and that they could take up residence in the souls of men. This, surely, was the case here. The prisoner appeared calm, poised, despite the overwhelming evidence which convicted him of bloody and blasphemous murder on at least two, if not four, occasions. The prisoner was mocking him, daring him to do his worst.

Amerotke stared round the court. On his left, through the porticoes, he glimpsed the gardens and fountains of the temple: the green meadows where the flocks of Ma'at grazed and the ibis bird sipped at the holy water under the shade of the palm and acacia trees. Amerotke wished he was there. He wished he could think, reflect, but everyone was waiting. On his left, squatting on cushions, writing trays resting on their thighs, were his Director of the Cabinet and Keeper of Petitions and their six clerks, including his kinsman young Prenhoe. They all sat, styli poised, tense, waiting for judgement to be given.

At the far end of the court, near the doorway, clustered the temple guards led by the brawny Asural; he now stood as if he was on parade, leather helmet couched under his arm. On Amerotke's right was Maiarch, the queen of courtesans, leader of the Guild of Prostitutes. She knelt, hands extended, her fat, painted face wet with tears which made the mascara and kohl run in dark rivulets down her quivering cheeks. Amerotke repressed a smile. Maiarch was a consummate actress. Since the case had ended she had knelt like that, her wig slightly awry, stubby fingers raised as if she wanted to drag divine justice from the heavens. Now and again the effort would be too much and she'd move in a jingle of bangles and the small bells sewn onto her robe.

'My lord,' Maiarch quavered, her reedy voice breaking the silence. 'We cry for justice!'

'Nehemu.' Amerotke leaned forward, his left hand touching the small statue of Ma'at on its plinth at the side of his chair. 'Nehemu, I ask you once more, is there any reason why sentence of death should not be passed against you?'

The reprobate just grinned back. 'Amerotke!' he sneered.

A collective hiss ran round the court. Nehemu was intent on blasphemy, depriving the judge of all his titles and proper courtesy.

'You will address the court in a proper fashion!' Amerotke snapped.

'Amerotke, Chief Judge in the Hall of Two Truths,' Nehemu snarled, 'do *you* have anything to say before sentence of death is passed against you?'

Amerotke didn't move but Prenhoe and the other scribes sprang to their feet. Asural came forward, hand going to the copper wire handle of his sword.

'If you wish to add to your list of crimes,' Amerotke's voice thundered. 'Then do so!'

Nehemu's head tilted back, eyes half closed. 'I am of the Guild of Amemets,' he rasped.

Amerotke repressed a shiver of fear. The Amemets were a guild of assassins; they worshipped the terrifying killer goddess Mafdet, who was represented as a cat. Was Nehemu one of their survivors? Nehemu clicked his tongue, savouring the consternation he was causing.

Amerotke made up his mind. 'Nehemu, you are a wicked man! You live and skulk in the Necropolis, the City of Dead, like the jackal you are. On at least two occasions you have taken a heset girl, a singer, a dancer, a member of the Guild of Prostitutes—'

'Dirt under my feet!' Nehemu sneered.

Asural was now striding forward, a broad leather belt in his hand. He quickly placed this round Nehemu's neck, pulling it tight.

'Shall I gag him, my lord?' he asked.

'No, no, not for the moment.' Amerotke waved his hand. 'Nehemu, listen, this court will have its say.'

'And so will I! And so will my guild!' Nehemu taunted, finding it difficult to talk with, the broad leather strap round his throat.

'Take the strap away,' Amerotke ordered.

Asural did so reluctantly. He remained behind the prisoner close, ready to restrain any outburst or sudden movement. Such scenes were rare. Prisoners, particularly those like Nehemu charged with dreadful crimes, usually hoped for a merciful death – a cup of poisoned wine or the quick release of the garrotte string. Nehemu had now forfeited these.

'You took these young women,' Amerotke continued, 'you slew them for your own pleasure. You strangled them and tossed their corpses into that part of the Nile where the crocodiles gather and feast.'

Nehemu tutted as if in self-mockery.

'You deprived them of life and, in desecrating their bodies after death, deprived them of a safe journey into the West,

18

to the Fields of the Blessed.' Amerotke leaned forward. On
the small sycamore table before him lay the papyrus rolls
containing the judgements of Pharaoh as well as the insignia
of his high office. He picked up a rod made out of terebinth
wood, its end carved in the shape of a scorpion. The court
breathed a collective sigh of relief: sentence of death was
about to be pronounced.

Maiarch lowered her hands and touched the floor with her
forehead in grateful submission.

'This is my sentence.'

The clerks were now busy writing.

'Nehemu, you are a wicked and vile man. Your crimes are
terrible. The captain of the guard is to take you to the same
place where you slew your victims. You are to be bound and
tied and sewn alive in the carcase of a pig still wet with blood.
This carcase is to be taken and thrown into the Nile.'

Nehemu's face sagged. He blinked at the hideous sentence
passed against him.

'You will know the full horror of your own crimes,'
Amerotke continued. 'Captain of the guard, take him away!'

Nehemu had regained his wits. He lurched forward, mouth
snarling. Asural, helped by the other guards, picked him up
and dragged him away. Amerotke lowered his head, placing
the scorpion wand back on the table. He wished things had
been different but what could he do? Life had been taken in
a sacrilegious way. Pharaoh's justice had been mocked.

Amerotke heard a shout and looked up. Nehemu had
broken free of his guards. He'd seized a dagger from one
of their sheaths and was running towards the judge, arm
raised. Amerotke didn't move. He didn't know whether it
was courage or fear. All he could see was Nehemu racing
towards him, knife in his hands, face contorted with rage. A
bow twanged. Nehemu was almost upon him when he flung
his hands up, dropping the dagger. He staggered forward,
one arm going behind his back as if to pull out the feathered
shafts embedded there. He slumped to his knees before the

table, blood mixing with his spittle, eyes rolling. He opened his mouth to speak, a gargling sound, then muttered a word; Amerotke wasn't sure whether it was 'Revenge' or 'Remember'. Then Nehemu crashed down against the table, knocking the scrolls and books onto the floor.

For a short while confusion reigned. Amerotke stood up, clapping his hands.

'This matter is ended. Justice has been done.' He smiled thinly. 'Albeit speedily and unexpectedly. Captain Asural, clear the court. Take this corpse down to the river and let sentence be finished. There will be a short adjournment.'

The court remembered itself and bowed. Amerotke bowed back and left. Once inside the small side chapel he closed the door, leaned against it, sighed and let his body sag.

'You should have been an actor, Amerotke,' he whispered.

His right leg wouldn't stop trembling, his stomach pitched, he felt slightly sick, hot and cold at the same time. He glanced down at his robes and thanked the gods there was no sign of blood. He took off his sandals, pectoral, bracelet and ring of office and placed them on the small draught-board table just inside the doorway. He then took a pinch of natron salt, mixed it with holy water from the stoup and liberally cleansed his hands, mouth and face. He sat down on the cushion before the Naos. Its doors were open; the statue of Ma'at knelt there, hands joined, serene-faced, ostrich plumes, the symbol of truth, sprouting from the stone coronet round her brow. Amerotke found this the easiest place to pray. He had deep reservations about the gods of Egypt; deeply interested in theology, Amerotke was more and more attracted to some of the theologians who argued that God was an eternal spirit, the Father and Mother of all creation, manifested in the sun, the source of all light. Ma'at was part of this and the truth remained constantly pure. Amerotke closed his eyes and whispered his favourite prayer.

'Oh, Lady of the Land of Nine Bows, Beloved Word of God.

Keep me in the truth, consecrate us in the truth. I give you thanks for my life and for that of Norfret my wife and my two sons Curfay and Ahmose.'

Amerotke opened his eyes. The high cheekbones of the goddess, her slanted eyes and smiling mouth always reminded him of Norfret. So serene and yet, when they were in their secret room, so ecstatic in her lovemaking. Amerotke hastily remembered himself and, leaning forward, arranged more tidily the vases of flowers, jars of perfumes and small dish of food which one of the priests had placed in front of the Naos. He heard a knock on the door.

'Come in!'

The door swung open. Maiarch, queen of the courtesans, stood on the threshold, fleshy jowls quivering, eyes beseeching.

'I come to give thanks, Lord Amerotke.'

He smiled. 'Come in.'

'I am not pure, I am not purified.'

'The same could be said of all of Egypt,' Amerotke replied.

The fat courtesan beamed with pleasure at the compliment. She bustled through the door in a wave of costly perfume, bangles jangling. She lowered herself onto the cushions against the wall, reminding Amerotke of a hippopotamus sliding with pleasure beneath the water. He had considerable time for this fat actress of a courtesan. She was kind, looked after her girls and bore herself with pride.

'I came to thank you, my lord.'

'There is no need. I am sorry for the girls.' He gestured at the shrine. 'The gods are all compassionate. Maybe their Kas will reach the Field of the Blessed, be taken over the Far Horizon.'

Maiarch nodded, blinking back her tears. Now and again she delicately wiped one of her eyes. Amerotke noticed how her fingernails were painted a brilliant red; they were so long they turned her hand into a claw.

'You'll always be welcome, my Lord Amerotke, at our house

of pleasure.' Maiarch's fat face creased into a smile. 'My girls could play a game with you . . .'

Amerotke shook his head. 'I thank you, my lady, but I have one woman, one wife.'

'Ah, yes, the Lady Norfret. Beautiful as the moon on a starlit night.' Maiarch waggled her plump shoulders and rose in a jingle of bells and bangles. 'In which case, my lord . . .'

She had hardly shuffled out when Asural marched in, Prenhoe behind him. The captain of the temple guard didn't stand on ceremony; his eyes, small and black as pebbles, glared furiously at the chief judge.

'The mess is cleared up but you shouldn't have allowed that. I've told you before, Amerotke, prisoners should be bound.'

'He died a quick death.'

'Was he a member of the Amemets?' Prenhoe asked anxiously. He sat down on the cushions, a woebegone expression on his face. 'I dreamt last night I was swimming in the Nile with a naked girl on my back. Her breasts were small and firm—'

'I wish I had dreams like that,' Asural interrupted.

'No, no.' Prenhoe's thin, narrow face was a picture of anxiety. 'I was swimming and a snake entered the water. I asked Shufoy what he thought of it. He replied that the dream was an augury of great danger threatening someone close to me.' He stared round-eyed at his kinsman. 'Shufoy was right,' he whispered.

'Shufoy is always right,' Amerotke declared. 'You haven't told him, have you?'

'I couldn't find him,' Asural answered. 'I suppose he's busy somewhere selling amulets and scarabs.'

'He's not interested in that any more,' Prenhoe said. 'He says the markets have become too crowded with tinkers and traders and the Scorpion Men have the monopoly on the sale of precious trinkets.'

'So, what's he selling?' Amerotke asked. 'Come on, Prenhoe.'

'He's bought an old papyrus on medicines.'

'Oh, no!' Amerotke put his face in his hands.

'He's offering a wide range of remedies,' Prenhoe continued. 'For burst lips, sore ears—'

'What about the Amemets?' Asural cut across the chatter. He glanced disdainfully at the young scribe. 'And, by the way, wasn't your pallet of writing pens upset? Shouldn't you be looking after it?'

Amerotke nodded at the door as a sign for Prenhoe to leave. The scribe made an obeisance towards the tabernacle, sighed and left, muttering under his breath.

Asural closed and locked the door behind him. 'The Amemets,' he repeated. 'Was Nehemu a member of that guild of professional killers?'

Amerotke stared across at the statue. 'I thought they had all been destroyed.'

'Why did you think that?' Asural demanded as he knelt down across from this enigmatic judge.

'No reason.' Amerotke closed his eyes. 'I've clashed with them before.' He recalled those dark galleries beneath the pyramids at Sakkara, the crumbling masonry, those black-garbed figures hastening towards him, only to be crushed by falling slabs of granite.

'There's more than one guild, you know,' Asural warned. 'What if Nehemu was one of them?'

'He murdered a temple girl,' Amerotke snapped. 'He killed alone.'

'I don't know.' Asural got to his feet. 'The motto of that guild of snakes is an attack on one is an attack on all. But if Nehemu was bluffing,' Asural shrugged, 'then it was nothing but sand in a desert wind.'

'And if he wasn't?'

'Look out for a carob seedcake smeared with cat dung and the blood of some animal,' Asural replied. 'The Amemets send it out as a warning that their goddess Mafdet is hunting you.'

'So they at least extend the courtesy of saying they are coming?' Amerotke joked, hiding his fear. 'Can't they be bought off or threatened?'

'No.' Asural walked towards the door. 'They have their own bloodthirsty rules. If they send a sign, they will try twice to kill you. If they don't succeed, they will regard you as sacred to Mafdet and never again will they raise their hand against you.'

'But I've got you to protect me, Asural,' Amerotke teased.

'And I am your loyal guard dog. But remember, my lord, Mafdet always hunts by night.' Asural left.

Amerotke knelt back on his heels; the threats of the Amemets did not concern him, not really. He put his trust in Ma'at. He was used to fighting in the battle line and, as a judge, he faced threats every day.

Somewhere in the temple a conch horn blew, a signal that the court was being reconvened. Amerotke bowed his head towards the statue, rose and put on his insignia of office, the pectoral, ring and bracelet. He adjusted his robes and, moving across, opened a sandalwood box and picked out a small turquoise-glazed hand mirror.

'The face of a judge,' he whispered. Amerotke remembered the advice of his teachers: 'A judge will feel many emotions but he must not show them.' He straightened the pectoral and applied two rings of kohl round his eyes. He heard a knock on the door. The Director of his Cabinet came in.

'All is ready, my lord. The three supplicants are waiting.'

Amerotke looked askance.

'The case concerns a woman who has two husbands,' the Director explained.

'Ah yes.' Amerotke rubbed his hands. He had read the papyrus scroll on this case. He walked back into the court. All sign of the chaos caused by Nehemu had been removed. The black marble floor shimmered, catching the reflection of the silver flowers painted on the green ceiling. The table stood straight before the judgement chair and the scribes were sitting between the pillars, Asural and his guards taking up their positions near the door at the far end.

Amerotke took his chair and stared at the people kneeling before him.

'Your names?'

'Antef, my lord,' the man on Amerotke's right spoke up. He was tall, sunburnt, with a soldier's face, a wiry body. He held himself proudly but his eyes were arrogant as if he not only expected justice to be done but done quickly.

'And you are?' Amerotke asked.

'I was, my lord, an officer in the Nakhtuaa.'

'Ah yes.' Amerotke smiled. He knew all about the 'strong-arm boys', veteran foot soldiers who followed the chariots into battle. 'Of what regiment?'

'The Anubis, my lord. I fought with the Vulture squadron at Pharaoh's great battle in the Delta.'

'I was there,' Amerotke replied slowly. He wanted to win the confidence of all three people, as well as show the court that Nehemu's attack had not disturbed him.

Amerotke placed his hands on his knees and stared at the soldier; memories flooded back of that long, thirsty march and the bloody clash of battle when Hatusu, ferocious as the lion goddess Sekhmet, had smashed into the Mitanni and crushed their power.

'And your name?' He turned to the young woman, a pretty little thing with a doll-like face, cheeks heavily painted, eyes rimmed by kohl. She wore a silver-edged wig, the long tresses almost touching the white shawl across her shoulders.

'Dalifa.'

'And you are?'

'She's my wife,' the soldier answered for her.

The young man on Amerotke's left lifted his hands as a sign to speak. 'My lord, she isn't!

'I am Paneb,' he added hastily. 'Scribe in the Hall of Truth at the Temple of Osiris.'

The young man reminded Amerotke of Prenhoe. He could

see that he and the young woman were deeply in love. Amerotke sat back. He loved such cases; no killing or bloodshed but deep, tangled relationships which either held people together or cut them asunder.

He made a sign and the chief scribe read out the background to the case. How Antef, in the Season of Planting six months previously, had marched north with Pharaoh's armies where he had received a blow on the head, lost his memory and stayed in the Delta until he recovered. Months later he returned to Thebes only to find that his pretty young wife, believing she was a widow, had, with the permission of the priests, now married young Paneb.

Amerotke scratched his chin. 'And I am to rule whether the first marriage is still valid and the second should be dissolved?'

Antef nodded vigorously.

'Do you love Antef?' Amerotke asked Dalifa.

'I never loved him.' Her voice rose. 'My marriage was arranged by my father.'

'And where is he?'

'He was an incense merchant,' the woman replied. 'He died two months ago of a rotting disease in his lungs.'

Amerotke nodded sympathetically. He saw a look of desperation in Paneb's face.

'Was your father rich?'

'Yes, my lord,' Dalifa replied. 'And I am his sole heir.'

A sigh ran round the court. Amerotke smiled. Antef didn't just want his wife back, he thought, he also wanted a share of her inheritance.

'Is this a matter of love?' Amerotke asked. 'Or wealth? Antef, would you be satisfied with a portion of your wife's inheritance?'

'It is not his,' the young woman interjected.

Amerotke raised his hand to silence her. Antef was too wily to step into the trap. 'This is a matter of love,' he replied coolly, 'Not treasure, my lord. I wish my wife back.'

'He wants the money!' Paneb screamed, his face suffused with fury. 'You know that, my lord.'

'I know nothing,' Amerotke replied. He thrummed his lower lip. If he decreed that the young woman could stay with her second husband, Antef would appeal, using the influence of his officers. Senenmut, liked to overturn a judgement now and again, just to make his influence felt.

Amerotke studied Antef. 'Where was this wound to your head?'

The soldier turned and Amerotke glimpsed the scar on the left side. 'A Mitanni war club,' he declared proudly.

'And what happened then?'

'I was knocked unconscious, my lord. When I came to, I had been left for dead. A woman combing the battle field found me and took me to her village near the oasis. I stayed there before travelling to Memphis. I gave thanks to the gods that my memory returned. I remembered my wife and journeyed home to Thebes.'

Amerotke glanced down to hide his unease. He had been on that battlefield. The Maryannou, the 'Braves of the King', had supervised the collection of the penis of every dead enemy warrior. Hatusu herself had insisted on this. She had sent them as a mocking, grisly trophy to her opponents in Thebes as well as to show how many Mitanni warriors she had slaughtered.

'I find it strange.' Amerotke lifted his head and caught the shift in Antef's eyes. Was the soldier telling lies?

'Why is that, my lord?'

'Well, you were a member of the strong-arm boys, brave warriors all. You wore the arms of the Anubis regiment. Why didn't they, when they combed the battlefield, find your body?'

'I was away from the rest, my lord,' Antef replied. 'You may remember, the battle spilled out across the desert.' A corpse was discovered and they thought it was mine.'

Amerotke nodded.

'I am a soldier,' Antef continued. 'I fought for divine Pharaoh. Is this the thanks I receive? Dalifa is my wife.' Anfet glanced round the court for support. 'Cannot the warriors of Thebes leave their wives to fight Egypt's enemies without finding another in their bed and sitting at their table when they return?'

Amerotke saw the look of pain in Dalifa's eyes.

'I do not love him.' She stretched her hands forward beseechingly. 'He was a cruel man, a bully. My lord, I have found my heart's desire. I would share my wealth to stay with Paneb.'

Amerotke nodded. 'The justice of Pharaoh will not be hurried. A man's wife is a man's wife,' he declared.

Dalifa put her face in her hands and began to sob.

'But which man's?' Amerotke added mischievously. 'It is a matter for this court to decide. And, until it does, I declare Dalifa's house be sealed. The young woman is to stay in the Hall of Seclusion in the Temple of Isis.' Amerotke glanced quickly at Antef and, for the second time that morning, saw murder in another man's eyes.

Pehtes: the Egyptian black hound.

CHAPTER 2

Out on the Red Lands, the broad-winged vulture, feathers ruffling in the desert breeze, hovered like a herald of death above the small oasis near the sprawling Hall of the Underworld. The vulture could sense the spilling of blood even before it happened. Trained in the ways of the desert, constantly hovering over the killers, the vulture had glimpsed the man-eater, the cruncher of bones, slinking its belly along the ground. The lion was stalking a pedlar who had stopped at the oasis to water his donkey and wipe the sand and grime from his own eyes and mouth.

The pedlar, a former soldier from Memphis, journeyed up and down the Nile selling copper rings and other ornaments. He was totally unaware of his approaching death. True, the oasis was quiet. The palm leaves above him hardly stirred as the heat haze shimmered, distorting the desert landscape. The donkey, however, was restless. The pedlar glanced up, narrow-eyed at the vulture.

'Not today, Pharaoh's hen,' he muttered.

He leaned down and lapped at the water like a dog, letting its coolness soak his face. He pulled his head up, opened the linen parcel on the rock beside him and chewed some of the dried dates. The donkey, a grey-muzzled veteran of the trackways, stood with its ears pricked. Now and again it threw its head up in a whinny. The pedlar got to his feet.

He retied his shabby head shawl so it would cover both his nose and mouth and walked out to the edge of the oasis.

Sand dwellers, desert wanderers, he wondered? To be sure, such thieves could attack but this oasis was not far from the city. He gazed up: the vulture was still hovering. The trader felt uneasy and returned to the pool. He squatted and listened carefully. He recalled the stories about the demons who lived out in desert: the gobbler of blood, the plucker of eyes, the taster of flesh. His mouth became dry so he removed his head cloth and once again immersed his head in the pool. It was so enjoyable. He lifted his face and stared. For the first time he noticed something lying between the oasis and that ominous labyrinth. Were they fragments of bone? Was that the remains of a chariot? It looked as if it had already been pillaged by those who lived out in the sandy wastes.

The pedlar got up. Suddenly his donkey whinnied. He swung round. He went cold with terror, even as his donkey brushed by him and galloped furiously away. A huge, tawny-maned lion seemed to have emerged from the heat haze. Was it a lion or Sekhmet the Destroyer? The beast just stood, one paw slightly forward, its whole body frozen. It wasn't a vision but a skilled hunter who had slunk slyly up so the wind couldn't carry its stench. The pedlar had never seen such a fearsome beast.

The lion sank down. It was cautious. It had hunted man before and knew the danger of the sword, dagger or bow, its scarred flanks bore the traces of such weapons. However, the lion knew the panic it could cause. A fleeing victim was easier prey. Its upper lip came back and it roared. The pedlar broke free from his fear and fled. He had never run so swiftly. A second roar shattered the silence. He looked round. The lion had become trapped in the bundles and harness he had left on the ground. The pedlar fled on. He was now out under the blast of the sun, the sand burning his ankles and feet. He ran towards the labyrinth. He knew the stories and legends but what else could he do? He turned quickly, the lion was in pursuit.

The pedlar reached the mouth of the labyrinth almost welcoming the cool darkness of its awesome black stone. He didn't care where he would go or what he would do. If he could only get lost, hide from the fury now roaring behind him. He fled deeper into the maze. He could tell from the sounds behind him that the lion had followed. The pedlar cursed and sobbed as he tripped and crashed against the stone walls.

Above hunter and hunted, the great vulture soared. There would be blood-letting, flesh and scraps to eat. It was always the case with the man-eater. The vulture could see both quarry and pursuer. A draught of air caught it so it rose, wings and head steady, neck out. The vulture circled and swooped but, confused, broke free of its fall and climbed again. The vulture couldn't understand. Any quarry, be it a rock rabbit or a baby gazelle, hid and took refuge. This was different. The labyrinth below him was quiet. The vulture could no longer glimpse the running pedlar or the pursuing lion. It was as if both hunter and victim had disappeared from the face of the earth. Nothing: no sound, no fight, no struggle. Only the labyrinth, the Hall of the Underworld, sprawling silently under the searing heat of the sun.

In the Hall of Two Truths Amerotke, Chief Judge of Thebes, stared down at the floor. He was trying to control his temper. In the space of a few hours, he had been insulted, almost killed, and now this arrogant soldier was refusing to accept his verdict. Antef knelt, staring hot-eyed at him. Amerotke took a deep breath and glanced up. He could dismiss Antef . . .

'You were an officer in the Nakhtu-aa?'

'Yes, my lord.'

'And you served under General Omendap in the Anubis regiment at the great battle against the Mitanni?'

'Yes, my lord.'

'How old are you, sir?' Amerotke tried to remain polite.

'About twenty-seven summers.'

'And you, Dalifa?'

'I have just passed my twenty-fourth summer. I was born—'

Amerotke gestured for silence.

'And how many years have you been married? At least,' he added hastily, 'before this happened?'

'Nine years.' Antef replied.

'Nine years?'

Amerotke, intrigued, forgot his temper. He studied Dalifa. She was very pretty with her smooth cheeks, soft neck, plump breasts and narrow waist. She knelt elegantly and stared shyly at him from under long eyelashes. Shufoy would call her a 'toothsome piece' or 'a merry bed fellow'. Paneb, the young scribe and her new husband, looked innocent enough. Amerotke caught a slyness in Dalifa's face. There was undoubtedly a bond between her and Antef: Amerotke was determined to discover what it was.

'You've been married nine years,' he declared. 'And were they happy years? Have you ever been to court? Have the police been called to your house? Have your kin intervened in any quarrel?'

'My only kin,' Dalifa spoke up quietly, eyelids blinking, reminding Amerotke even more of a lovely turtle dove, 'was my poor father. He has now died.'

'And you, Antef?'

'I am not from Thebes, my lord. I come from the Delta.'

'Your kin?' Amerotke asked.

The judge noticed how Dalifa became agitated, just a little as she moved on the cushions, fingers up to her mouth. Antef, too, looked disconcerted.

'What is the matter?' Amerotke asked, his curiosity aroused. 'Antef, you have kin?'

'I was brought here by an aged aunt, together with my twin brother.'

Amerotke stared back. The rest of the court, the scribe, the

Director of his Cabinet, the police near the door, caught the judge's impatience and stirred restlessly.

'I wish you'd answer my questions bluntly,' Amerotke demanded. 'So, you had a twin brother. Where is he now?'

'My lord.' Antef spread his hands. 'I have been waiting in your court for some time. I have heard the gossip . . .'

'Would you please answer my question?'

'I had a brother,' the soldier replied quickly. 'He was a gambler, a wastrel. I joined the regiment: he became a mason but spent most of his time in the taverns and the brothels along the quayside. He was drawn into a quarrel and picked up a wager.'

'Yes?' Amerotke asked. 'What was this wager?'

'That he could pass safely through the Hall of the Underworld.'

A loud sigh swept the court. The scribes, their writing trays on their knees, looked at each other and smiled. Amerotke kept his face impassive.

'You know about the Hall of the Underworld?'

'Yes, my lord, I do.'

Amerotke raised his hand. 'We do not wish for one case to run into another. I do not wish for a description or an explanation about that labyrinth, just the outcome of your brother's wager.'

'He went out to the Hall of the Underworld. I took him there at night. I gave my word as an officer that he would go through whilst I would wait for his return.'

'And?'

Antef spread his hands. 'My lord, he never came out. He was the last of my kin. I cannot see what he has to do with my marriage.'

'Yes, let's return to your marriage.' Amerotke agreed. 'You were married nine years. You saw service with Pharaoh's army?'

'Yes, my lord, minor campaigns in the Red Lands.'

'But the battle against the Mitanni?'

'That was different.'

'Yes it was,' Amerotke agreed.

How could anyone forget that long, hot, dusty march: Hatusu desperately seeking out the Mitanni army: the treachery of some of the Egyptian troops. Hatusu, fierce and relentless as a panther, had shown she was her father's daughter. She had crushed the enemy, returning in glory to Thebes but, this man hadn't. Amerotke sat, fingers to his mouth, and stared at the couple. Something was very, very wrong. Here was a young soldier who had covered himself in glory but had lost his memory, wandered about the cities of Egypt before he returned to find his wife, now a wealthy woman, had married someone else.

'And you, Dalifa?' Amerotke smiled at the young woman. 'Let us examine what your husband has said.'

'He is not my husband!'

'That is for this court to decide!' Amerotke snapped. 'So, let us go back to those frenetic days when the army left Thebes. You said farewell to Antef? You kissed him sweetly?'

The young woman nodded.

'You wished him well? Please answer.'

'Yes, my lord, I wished him well.'

'And in which temple did you pray for his safe home-coming?' Amerotke continued sweetly. 'That, surely, is the custom of soldiers' wives, isn't it?'

'My father gave me incense to pray.' The words came out in a rush. 'I made an offering at the Temple of Osiris.'

Amerotke ignored Prenhoe's grin.

'Ah, that's where you met young Paneb?' Amerotke asked. 'Though he's a scribe, not a priest.'

'I was very concerned,' Dalifa replied. 'I wanted to find out where the army had gone. He showed me maps. He was kind to me.'

Amerotke looked threateningly at the scribes, now laughing behind their hands.

'Paneb.' He smiled at the scribe. 'Did you know Dalifa

was a married woman? The wife of one of Pharaoh's brave soldiers?'

The young man sat, tongue-tied.

'He was honourable in all his dealings,' Dalifa broke in.

'How's this?' Amerotke asked. 'He is now your husband, at least in your eyes. True, it is the custom for a widow to marry again, especially one as young and comely as you.'

Dalifa simpered back.

'But why the haste?'

'I waited for news,' she replied tearfully. 'We heard of glorious Pharaoh's marvellous victory. When the Anubis regiment returned and camped outside Thebes, I discovered Antef was not among them. An officer informed me he'd been killed.'

Amerotke held his hand up.

'I am sorry,' he said. 'You were definitely told that your husband had been killed? So a corpse had been found? Where is this officer?'

Dalifa fluttered her pretty fingers.

'I cannot tell you, my lord. I . . .'

The Director of the Cabinet rose to his feet, a sheet of papyrus in his hands.

'My lord, I have a list of the dead from the Anubis regiment.'

Amerotke nodded and the scribe walked across. The judge studied the list closely. He made out the hieroglyphics for Antef, beside it 'mutilated: killed in action'.

'What does this mean?' he asked. 'Mutilated: killed in action?'

'It describes the state of the corpse, my lord,' the scribe answered. 'As you now know, we try to give an honourable burial to all our dead.'

'So, Antef's corpse was recognised?'

'Oh yes, my lord. We have summoned the regiment's doctor.'

Amerotke had to wait while the ponderously girthed physician lumbered into court, holding an ornate hand fan and a small bowl of perfume. He kept sniffing at this as if he found the rest of the world unclean and contagious. One of his sandals had broken and this slapped against the floor. It gave him the appearance of a clown. He stared threateningly around at the murmur of laughter which greeted his appearance. He bowed towards Amerotke who waved him to the cushions set aside for witnesses. Wheezing and gasping, the physician lowered himself down. Amerotke found it difficult to imagine such a man marching with the regiment, enduring the burning dry wind, the glare of the sun, the haste and terror of an army deploying for battle. Then Amerotke remembered seeing him during the campaign. Of course, the man had never marched but been carried like some regimental trophy in one of the carts.

'Your name?' Amerotke asked.

'Baki, regimental physician.'

Amerotke lifted his hand to hide the smile. Baki spoke like a professional officer.

'And you were with the Anubis?'

'My lord, I was with the regiment, it was a great victory.'

'And afterwards?' Amerotke asked.

'As you know, my lord, we soldiers, after such a great victory, rest and rejoice . . .'

'Yes, go on!' Amerotke urged.

'My task was to tend the wounded. These are divided into serious cases—'

'And not so serious.' Amerotke finished the sentence for him.

'Most perceptive, my lord,' Baki murmured.

'And the dead?' Amerotke glared at him.

'They are brought in on stretchers, arranged in rows according to regiment and brigade, we then try to identify them. Sometimes it's easy, an arrow wound, a sword thrust but, in other cases, the body may be crushed by a chariot or the face pounded by the hooves of a horse.'

'And the soldier known as Antef?'

Baki stared at the soldier kneeling not far from him.

'Well, my lord, for a corpse he looks remarkably alive and vigorous.'

Amerotke waited for the laughter to subside. 'But you recognised this corpse?'

'No, my lord. I thought the corpse was Antef's. Remember the battle had taken place near an oasis then it spilled out, followed by the rout and pursuit of the Mitanni. Corpses were strewn for miles. The task of collection didn't begin till the following dawn. During the night, the hyaena and lion packs had been very busy. Several of the Nakhtu-aa from the Anubis regiment were missing. Corpses were brought in wearing their insignia and we had to fill the gaps. I thought one was Antef's.'

'My lord, that can't have been.' Antef held up his wrist guard depicting the jackal head of the Anubis regiment. He also tapped the small copper gorget round his throat.

'Are they personal insignia?' Amerotke asked.

'Yes, my lord, they give my name and former regiment.'

'So, these couldn't have been found upon the corpse?' Amerotke asked Baki.

'No, my lord, they couldn't have been. I made a mistake.'

'Before you go.' Amerotke stretched out his hand. 'How was the corpse?'

'Cut and mutilated.' Baki narrowed his little eyes. 'Especially the face and side of the head. One sandal was missing. He certainly wore the loin cloth and kilt of the Anubis regiment. Somebody else thought it was Antef. I can't remember who, but you know what clerks are like?' He smiled falsely across at the scribes busy recording his words. 'Every corpse must have a name and that was given Antef's.'

Amerotke thanked him. The little doctor got to his feet and

waddled out. The judge stared down the court as if lost in thought. In reality he was trying to hide his own unease. There was something very wrong here. Taken separately, each part of the story made sense yet, put together . . . ?

'Antef, how long were you away from Thebes?'

'A matter of months, my lord.'

'You were surprised to return and find your wife married?'

'Very,' the soldier scoffed.

'And Dalifa? You recovered quickly from your mourning?'

'I spent the prescribed seventy days.' She retorted haughtily. 'But I was distraught. My father had died and Paneb did prove,' her sloe eyes shifted to her new husband, 'to be a source of comfort and support.'

'I am sure he was!' Antef roared.

'Silence!' the chief scribe bellowed.

'Where are you staying?' Amerotke asked the soldier. 'Have you returned to your regiment?'

'No, my lord, I have an honourable discharge.' Antef waved his hand. 'The faces of my companions provoked memories I would like to forget. I have hired a chamber above a wine shop while I await the decision of the court.'

'It will be a difficult one.' Amerotke scratched his chin. 'I mean, you may want your former wife but she certainly doesn't want you. The court could grant a divorce?'

'In which case,' Antef's voice was almost a snarl, 'I would demand heavy compensation from my former wife.'

Amerotke stared at the Director of his Cabinet, an expert on such matters. The scribe only pursed his lips and shook his head sorrowfully. Amerotke studied both Dalifa and Antef. Paneb he dimissed as a bright-eyed young scribe much taken by this nubile, wealthy widow. But Antef and Dalifa? A loving couple? He went off to war and returned to find his so-called widow someone else's wife. Amerotke noticed how the couple hardly looked at each other. Was Antef so in love? Or was he just after his wife's new found wealth? This matter certainly needed further investigation.

He gestured at Prenhoe to bring across one of the transcripts of the case. Amerotke read this quickly.

'Antef, you describe how you fought and received a head wound? A local woman found you and took you to her village?'

'Yes, my lord.'

'And what did you do there?'

'I tilled the ground, tended goats.'

'And how long for?'

'Three or four months,' Antef replied.

Amerotke caught a betraying flicker of the eye.

'My memory came back.' Antef snapped his fingers. 'Not immediately, more like water trickling through a wall, at first little drops, then it gathered apace. I had poor sleep and nightmares. However, once I recalled who I was, I decided to leave.'

'And can you produce witnesses for this?' Amerotke asked. 'Or?' he added with a smile, 'is your memory still impaired?'

'My lord, the woman who found me has since died. I tried to thank her.'

'But the village is still there. Someone will remember you.'

Amerotke made a gesture for silence.

'My original decision still stands,' he declared.

This time Antef looked at the floor. Dalifa glanced at her former husband, her eyes full of a passionate hatred. Paneb put his face in his hands as Amerotke pushed back his chair.

'The session's ended.' The judge announced. He spread his hands in a form of prayer. 'May the power of Pharaoh be sustained and strengthened.'

'Amen!' The line of scribes chorused.

Amerotke walked into the side chapel. He closed the door behind him and leaned against it. Somewhere in the temple a priestess was singing. Amerotke smiled, it was one of his favourite chants.

'Speak truth for the Lord of Truths.
Avoid doing evil.
The righteousness of a good man
Goes out before him then dies
But, truth itself, lasts for an eternity!'

Amerotke stared across at the carvings on the wall: a mummy-case of gold with a mask of lapis lazuli was being taken into a tomb chamber, its pillars were made of red and green stone. Amerotke recalled the reference to the Hall of the Underworld. He would soon have to deal with that but what about Dalifa and Antef? If truth was more than a matter of words, a being, an essence, an entity, a goddess? Did not the same apply to the opposite? Did a lie have a life of its own? Exude its own dreadful fragrance? Amerotke was sure this was the case here, both Dalifa and Antef were lying and bound by that lie. Amerotke chewed the corner of his mouth. He would need help, it was time to seek out little Shufoy.

Apophis: the Dweller in Darkness, enemy of the
Egyptian Sun God.

CHAPTER 3

Amerotke, fly whisk in hand, walked out of the Temple of Ma'at onto the great paved concourse which lay baking under the hot noon sun. Prenhoe had checked the water clock and proclaimed the hour, and Amerotke had announced a recess during the heat of the day. The crowds thronging the stalls had also thinned as people hurried home, down to the riverside or into the public gardens for shade and respite from the heat.

Amerotke paused to watch the Viceroy Kush walk by in solemn procession, a golden parasol held above his head, to the House of a Million Years, the royal palace near the river. The Viceroy's bodyguard, white earrings glittering about their broad, swarthy faces, swaggered alongside, dressed in white pleated garments with panther skins hanging down their backs. Short, green and gold wigs, adorned with feathers, covered their shaved heads. The Prince of Kush, dressed in costly lynx, was ostentatious in his finery; silver bangles covered his arms and, on top of his golden wig, sat an absurd little crown like a clown's cap. In front of the Viceroy, professional flatterers announced who he was and, every so often, would throw themselves on the ground, arms raised, shouting their deference.

'Hail to you, Prince of Kush! Beloved of Pharaoh! Grant us breath! Grant us life!'

Amerotke watched them go and then moved among the stalls. A courtesan in a gorgeous wig and white diaphanous gown, a baby cheetah on a silver leash trotting behind her, came up to whisper sweet salutations. She recognised Amerotke and turned hastily away. The judge walked deeper into the market, sniffing at the air sweet with the fragrant odours from the aromatic balm, bark, cinnamon, herbs and other costly products on sale. This was the wealthy part of the bazaar where precious ornaments and costly cloths were available at exorbitant prices. Amerotke wondered if he could buy something for Norfret and decided on an ivory statuette of a leaping panther.

He moved out of the market across the concourse. Shufoy should be here. At last Amerotke found him beneath a palm tree on the corner of one of the thoroughfares leading to the temple area. The little man was asleep, arms crossed, his parasol tied by a rope to his wrist. Amerotke crouched down. He studied the dwarf's rather wizened face, the hideous scar where his nose had been. Shufoy had been the victim of a terrible injustice. Amerotke had taken him into his household as an act of reparation and Shufoy had repaid this with loyalty and good humour. Amerotke was amazed at Shufoy's knowledge, his determination to amass a fortune through one scheme after another.

'I am not asleep, my lord.'

'Then why don't you open your eyes?' Amerotke teased.

'Is my lord well?'

Amerotke sighed with relief. Apparently Shufoy had not yet learnt about Nehemu's murderous attack.

'I am always better when I see you, Shufoy.'

The dwarf opened his eyes and bared his lips in a gap-toothed grin. He stared around and tapped the leather purse tied on a cord round his bulging middle.

'A good morning's work, master.'

'What have you sold?' Amerotke made himself comfortable.

46

'A cure for loose bowels. Take a beetle, cut off its head and wings, bake it in snake fat, mix it with honey.' The dwarf clapped his hands. 'It will keep you away from the latrines for days.'

'Aye,' Amerotke smiled. 'And what's the cure for that?'

'Take a beetle,' Shufoy declared, 'remove the head and wings, bake it with wheat sprouts, mix it with juice of figs . . .'

'And you are back on the latrines?' Amerotke asked.

Shufoy sighed and got to his feet. 'Everyone's gone, everyone's resting. It's true what they say, master, trade and gold depend upon the weather. Have you eaten?' He looked at Amerotke. 'You only had some cake this morning.' He wagged a finger. 'The Lady Norfret was strict—'

'I have eaten,' Amerotke replied.

A merchant passed, leading a sumpter pony, the panniers on either side decorated with bells which jangled noisily.

'I could sell you some earplugs,' Shufoy offered. 'Master, why have you come to see me? Soon the crowds will return. I must do business.'

'One favour, Shufoy. You know the boatmen along the river?'

'One or two,' Shufoy replied.

Amerotke grasped the dwarf's hand and squeezed it gently. 'They collect more gossip than fishermen do fish. I want you to ask them about a soldier. His name is Antef. He fought in the great battle to the north. He apparently lost his memory, stayed for a while in Memphis then came back to claim his wife and her new-found wealth.'

Shufoy pursed his lips and blew his cheeks out. He reminded Amerotke of the little god Bes, the mischievous sprite who was supposed to look after children and animals.

'Can you do that for me, Shufoy?'

'They'll need paying.'

'A precious stone,' Amerotke offered. He glimpsed the hurt in Shufoy's eyes. 'Two precious stones, one for you and one for the man who brings me news.' He turned to go away.

'I'll be here at dusk, my lord,' Shufoy called out.

Amerotke didn't turn.

'There goes the great judge, the Lord Amerotke! Chief Justice in the Hall of Two Truths!' Shufoy's voice boomed. 'A man who has just come to congratulate me on distilling a remedy for a sickly stomach. Come close! Come close!'

Amerotke hurried on as Shufoy attracted the attention of a group of priests.

'I hope they like beetles,' Amerotke muttered to himself. He quietly prayed that Shufoy would be careful. On a number of occasions Amerotke had punished quacks and pedlars who sold potions which did more harm than good.

He walked into the coolness of the temple, along the marble-paved corridors which led round to the back of the Hall of Two Truths. Prenhoe was waiting, hopping from foot to foot. He held a small papyrus scroll sealed with the royal cartouche of Pharaoh.

'I've been waiting, master. The messenger said it was urgent.'

Amerotke took the scroll, kissed the seal and broke it. The message, written in Senenmut's own hand, was curt. 'Amerotke is summoned to the House of a Million Years. He must present himself for an audience just before sunset.'

'Is it trouble?' Prenhoe asked. 'I had another dream last night, Master. Shufoy and I were sharing a girl . . .'

Amerotke went into the small shrine and closed the door on Prenhoe but the scribe didn't give up so easily; in fairly colourful terms he shouted an account of his dream through the door. Amerotke quickly tended to his toilet, purified his hands and mouth, put on his insignia and opened the door.

'One more word about your dreams,' he warned Prenhoe, 'and I'm going to send you back to the House of Life.'

'Master, you can't do that. I am taking my exams at the end of the Planting Season.'

'Then study hard. Prenhoe, the court awaits!'

As soon as he took his seat and stared at the papyrus sheets his Director of the Cabinet handed to him, Amerotke knew the case before him was both serious and sensitive. He glanced up. Everyone was in position; unusually, they were not looking at him but staring at the young chariot officer kneeling on the cushions in the place of judgement. Amerotke smiled at him. The young man looked nervous. He kept plucking at his tasselled robe or playing with the copper bracelet round his wrist which proclaimed he was an officer in the Panther squadron of the Anubis regiment. Amerotke had heard the rumours; Norfret herself had relayed the gossip, learnt from visiting friends in the city. Amertoke always tried to keep his mind clear of such tittle-tattle; he was wary of being drawn into conversation, of saying something which could be twisted. He glanced at his Director of Cabinet.

'I thought this case was not ready to come before this session.'

The Director of Cabinet, a severe-faced man, shook his head and pointed to the judgement chamber. 'I left a message there this morning, my lord, but the attack by that malefactor . . .' His voice trailed off. 'This matter,' he added, 'cannot wait any longer.'

Amerotke studied the piece of papyrus in his lap. The news of this case had swept Thebes, delighting the gossips and rumour-mongers. The young man before him, Rahmose, was the youngest son of Omendap, commander-in-chief of Egypt's armed forces, a personal friend of Senenmut and Hatusu and a man who had played a vital role in Hatusu's coup and subsequent seizure of power. According to the summation, Rahmose had been a close friend of two other young officers, Banopet and Usurel. These were the twin sons of Peshedu, overseer of the House of Bread and of the House of Silver. One of Egypt's wealthiest men, Peshedu managed both the sale of grain and the silver supply from the Nomachs and principal cities of the kingdom. According to the report, Peshedu's sons had quarrelled with Rahmose. They had taken their chariot out into the Red Lands to the Hall of the Underworld, the great labyrinth built in the desert by the Hyksos. Rahmose had, allegedly, followed them into the desert to make his peace. He had driven his chariot to the Hall of the Underworld only to find his two companions had gone into the maze. Rahmose, as a joke, decided to unharness the horses from their chariot and bring them back to Thebes.

A day passed and the two young officers did not return. A search was made and the chariot was found, as well as the remains of a sand-wanderer who had been attacked by some wild animal. Scouts, despatched into the Red Lands, discovered the prints of a large lion. According to gossip around the oasis, this beast, nicknamed the 'Cruncher of Bones', or the 'Eater of Flesh', was terrorising the area. More importantly, however, no trace had been found of the two officers so Peshedu had accused Rahmose of killing them. Amerotke finished reading and glanced up.

'Are you an assassin, Rahmose?'

'No, my lord.'

The judge lifted a hand. 'Why did your friends go out to the labyrinth? Did they take weapons?'

'Yes, as well as wineskins and food,' Rahmose answered nervously. 'At a party recently they had boasted that they would go through the maze and come out.'

'That shouldn't be difficult.'

'My lord judge, have you ever been to the maze?'

'I've been near there.' Amerotke glanced across at his chief scribe. 'What is known of this maze, the Hall of the Underworld?'

'According to legend, my lord,' the scribe answered, 'before the Divine House expelled them, the Hyksos built a great fortress out near the oasis of Amarna.'

The chief scribe, a pompous, squat man, preened himself at

being able to display his knowledge. Amerotke beat a tattoo on his knee, a sign he was becoming impatient. The chief scribe, however, would have his moment of glory.

'The gods of Egypt intervened,' he declared sonorously. 'The great earth snake, Apep, shuddered—'

'In other words, there was an earthquake?' Amerotke snapped.

'The great snake shuddered,' the chief scribe continued. 'The fortress collapsed but the Hyksos King had a dark soul. Slaves and prisoners of war were driven out into the Red Lands and the blocks of granite were re-arranged to form a huge labyrinth. The Hyksos revelled in blood. Men, women and children were driven into the labyrinth without food, water or any form of sustenance. Many died, their skeletons whitening the gloomy alleys of the maze.'

A murmur of disgust rose at such sacrilegious practices. To kill a man then deny his body proper burial was the ultimate cruelty for it denied the soul the power to travel into the West across the Far Horizon.

'Sometimes,' the chief scribe continued, 'wild animals were released into the maze. They, too, became lost or had to depend on human flesh for sustenance.'

'And now?' Amerotke intervened. 'Is it possible that wild beasts still occupy the maze?'

Prenhoe raised his stylus. 'I doubt it, my lord.' He smiled in embarrassment as the chief scribe clicked his tongue disapprovingly.

'Continue, Prenhoe,' Amerotke said.

'The Hall of the Underworld is a tortuous labyrinth,' the young scribe explained. 'A wild animal, such as a lion or a hyena, might be able to get out but,' Prenhoe put his stylus down on the writing table, 'I doubt if they'd go in there in the first place.'

The chief scribe, eager to assert his authority, lifted his hands as a sign to speak. 'There is one other factor.'

Amerotke nodded.

'The House of the Underworld is a lonely place with an evil reputation. The desert dwellers and sand-wanderers never enter. But, over the years the young blades of the court, mischievous youths,' his face creased into a disdainful smile, 'sometimes go there to test their courage.'

'And?'

'Some come out, my lord. Others do not.'

'What do you mean?'

'They just disappear. Rumour has it that demons lurk there to capture both body and soul.'

Amerotke stared at the sunlight streaming through the portico, a ray of warm gold in which the dust motes danced. He would like to say he didn't believe in demons, men didn't just disappear from the face of the earth.

'And has a search been made for these lost ones?' he asked.

'Oh yes, my lord judge, but no trace has ever been found. Only the skeletons of those the Hyksos killed.'

'And this time?' Amerotke tapped his foot impatiently.

'Two young officers, the twin sons of one of Pharaoh's chief ministers, have disappeared.'

Amerotke stared at Rahmose. Undoubtedly this man had acted foolishly but was he guilty of murder?

'A thorough search has been made?' he demanded.

'Yes, my lord. I would call the officer in charge, with your permission.'

Amerotke agreed and the chief scribe rose to his feet and clapped his hands. 'Let Kharfu present himself before the court!'

There was a movement at the back. Asural stepped aside and a tall, wiry man strode forward. He was dressed in a leather cap, riding boots which came up to his knees, a war kilt with bronze clasps and buttons, and across his naked chest a thick leather belt. Its pouches and sheaths were empty. Witnesses were not allowed to bring arms before the Chief Judge of Thebes. Amerotke pointed to the scarlet cushions near the small shrine of Ma'at. The man crouched down, put his fingers on the shrine and, closing his eyes, repeated the short oath a scribe read out. Amerotke studied Kharfu intently. A typical soldier, weather-beaten face, hollow cheeks, eyes narrowed from constantly gazing against the hot sun and desert winds. His muscular body showed scars now healed into pink welts. Amerotke noticed the tasselled wrist guards, the blue and red feathers attached to the belt on his kilt. A soldier but also a dandy, he concluded. A man who liked to show off in the beer shops and catch the eye of the dancing girls.

'You are Kharfu?'

'Yes, my lord.'

'Remove your cap in court,' Amerotke said softly.

The soldier hastily obeyed.

'You are a soldier?'

'Chief scout in the Isis regiment, the Gazelle brigade.'

'And you were sent out to search for the missing men?'

'I and a dozen others from the brigade. We left early in the morning following their disappearance.'

'And what did you find?'

'A chariot. Its spear, sheath and arrow quivers were empty.'

'So the two officers took arms into the labyrinth?'

'It would appear so, my lord. There were the remains of a fire, a broken cup, an empty wineskin. We also found the remains of what must have been a sand-wanderer, some blood, bone and tattered clothing, next to the tracks of a lion. The sand-wanderer had come from the nearby oasis, his dromedary had fled.'

'Could this lion have attacked the missing men?'

The scout shook his head. 'I sent one of my men around the labyrinth. We found no trace of any animal spoor.'

'How many entrances are there to the maze?'

'Five or six. We discovered no tracks except one, the nearest to where the chariot had been left.'

53

'Continue.'

'The tracks had faded but my boys are good. They detected that two men had entered.'

Amerotke pointed at the accused. 'Could he have gone in?'

'Perhaps, but we found no trace.'

'How do we know that the two officers are not still in the labyrinth wandering around lost, weak, hungry, or crazed with thirst?'

'I don't think they are alive, my lord. Apparently Usurel carried an ornamental hunting horn. If they were lost he would have blown it. More to the point, I told some of our scouts to blow theirs. There was no reply.'

'And then what did you do?' Amerotke asked.

'We were wary of going in. We were not frightened of the legends but there was a possibility that the man-eating lion was sheltering there. But some of my men fought in mountainous regions, they are good climbers, and the blocks to the maze are a man's span apart.'

'Ah.' Amertoke smiled and shifted on the seat. 'So you sent scouts on top of the blocks?'

'Yes, my lord. They skipped and jumped from one to another. It was tiring but they could do it. They covered the whole maze. They found other skeletons, unfortunates who died there years earlier. But of the two officers Banopet and Usurel there was not a trace.'

'So.' The chief judge turned to Rahmose. 'And your version of events?'

'Two days ago, my lord, I and my two friends had an argument.'

'About what?'

'About courage. They wanted me to join them in threading the labyrinth. I refused. They called me a coward.'

'Where did this quarrel take place?'

'In a beer shop down near the Sanctuary of Boats. They said they'd go without me.' The young man nervously fingered the gold chain round his neck. 'The following morning they called at my house. I again refused. They drove off in their chariot laughing and jeering.'

'And so you decided to follow?'

'I did, my lord, but when I reached the Hall of the Underworld, it was late in the day. There was no sign of my two friends. But I heard singing – I think it was Usurel.'

'Singing?' Amerotke leaned forward.

'Just the faint traces of a song on the breeze. I became angry. I thought I'd teach them a lesson. So I unhitched their horses and drove back to Thebes.'

'Wasn't that rather foolish?'

'On reflection, yes, my lord, but it was meant as a joke. They'd proclaimed how tough and hardy they were. I thought a walk home would cool their pride. They were soldiers, well armed.'

'But the lion?' Amerotke asked. 'The sand-wanderers?'

'Sand-wanderers never attack well-armed soldiers,' Rahmose replied. 'And, as for the lion, my lord, I knew nothing of it.'

'Still it was foolish.' Amerotke tapped his finger and lifted his hands as a sign that he was going to pronounce judgement. 'There is no doubt these two young men have been killed. They are not the sort to flee, there is no good reason why they shouldn't have returned to Thebes. Evidence indicates they entered the Hall of the Underworld, none exists that they ever came out. You, sir,' he pointed at Rahmose, 'acted foolishly and stupidly. It is my decision you have a case to answer.' He waved a hand dismissing the scout.

Rahmose leaned back on his heels, fingers to his face. The clerks stirred, whispering among themselves, nodding in agreement with Amerotke's judgement. There were murmurs from the onlookers at the back of the court. Amerotke gestured to his cup-bearer who hastened across with a cup of Maru, a cool white wine. Amerotke sipped and handed it back. The clerks hurried forward to prepare the court for a formal hearing. Large cushions were arranged on the floor.

Amerotke glimpsed a movement at the back of the court. Valu, the royal prosecutor, dressed rather ostentatiously in a white gauffered linen robe, a brocaded shawl round his shoulders, waddled forward, his silver-tipped sandals slapping the floor. Valu was squat, he had hardly any neck and his face was creased into rolls of fat which almost hid his dark bright eyes. He always reminded Amerotke of a sparrow, constantly searching about. His arrival caused some muted laughter. Valu always painted his face like that of a woman, black kohl under his eyes, the eyelids daubed green, carmine on his lips and more rouge on his cheeks than any courtesan. He wheezed and puffed, knelt on the cushion provided and bowed towards Amerotke. The chief judge noticed how his fingernails were painted a dark green to match the bracelets on his wrists.

'My lord,' he simpered. 'A true and wise decision.'

'Welcome, Lord Valu,' said Amerotke.

He studied the royal prosecutor. Valu would not let his guard slip. He loved to play the fool but he was a ruthless, ambitious lawyer, whose appearance belied a reputation for cunning that a mongoose would envy. Since he had left the College of Life, Valu had proved himself to be one of Thebes' most eminent lawyers, the eyes and ears of Pharaoh, the searcher-out of conspiracies, the harrier of any enemy of the Divine House. The royal prosecutor presented all important cases. Valu did not care whom he offended. He'd turn and twist like a snake and claim he was only obeying Pharaoh's will, and who could challenge that?

'A good and wise decision, my lord judge,' Valu repeated, 'befitting one who holds high office in the Hall of Two Truths.'

'I do not think it is a wise or a good decision,' Amerotke retorted. If he had agreed that it was a good decision, that would have betrayed bias and deeply upset General Omendap.

'My lord?' Valu's shaved eyebrows lifted in mock surprise. 'I fail to follow you.'

56

'What is wise and good the court will decide. My decision is just the result of cold logic. So, what have you to say, eyes and ears of Pharaoh?'

'I have read the evidence,' Valu responded, licking his lips, rubbing his hands together. He leaned back on his heels.

'And?'

'We know, my lord, that two young officers went out to the Hall of the Underworld. We have reasonable proof that they encountered no wild beast or any other enemy in the Red Lands. We accept that they may have entered the labyrinth. But, if that is the case,' Valu spread his hands, 'they would either have been able to thread their way out again or become lost. We know they didn't come out.' Valu smiled. 'And we know from the scouts that they are no longer there.'

Amerotke felt a chill of apprehension. The young man Rahmose could be accused of stupidity, of a foolish act but Valu was leading the court down a different path. He was teasing out a much more serious accusation.

'I will not comment,' Amerotke declared. 'Lord Valu, state your case.'

Valu sighed and ticked the points off on his stubby fingers. 'These two young officers did not come back to Thebes. They are not in the labyrinth. There is no evidence that they were attacked by man or beast. We have Rahmose openly admitting a serious quarrel, how jibes and taunts were passed between him and the two missing men.' Valu raised his head. He leaned back, hands on his thighs. 'I, the eyes and ears of Pharaoh, maintain that Rahmose did not only take away their horses, he went out and killed these two young men and their corpses still lie in the hot sands of the Red Lands.'

'You accuse him of murder?' Amerotke asked, stilling the clamour with his hands.

'Yes, my lord, murder twice over!'

Amduat: the Book of the Egyptian Underworld.

CHAPTER 4

In the garden tower of the Temple of Horus, the priest's servant and guard Sato wearily pulled himself up the winding stone steps to the stairwell outside the top chamber. Sato was truly tired. Earlier in the day he had drunk more beer than was wise and then frolicked with a young whore in a pleasure house. She had been energetic and vigorous, her oiled body slipping and writhing beneath him. Sato could smell her perfume, still recall her smooth face and the oiled wig on her head.

Sato had come up here once already but then remembered the cakes and beer; he'd gone back to the kitchens and collected the tray which he'd left in a small cupboard at the foot of the steps. He was so tired!

'I should be in my bed,' he moaned.

But darkness was falling and the old priest, Father Prem, would be studying the stars before coming down to sleep. Sato would do the night watch. Sometimes Prem would wake in the early hours having seen visions in his dreams and would wish to consult the sacred books. On such occasions Prem always demanded a jug of beer and some honey cakes. He had explained how astrology and astronomy, not to mention visions, sharpened the mind and whetted the appetite, but he had said this with a toothless smile and Sato wondered if he was laughing at him. A strange one, Prem. Such a little

61

head, vein-streaked and bony, but a veritable treasure house of knowledge and learning. A man of ancient years who had studied in the House of Life and prayed in the Temple of Horus since he was a boy.

'We need Horus,' the old priest would say. 'The Golden Hawk of Egypt with his diamond eyes. He is our protector. With silver wings outstretched, Horus protects Egypt against the sudden swoop of the Angel of Death, that black-ringed demon who comes hurtling out of the skies to spread pain, famine and war!'

Sato paused in his climbing, peering up into the darkness. This tower was old; built of sheer stone surrounded by gardens and trees, it soared up to the sky. Some said the Hyksos had built it as a fortress to keep the people of the Nine Bows subjugated. Now it was part of the academy used by those who studied the skies.

'Ah well,' Sato breathed.

He reached the stairwell, put down the leather bag he carried, undid the shabby war belt and threw it into a corner. Prem was a strange one. Some said that as a young man he had fought the last of the Hyksos; certainly he was frightened of this tower and the ghosts and demons which might haunt it.

Sato knocked on the chamber door. 'Divine Father?'

No answer.

'He must be up on the top,' Sato whispered.

He climbed up. Sure enough, the door at the top of the tower was open. Sato pulled it aside and peered out. The night sky was blue-black, the stars quite clear. Prem was there, his back to him. His straw hat was on his head, protecting him against the cold night breezes, and a thick white shawl was wrapped about his hunched shoulders.

'Divine Father, I am here.'

A hand came up in acknowledgement, the head went down. Sato sighed, closed the door and trudged down the steps. Prem was busy with his charts, his map of the heavens showing the different constellations. This was a lucky night, one marked by the temple as fortunate for such study. Prem would be searching for the 'Head of the Goose' or the 'Star of the Thousands' or even for one of those great shooting stars, licks of eternal fire, as Prem described them.

Sato eased himself onto a stool and stared at the strange paintings on the wall. Griffins with fiery eyes and darting black tongues chased lions and other creatures across a blood-red landscape. Men in strange armour rode chariots behind. Sato wondered if these were the Hyksos, cruel hunters, rapacious men. He heard a sound and drew himself up. Was it the night wind? Or some animal slithering on the steps? Sato gathered up his robes and anxiously looked around, searching the darkened stairwell and the steps leading to it for snakes, asps or scorpions. Nothing there. Or were they ghosts? The concubines, those chattering women, were always frightening the children with stories about the temple's past, about the dark caverns and passageways beneath, which were said to be thronged by the ghosts of those the Hyksos had slaughtered. Hadn't he heard how the Hyksos had used panthers to hunt men? Sato sniffed. He wished old Prem would come down; they could both sleep and get some peace, for they were living in uneasy times. The high priests of the other temples had gathered, ostensibly to discuss theology, though everyone knew the real reason. Hatusu the Queen had proclaimed herself Pharaoh. Could the priestly caste accept this? The army adored Hatusu because of her victory. The merchants, bankers and traders fawned on her because trade had been restored and expanded. But the courtiers, those who had followed the now disgraced Grand Vizier Rahimere, still hoped to undermine her. Let her rule, they jibed, but did the gods favour her?

Sato heard the door at the top open, Prem's wheezing breath and the sound of footsteps as he made his way carefully down. Sato got to his feet. Something clinked and rolled down the steps. Sato hastened after it, the ring bouncing ahead of him. It stopped. Sato picked it up and clambered back. Prem had already unlocked the door to his chamber and entered.

'Leave it on the table,' Father Prem whispered. The old priest was sitting on a stool with his back to the door. With his hand he indicated the table just inside the room.

Sato obeyed. He left the room and closed the door behind him and the old priest, as usual, pulled the bolts across. Sato settled down. He opened his leather bag and bit into the wheaten cake it contained and almost choked at the terrible scream which came from the priest's chamber. Sato had never heard any human being cry out like that. The sheer agony and horror! Sato dropped the cake, leapt to his feet and hammered on the priest's door.

'Divine Father! Divine Father!'

No reply. Sato hurried down the steps. He slipped and hurt his ankle. Cursing and swearing, he reached the bottom, threw open the door and ran out into the garden, screaming for help. He daren't leave the tower. What if the assassin was still in there and tried to escape? He ran back to the doorway and stood bellowing at the top of his voice, only pausing when guards came racing across the grass, swords drawn. Others, too, were hastening towards him – priests from the different houses in the temple grounds.

'It's divine Father Prem!'

The guards shoved by him and up the steps. Sato followed. The staircase became thronged. Sato pushed at the door. It was still locked and barred.

'Divine Father has been attacked,' he gasped. 'I heard him scream.'

'The window!' one of the guards shouted out.

'Impossible,' another shouted. 'It's at least ten spans from the ground.'

'Haven't you heard of rope?' the captain of the guard sneered.

The guards hurried down. Sato was pushed out of the way,

a sycamore log was brought and, under the direction of the captain, the door was pounded. The wooden lock on the other side snapped, the bronze bolts buckled and the door sagged inwards on its leather hinges. The guards clambered in, Sato behind them.

The chamber smelt of rose water, parchment and something else, the iron tang of the slaughterer's yard. Prem was sprawled on the bed; his old straw hat had rolled off onto the floor and that clever old head was drenched in blood which seeped out over the headrest and linen sheets. Sato turned away to be sick in a copper bowl in the corner. The priests arrived, led by Hani, high priest of the temple.

'By Horus's breath,' Hani whispered loudly. 'His head has been caved in.'

Sato came back to the bed. Lord Hani was correct: the old priest's forehead had been crushed inwards. On either side of his face were long gouges like those from the claws of a huge cat.

'It's as if some animal was here,' the captain of the guard declared.

'But how?' Hani asked.

Sato looked over his shoulder. The wooden shutters were closed. He went across and pushed them open. He gulped in the night air and looked down the dizzying drop. Guards holding torches peered up at him.

'There's no sign of anyone or a rope ladder,' a soldier shouted. He pointed to the base of the tower. 'The ground is wet and muddy but there are no print marks.'

Sato closed the shutters.

'What did the guards say?' Hani asked.

'Your holiness, whoever killed the divine Father did not leave by the window.'

'But that's impossible,' the captain snapped. 'The door was still bolted on the inside.'

'Check the top of the tower!' Hani ordered.

The guards hurried out, clattering up the steps. They returned, their faces dejected.

'Nothing, your holiness, but a small table and two cushions.'

The chamber fell silent. Sato could see what the soldiers were thinking. Demons haunted this tower. Had some force, some dark shadow of the underworld risen up and killed the divine Father in such a horrid fashion? Hani went over and drew a sheet gently over Prem's blood-spattered face.

'Have the corpse removed to the House of Death,' he instructed. 'Let the embalmers do their work.'

Hani swept to the doorway then turned round, head tilted back. His sharp nose scythed the air, heavy-lidded eyes sweeping the chamber.

'I shall go to the palace,' he declared. 'This is the second death in our temple. Divine Pharaoh must be informed.'

> Thy upper lip is Iris,
> Thy lower lip is Nephthys.
> Your neck is the goddess,
> Your teeth are swords,
> Your flesh is Osiris,
> Your hands are divine souls.
> Your fingers are blue serpents,
> Your sides are two feathers of our moon.
> You are our father and we are thy sons.
> You are the staff of the old man,
> You are the foster father of the child.
> You are the bread of the afflicted.
> You are the wine for the thirsty.
> You are Egypt's golden shield.

Amerotke knelt, forehead to the ground in the great Hall of Audience which ran parallel to the banqueting hall in the House of a Million Years. White clouds of incense rose from silver pots to mix with the bitter-sweet smell of herbs and the cloying fragrance from the roses and countless garlands placed around the walls. Before him on a dais, shaped like a shrine with stuccoed pillars, painted blue-green and yellow on either side, with a serried row of gold cobras along the top, sat Hatusu, Pharaoh-Queen of Egypt.

Amerotke half listened to the choirs standing on either side of the Divine Shrine. He felt uncomfortable but, to observe protocol and etiquette, kept his head down. The walls on each side of the hall glittered with precious stones, the silver stars on the light-green ceiling reflected and mingled with the sunbursts on the blue marble floor.

Amerotke realised that he was being shown great favour. Pharaoh had summoned him to this splendid audience so all Egypt might see how highly she regarded her chief judge in the Hall of Two Truths. The singing stopped, fading away like a song on the breeze.

'You may kneel up.'

Amerotke did so, shifting for better comfort on the feather-down cushion beneath his knees. Hatusu sat on the great throne of alabaster ornamented with gold and ivory and studded with dazzling gems. Her jewel-encrusted sandals rested on a lion-footed stool. Over her shoulder, above the white sheath dress, hung the precious Nenes, the divine coat of the Pharaohs of Egypt. She had, this day, chosen to wear the vulture head-dress with its gold disc in the midst of gorgeously dyed ostrich plumes. Amerotke studied the olive-skinned, beautiful yet impassive face. Hatusu was only just past her twentieth summer yet she wielded the crook and the flail over the Land of the Two Kingdoms. Her kohl-ringed eyes stared out at a point further down the hall; her fingernails, painted an oyster pink, clawed at the arms of the throne, shaped in the form of leaping cheetahs. On her right stood Senenmut dressed in a white robe, his muscular, strong face wreathed in smiles. One hand lightly touched the throne, the other tapped the precious gold pectoral round his neck, proclaiming him to be Hatusu's First Minister, Grand Vizier of Egypt.

Senenmut coughed and winked at Amerotke. The chief judge coloured in embarrassment. He had been shown great favour and he must respond.

'I see your face, oh Divine One. Your radiance touches my heart. My soul is filled with pleasure at gazing on your majesty.' Amerotke bowed.

Senenmut clapped his hands softly, a sign that the audience was over. The guards in their stiffened blue and white head-dresses, bronze cuirasses and metal-studded leather kilts turned and marched towards the door, spear in one hand, shield depicting the emblem of the Ibis regiment in the other. Amerotke remained kneeling. Two servants appeared and pulled a gold silk curtain across the dais, screening divine Pharaoh from mortal eyes. Still Amerotke waited. The hall was now being cleared of the keeper of the perfumes, the custodian of Pharaoh's slippers, the royal fan-bearer, the chamberlains and other court flunkeys. Amerotke peered over his shoulder. Only a few guards now remained near the silver-plated doors. Senenmut appeared, walking between the pillars towards him. He stretched out both hands and raised Amerotke to his feet.

'A little trying,' the Grand Vizier grinned, 'but Her Majesty insists on showing her divine effulgence, as well as demonstrating to all of Thebes how much she treasures her chief judge of the Hall of Two Truths.'

'It can be painful on the knees,' Amerotke replied. 'But it's bearable.'

'Hatusu will see you now.'

Senenmut led him along a narrow gallery, the walls decorated on either side in brilliant colours. Amerotke noticed with amusement how all the paintings were fresh, depicting Hatusu's great victory over the Mitanni in the north a few months earlier.

Hani, High Priest of Horus, was waiting in an antechamber. Beside him sat his wife, Vechlis, tall and sharp-faced, her eyes heavily painted, her cheeks covered in rouge. A black, oily wig hung down to her shoulders, each tress tied in small silver tubes. She was an imperious, hawk-faced woman with glittering eyes and prim mouth. Amerotke had known her from childhood. He stopped and bowed.

'It's good to see you, my lady.'

Vechlis acknowledged the greeting with a smile. 'And you, Amerotke. Your deeds and words are now famous throughout Thebes.' Vechlis came forward and cupped his face in her hands. Her eyes were bright with tears. 'It seems only yesterday,' she murmured, 'when I walked with you, Amerotke, through the temple gardens to show you a singing bird. Such a quiet boy with eyes for everything! We need you, Amerotke. You must join the meeting in the Temple of Horus. Your presence will help both divine Pharaoh's and my husband's cause.'

Amerotke bowed and followed Senenmut into Hatusu's private chamber. The walls were of unadorned white limestone. Hatusu had set aside all royal regalia. She was sitting on a cushion on the floor, her back against the wall. The window above her was open and she was plucking at her gown to catch the evening breezes.

'By all that's holy,' she grinned, 'power and majesty can be very tiresome! Senenmut, close the door.' She raised her hand for Amerotke to kiss then gestured at some cushions. 'Make yourself as comfortable as possible.'

Amerotke and Senenmut both squatted on the floor facing their Pharaoh. The chief judge felt slightly embarrassed. Hatusu now looked like any young woman, eyes bright, lips parted as if she had been dancing at some feast and had come here to relax. He recalled how, years ago, he used to meet her at her father's court. They'd sit like this and tell each other stories. Now this young woman who had assumed the crown of Pharaoh, a veritable stickler for being accorded every dignity, sat like a woman in the marketplace ready to discuss neighbourhood gossip.

'Do you wish something to drink?' Hatusu asked. 'We have white wine or ice-cold sherbet.'

Amerotke shook his head.

'You didn't kneel too long?' she added mischievously.

'Your Majesty,' Amerotke replied airily, 'it was worth every second.'

Hatusu threw her head back and laughed. She leaned over and poked his shoulder. 'You are such a bad liar, Amerotke.' Her face grew serious. 'I heard about the attack in the court by that villian Nehemu. I've ordered his corpse to be displayed on the walls.' Her eyes were now hard. 'A clear warning that no one lifts his hand against Pharaoh's officials!' She picked up a fan and waved it against her face. 'So, Omendap's son has been accused of murder?'

'That's what the royal prosecutor maintains. He alleges Rahmose's two companions did not become lost in the maze of the Hall of the Underworld but the young man killed them and buried their bodies in the desert. A short while later one of the sand-wanderers came, probably to strip the chariot of anything valuable, and was killed by a lion.'

'And Rahmose took their horses? An assassin would not have done that,' Hatusu said. 'He admits he went out into the Red Lands looking for his two companions. Again, it is highly unlikely an assassin would confess to that.'

Amerotke shook his head. 'That, my lady, is not the truth. Before I left the court, I studied evidence submitted by the prosecutor. According to this, Rahmose took the horses and rode back to Thebes. Night was falling. In the normal course of events he would have reached the city and no one would have been any the wiser. The royal prosecutor says he can produce witnesses that Rahmose told no one where he was going or what he was going to do. He simply informed one of the servants that he was going for a short ride along the Nile and would not be away long.'

Senenmut's face became grave; he glanced quickly at Hatusu.

'But Rahmose's chariot suffered some mishap on his return,' Amerotke continued. 'Nothing serious, a wheel became loose and he had to stop. One of the horses he had taken bolted and ran straight into a cavalry patrol. The scout seized it, followed the tracks back and encountered Rahmose who was on the point of leaving. According to the officer's testimony, Rahmose tried to flee. He loosened the other horse he had taken and drove away as if chased by all the demons of the underworld.'

'But the wheels became loose again,' Senenmut broke in.

'Yes, my lord, Rahmose was forced to stop. The cavalry patrol were now highly suspicious. They could see the horses Rahmose had taken were of high quality. In fact, one of them bore Peshedu's brand.'

'Why didn't the officer responsible send out a patrol to this Hall of the Underworld?' Hatusu asked sharply.

'It was nightfall,' Amerotke replied. 'Their horses were winded and tired. They carried little provisions and they wanted to question Rahmose further.'

'How many people know these details?'

'By now, my lady, most of Thebes. It would appear that Omendap's son tried to lie.'

'So, so.' Senenmut leaned his elbows on his knees and pressed his fingertips together. 'We have Rahmose's story and the royal prosecutor's allegations. I can see where that wily little brain will lead the court. He'll paint a picture that Rahmose left Thebes by stealth. He went out to the Hall of the Underworld, killed his two companions, buried their bodies in the sand and took their horses, intending to drive them off. If the cavalry patrol hadn't stumbled across Rahmose, the sand-wanderers, desert dwellers or Libyan raiders would have been blamed.'

'I think so,' Amerotke agreed.

'Some mention was made of the missing men's tracks being found leading into the maze,' Hatusu remarked.

Amerotke stared through the window. Norfret would be

waiting for him and he wondered where Shufoy had gone. Prenhoe had whispered that he had heard a rumour that Shufoy had been seen talking to the courtesan Maiarch. Amerotke sucked in his lips. He wondered if Maiarch had made the same offer to the little dwarf as she had to him.

'My lord judge,' Hatusu leaned forward, digging her painted nails into his knee, 'we are waiting with bated breath.'

'The tracks leading into the maze mean nothing,' Amerotke murmured. 'All they prove, if they are the footprints of the missing officers, is that they stood at the entrance.'

'But could Rahmose kill two soldiers?' asked Senenmut.

'Why not?' Amerotke wiped his mouth on the back of his hand. 'Let us say he drives up in his chariot. His two companions are tired, perhaps drunk, they had taken a wine-skin. They are at the entrance to the maze when Rahmose arrives. They come staggering out to meet him, jeering and cat-calling. Rahmose is a skilled archer. He pulls two arrows from his sheath; you could measure the time in heartbeats before both men lie dead. Rahmose then clambers down. He quickly takes the bodies and buries them. The same is true of their weapons. Remember, apart from the wineskin and the cracked cup, nothing else has been found. The royal prosecutor could argue that Rahmose left Thebes, not intending to kill the young men. But a quarrel occurred and blood was shed so the corpses had to be hidden and Rahmose fled.'

'So,' Hatusu concluded, 'the only way Omendap's son can escape sentence is if the two officers can be found either dead or alive. If alive, there's no further problem. If dead, Rahmose is still suspect until he is cleared of any involvement in their killing.'

'Is that why I am here?' Amerotke asked sharply. 'Is divine Pharaoh going to give me the benefit of her far-reaching wisdom?'

Hatusu drew in her breath in a sharp hiss. 'I do not interfere with my judges!' she snapped.

No, no, Amerotke thought, not unless you have to. He fingered his ring of office. If Hatusu tried to force him, he'd resign his post and that would be that. He did not want to become a laughing stock in the beer shops, dismissed as Hatusu's puppet, a man who had been bought and sold.

'Peace now, Amerotke,' Senenmut murmured, clasping his arm. 'Ask yourself one question. Is Rahmose a murderer?'

'I have met many a rogue, my lord, with a smiling face. They say the calmest waters hide treacherous depths. You are concerned, aren't you? If Rahmose is found guilty you lose the friendship and support of Omendap your commander-in-chief. If the case is dismissed, you lose the wealth and support of Peshedu, father of the two missing men.'

'There can be no compromises?' Senenmut asked.

'My lord, we should wait until we collect more evidence and see if a compromise can be made.'

'You'll go out there?' Hatusu asked. 'To the Hall of the Underworld and search the place yourself?'

'Of course, my lady. Only the gods know what lies in that labyrinth.'

'But not too soon,' Hatusu murmured. She pulled at her robe, letting it slip to reveal one perfectly formed breast tipped with gold paint. Amerotke looked away quickly and Hatusu laughed flirtatiously. 'The Lady Norfret keeps you busy, my lord judge.'

'Never as busy as you, my lady.'

Again a laugh, a girlish snigger.

'Omendap's son can wait,' she said slowly. 'I've ordered scouting patrols out into the Red Lands to see what they can find. I have other business for you, Amerotke. You've heard the chatter about the high priests?'

'Ah yes, their meeting at the Temple of Horus.'

'It is very important,' Senenmut declared. He took off his pectoral, placed it over one knee and ran his finger delicately along the gold tracery depicting the god Osiris. 'You know the situation, Amerotke. Hatusu is Pharaoh by divine decree.

73

She inherits the throne as the daughter of Tuthmosis I, as well as her divine conception by Amun in her own mother's womb.'

Amerotke kept his face impassive. Such propaganda had been proclaimed all over Thebes, in the temple paintings, on pylons as well as in prayers carved round the shrines and royal monuments. Hatusu was not only of divine descent from her father but owed her conception to the intervention of the god Amun himself.

'Our divine lady's great victory in the north,' Senenmut continued, 'the annilihation of her enemies, the acclamation of the people have all confirmed her true destiny.'

'You only await the assent of the priests,' Amerotke finished, 'and all will be complete.'

'I want you to join their meeting tomorrow.' Hatusu's dark-blue eyes were full of laughter. 'You will speak for me, Amerotke. You will champion my cause. You, the High Priest of Horus, together with his wife the Lady Vechlis . . .'

'You have no more ardent supporters,' Amerotke replied. 'True, the business in the Hall of Two Truths can wait but what else?'

'Why, Amerotke,' Hatusu smiled. 'One of your old friends has decided to intervene.'

Amerotke looked puzzled.

'Murder,' she explained. 'The hand of the red-haired god Seth!'

Ka: the ancient Egyptian for 'spirit of the dead'.

CHAPTER 5

Amerotke had to wait for a while. Senenmut piled the cushions and arranged the chairs to make things more formal.

'Appearances are everything,' he murmured mischievously.

Hatusu sat enthroned, Senenmut and Amerotke on two stools before her when High Priest Hani and Vechlis were ushered in. Hatusu quickly dispensed with the formalities, allowing the high priest and his wife to kiss her sandalled foot before gesturing at the stools before her.

'Your Majesty, we have come direct from the palace,' Vechlis said. 'The divine Father Prem has been horribly killed.'

She briefly described the circumstances surrounding his death. Her husband was visibly agitated. Officially known as Horus, Hani's close face bore little resemblance to the falcon god he served. Vechlis was of sterner stuff; harsh-faced, her eyes glowed whenever she glanced at Hatusu. Amerotke listened fascinated. Most murders were clumsy, malicious, with very little planning. This was different. When Vechlis finished, Hatusu looked at Amerotke.

'According to the evidence, Chief Judge,' she said, 'the divine Father was killed by the blow of some wild cat. Yet,' she glanced at the high priest, 'was there any sign of such an animal in his chamber?'

Hani shook his head.

'And would anyone want him dead?'

Again a shake of the head.

'He was much loved,' Vechlis spoke up. 'An ancient scholar. Who would want to kill an old man in such a hideous way?'

'And, of course, there's the other death.'

'Yes, my Lord Senenmut, there is,' Hani said. 'Neria, our archivist and chief librarian. He went down into the ancient passageways beneath the temple, a warren of galleries. At its centre, as you know, lies the tomb of the most ancient Pharaoh of Egypt, Menes of the Scorpion line. It was the day Her Divine Majesty visited the temple.' Hani paused. 'All our visitors and guests were resting after the feast. A servant saw smoke coming from the steps down to the tomb. The alarm was raised.' He shook his head. 'A terrible sight,' he whispered. 'Neria must have been returning up the steps. Someone opened the door, threw oil over him then set him alight. Nothing but charred, blackened flesh.'

'And you think these murders,' Amerotke said, 'have something to do with the meeting of the high priests at your temple?'

'Perhaps,' Hani replied. 'But they are holy men, my Lord Amerotke. They bear the names of Egypt's gods: Isis, Osiris, Amun, Anubis, Hathor. Five in all, six if you include myself.'

'But,' Amerotke insisted, 'the murders only began when they arrived. How long have they been there?'

'Two to three days. So far we've discussed mundane matters: revenues, taxes, the academies in the House of Life, the rites and rituals of different temples.' He looked shamefaced. 'We, er, began with divine Pharaoh's accession but, well, we could make little progress.'

'So, who insisted that Her Majesty's claim to the throne of Egypt be a matter for later debate?'

Hani shrugged. 'I don't really know, my Lord Amerotke.'

'Oh, come, come,' said Senenmut impatiently. 'It is well known, my Lord Hani, that the high priests, apart from you and your wife, have not been enthusiastic in accepting the will of the gods. We,' he glanced quickly at Hatusu, 'decided to press matters by asking for their opinion.' He shrugged. 'Some people consider that a mistake. We do not. At least the matter is out in the open but,' he added warningly, 'we demand their support.'

'They are traditionalists,' Hani protested. 'They have seen the turbulence caused by . . .' he hesitated, staring fearfully at Hatusu.

'Say it, my lord,' she said firmly. 'Spit out the words of your heart.'

'The Hyksos have been repelled,' Hani continued almost in a gabble. 'For the last sixty years the Land of the Two Kingdoms has known peace, security, power abroad. Why should they accept a queen as Pharaoh, when there is . . .' His voice faltered.

'Your husband's young son, Tuthmosis,' Vechlis finished for him. 'My lady, I merely speak as I find. The high priests believe that young boy should wear the double crown of Egypt.'

'Where did such rumours begin?' Amerotke inquired.

Vechlis smiled thinly. 'We women are regarded as gossips yet we are nothing to a gaggle of priests.'

'That is no way to speak of your brothers!' Hani snapped.

Vechlis glared contemptuously at him and glanced away.

'And how will the debate go?' Amerotke asked. 'What will convince this, as you call it, gaggle of priests that Hatusu rules by divine decree?'

'A study of the past,' Hani replied quickly. 'A critical examination of the archives, the ancient manuscripts.'

'Ah.' Amerotke held a hand up. 'So that is why Neria and Prem were murdered. They were scholars of Egypt's past, yes?'

Hani nodded.

'I would wager a pot of golden incense,' Amerotke said, 'that their sympathies were well known.'

'They thought the same as we do,' Vechlis responded. 'That Hatusu was divinely conceived, that her outstanding victory against the Mitanni, as well as her triumphs over her enemies at home, are signs enough of the divine Hatusu's right to rule.'

'Hatusu controls the army, the people,' Amerotke pointed out. 'What can this coterie of priests say? That she has no right? Are they going to take away the crook and the flail, the crown and the Nenes?'

'No, no.' Vechlis played with the silver-edged tassel of her wig. 'I am sure that they would not be so bold or so stupid. Her Majesty knows what will happen.'

'A whispering campaign?' Senenmut spoke up.

'Yes, my lord. Their opposition will not be a strong wind but a gentle, insistent breeze seeking out any discontent or dissent, looking for signs and portents.'

'And, of course, these murders,' Hatusu snapped, 'will be regarded as symptoms of divine disfavour.'

'Precisely, Your Majesty.' Hani leaned forward. 'Go into the marketplace, the quayside, the Sanctuary of Boats, the beer shops or cross the Nile to the Necropolis, even here in the House of a Million Years, and you will find the whisperers as busy as snakes, slithering about looking for their opportunity. They lie in wait.'

'And I am to root them out?' Amertoke asked. 'Your Majesty, I am not a scholar or a theologian.'

'You are a symbol of our divine will,' Hatusu told him. 'You have a sharp mind and a decisive wit. You will argue my claims and trap this murderer. Believe me,' Hatusu clenched her fists and sat up straight, eyes blazing, 'I'll see whoever's responsible crucified against the walls of Thebes!'

Amerotke turned his stool slightly to face Hani and his wife. 'These deaths have a number of things in common,' he said. 'Both victims were members of your temple. Both had an interest in the history of Egypt. Both died in very mysterious circumstances.'

'What are you implying?' Hani asked.

'That the killer must be someone who knows the Temple of Horus well.'

'But you forget,' Vechlis broke in. 'Every priest in Egypt has studied in our House of Life and its School for Scribes.'

Amerotke nodded; he had forgotten that. The Temple of Horus was famous for its scholarship and, because it housed the body of Egypt's first Pharaoh, the mysterious Scorpion God, it was regarded as especially holy, a shrine, a place of pilgrimage.

'You say,' Amerotke played with the ring on his little finger, 'that this debate about divine Pharaoh's succession has caused much controversy among the priests – except for you, my Lord Hani, and your wife, who are well known as her fervent supporters.'

'But who isn't?' Hani asked quickly.

'The other high priests,' Hatusu retorted. 'They do not conceal their hostility.'

'And who else?' Senemut demanded.

'You know full well, my lord,' Lady Vechlis replied. 'Sengi is chief scribe in our House of Life. He has made his opposition known among the scholars.'

Hatusu's face mottled with fury at the mention of Sengi's name. Even in the Hall of Two Truths, Amerotke had heard about this outspoken, brilliant scholar, patronised by Hatusu's dead husband, the divine Tuthmosis II. Sengi belonged to no party but constantly questioned how a woman could sit on the throne of Egypt.

'Sengi is helped,' Vechlis went on, 'by a wandering scholar, a man noted for his mastery of rhetoric and debate. This old friend of our chief scribe has hastened to Thebes to offer his assistance.'

'Pepy!' Hatusu exclaimed.

'Yes, my lady, Pepy.'

Amerotke narrowed his eyes. He recalled his own days in the House of Life at the Temple of Ma'at. Ah yes, Pepy.

A visiting scholar who flouted the fashions of priests and scribes by growing his own hair, beard and moustache; tall, thin, with mocking eyes and steely lips. The scholars whispered that Pepy believed in nothing. For him there was no Far Horizon, no gods, no Fields of the Blessed. He proclaimed the mummification of bodies was a waste of both time and precious treasure, that the dead became particles blown about by the desert wind.

'I know this Pepy,' Senenmut murmured. 'They claim he is an atheist.'

'My husband should have burnt him,' Hatusu jibed.

'He's too clever, Your Majesty.' Senenmut leaned over and brushed the back of Hatusu's hand, a sign for her to keep calm.

'Pepy is a brilliant scholar,' Hani agreed. 'Sengi paid for him to come from Memphis. Pepy is always attracted by gold, silver and precious stones.'

'But why did you allow him into your temple?' Hatusu exclaimed.

'My lady, what could I do?' Hani spread his hands.

Amerotke noticed how dry and wrinkled his long fingers were, like the claws of a cat.

'Pepy is famous, a master of debate. True, allegations and accusations have been levelled against him but nothing has been proved. If I turned him away, I would have been accused of bias.'

'Sengi,' Vechlis sniffed, 'is not a man who forgives easily. He'd claim the Temple of Horus was trying to stifle debate by your own silent decree.'

'This Pepy,' Amerotke asked, 'now studies at your temple?'

'He did so until a day ago,' Hani replied. 'Sengi and Neria allowed him into our library. Our archives hold precious manuscripts dating back many hundreds of years. It also has a collection of inscriptions, drawings, writings in languages we don't even understand.'

'You allowed such a rogue into so famous a library?'

Senenmut exclaimed. 'Come, come, my Lord Hani, Pepy may be a famous scholar but his love of gold and silver is also well known. He has been accused by other libraries, colleges and Houses of Life of being light-fingered with their manuscripts.'

'I thought the same,' came the hot reply. 'So, Pepy was only allowed into the library accompanied by two of the temple guards. They sat at the table with him, searched his bag and his clothing before he left. He did not come today.'

'What do you mean?' Amerotke asked.

'He was given a chamber but Pepy likes, how can I put it, the finer things of life. Two days ago he apparently hired an upstairs chamber in a tavern down near the quayside.'

'Typical of that whoremonger!' Hatusu snarled. 'A man of many tastes, so I understand.'

'He was supposed to come into the temple today,' Hani continued, now frightened by Hatusu's anger, 'but he did not.'

'And?' Amerotke asked.

'I sent a temple guard down to the quayside to see if all was well. Sengi insisted I did. Pepy was definitely there and, according to rumour, spending most liberally.'

'Have you checked the library?' Senenmut asked.

Hani looked frightened and shook his head.

'Are you saying that Pepy may have stolen something?'

'It's possible,' Senenmut answered. 'His fingers would itch at so many ancient manuscripts. Along the quayside he would find buyers – rich merchants, priests from other temples.'

'I was going to organise a search,' Hani stammered. 'But the death of Prem, my visit here . . .'

Hatusu clapped her hands softly. 'My Lord Amerotke, you have heard enough. The cases awaiting you in the Hall of Two Truths can, like a good wine, mature a little longer. Tomorow morning the council of priests meets again and you are to be present. You are also to make diligent search for this Pepy. Find him and you may find the assassin.' Her face became wreathed in smiles. 'And you, my Lord Hani and Lady Vechlis.' She stretched out her hand and opened her fingers.

Hani gasped. In the palm of Hatusu's hand lay two small cartouches wrought of pure gold. They showed the hieroglyphics of Hatusu's personal seal.

'They are yours.' Hatusu said softly. 'Marks and symbols of my friendship. Bring this matter to a successful conclusion and you shall be proclaimed from the Balcony of Audience as close friends of divine Pharaoh.'

She made a movement with her hand, a sign that the meeting was over. Hani, Vechlis and Amerotke hastily fell to their knees and made obeisance. Even as he did so, Amerotke hid his deep, cloying fear. Hatusu was correct. In the Temple of Horus lurked the destroyer, red-haired Seth, the god of sudden death and murder.

Shufoy believed he had crossed the Far Horizon and was in the Field of the Blessed. Maiarch, queen of the courtesans, had invited him to one of her select houses near the Sanctuary of Boats. This was no brothel or bordello but a true House of Love with cool halls and beautiful water basins set between the brightly-coloured pillars. Shufoy lay back on the couch. Concubines hovered about him, their slim, naked bodies carefully shaved and oiled, lips painted, eyes lined with kohl, finger and toenails coloured carmine. One brought him a bowl of faïence full of lotuses to gratify his nostrils, another offered sweet, iced melons to quench his thirst. Shufoy languidly thanked them both. He turned to where a group of naked ladies had placed a game board on a table and, with giggles and muted laughter, set out the enamelled terracotta pieces with the heads of gazelles, lions and jackals. Behind Shufoy, two concubines waved great ostrich plumes drenched in perfume. Shufoy gazed about and groaned with pleasure. The walls were covered in brightly painted scenes: birds fluttering over rose bushes, gazelles hiding among leaves, fish shooting through blue water.

From the back of this Hall of Love, harps and lyres echoed. A girl from the Land of Kush came, knelt beside him and began to sing:

> She led me by my hand.
> We went into her garden to walk.
> She made me eat honey taken from the heart of the honeycomb.
> Her reeds were green, her shrubs were covered with flowers.
> Gooseberries and cherries redder than rubies.
> Her shrubbery was cool and airy.
> She gave me a present:
> A necklace of lapis lazuli with lilies and tulips.

The girl finished her song and withdrew. The music grew louder; dancing girls appeared, their nipples painted blue, thick wigs tied back.

Shufoy closed his eyes. 'This is the life,' he murmured. 'A man must take his rest and the body needs as much pampering as the soul.'

'Shufoy!'

'I know that voice.' The dwarf opened his eyes.

Amerotke was bearing down on him, Maiarch trotting behind, fluttering her fingers.

'My lord judge!' she wailed. 'If we cannot please you then at least let us pleasure your servant.'

Shufoy glared up at Amerotke. 'Leave me here, master! Let me float like a lily upon a pond.'

'I'll give you lilies!' Amerotke snapped. 'Lady Maiarch?' He turned back to the courtesan. 'The chief judge cannot take presents and neither can his servants.'

As soon as the words were out, Amerotke knew they sounded both stupid and pompous. He turned back to Shufoy.

'You may stay if you wish. I must be going home.'

The dwarf swung his little legs off the couch. He grasped Maiarch's plump fingers and kissed them. 'Some other time, Madam. I have business with my master.'

Shufoy collected his parasol and little bag. He made sure none of the ladies had helped themselves to any of his cures and hastened after Amerotke. The streets and thoroughfares were still busy. Fine ladies and gentlemen were taking the cool of the evening, the great ones of the earth coming out to mingle with the people of the streets in a many-coloured, chattering throng. Great nobles displayed their pride and high birth in the insolent luxury of their clothes and ornaments. Officials returned from work, long sticks in their hands, newly shaved and rouged, clothed in pleated mantles and floating skirts. Bald-headed priests, thronging together like chickens, sauntered by in clouds of white drapery and ostentatious jewellery. A group of soldiers stood outside a beer shop, bawling a military song:

> Come and I will tell you of marching in Syria
> And fighting in distant lands.
> You drink foul water and fart like a trumpet.
> If you get home you are just a piece of old
>   worm-eaten wood.
> They'll stretch you out on the ground and kill you.

Amerotke pushed by these. Now and again he'd pinch his nostrils at the cloying, contrasting smells: the grease from cookshops, the oil from the seller of figs, who mashed the fruit and mixed it with olive oil and honey. In the narrow lanes and streets, muck-rakers cleaned open sewers and emptied latrines. Flies buzzed in great black hordes. Dogs barked, naked children ran out chasing each other with hollowed sticks. People shouted and yelled from upper storeys. Temple guards swaggered by. At last Amerotke and Shufoy were free of this throng and made their way down towards the city gates. Amerotke paused and stared sadly down at Shufoy.

'I am sorry,' he apologised. 'I truly am but I was tired.'

'And I'm sorry as well.' Shufoy, wrinkled his face in annoyance. 'The tongue should tell the truth, heart should speak to heart.'

'What are you ranting about, Shufoy?'

'You didn't tell me about the attack on you in the court this morning.' Shufoy banged the parasol and almost did a dance of rage. He stopped and peered up. 'I thought the Amemets were all dead.'

Amerotke took him by the shoulder and moved on. 'The Guild of Assassins has crossed my path a number of times.'

Shufoy nipped his master's wrist. 'But you said they were dead, killed out in the desert lands.'

'Some may have survived,' Amerotke replied. 'Pharaoh's spies from the House of Secrets have informed me that the Amemets are being re-organised, recruiting new members.' He tapped Shufoy on the head.

The dwarf struck his hand away and replaced his skull cap.

'You know more about them than I do,' Amerotke continued. 'You listen to the gossip in the bazaars and markets.'

Shufoy nodded. 'They worship Mafdet, the goddess who takes the form of a killer cat. If they pledge to kill you—'

'Yes, yes, I know all about the carob seedcake,' Amerotke interrupted.

'I'll make inquiries. The Amemets may love killing but they love gold even more.'

Amerotke fell silent as they approached the city gates. The captain of the guard bowed as he recognised the chief judge and they were let through untroubled, out onto the highway.

'Do you really think Nehemu was one of them?' Shufoy asked.

'He may have been bluffing,' Amerotke replied. 'We can

only wait and see. You've asked your friends along the river to make careful inquiries about Antef?'

'Oh, yes, I was coming back from there when Maiarch met me. And what about this other business out at the Hall of the Underworld?'

'We'll see. We'll see.' Amerotke stared out across the river, still busy as barges and ferries made their way to the city quayside. 'It will be good to be home,' he murmured. 'And once again, Shufoy, I am sorry about the ladies.'

Shufoy decided he had scolded his master enough and began to tell him a salacious story about a priest, a dancing girl and a new position she had offered him. Amerotke half listened. They passed the grey, crowded huts which housed the workers who flocked to the outskirts of the city looking for work and cheap food. An arid, smelly place. A few acacias and sycamores provided some shade; the ground was peppered with piles of refuse, the field of fierce battles waged by dogs, hawks and vultures. Men were at work rebuilding their frail brick houses damaged by a recent storm. Idlers stood along the path staring with swollen eyes or smiling in a display of teeth spoiled by bad flour and rotting meat. Amerotke paused to give alms. All the time Shufoy was talking.

They passed out into the countryside. Here stood the villas of Theban officials behind tall battlemented walls and doors of heavy cedar wood. Amerotke wondered if Hatusu had any plans to distribute the wealth, to restrain the rich and give the poorer a chance to improve. Would the matter be raised in the royal circle? He was lost in such thoughts when Shufoy plucked at his wrist. They were home and Shufoy was banging on the postern door with his parasol demanding entrance in the name of his master.

The gate swung open. Amerotke stepped into his own private paradise, feeling guilty at the poverty he had just glimpsed. This was his oasis of calm. Apple, almond, fig and pomegranate trees grew here in glorious profusion. Sun-baked plots full of onions, cucumbers, aubergines and other vegetables gave off a pleasant savoury odour. Amerotke, followed by Shufoy, walked along the path and up the steps into the entrance hall.

Norfret was waiting for him. She removed his sandals and brought water to wash his feet and hands and an alabaster jar of oils to anoint his head. She slipped a garland of flowers over his neck. Shufoy looked around. No other servants were present. The entrance hall was full of delicious perfume. Norfret was dressed in a simple white sheath dress and gold sandals. The dwarf became embarrassed. Norfret apparently wished to be alone with her husband so he mumbled his excuses and went looking for his two charges whose voices he could hear at the other end of the house.

Amerotke took Norfret's face in his hands and kissed her gently on the brow.

'Outside those walls,' he whispered, 'men are wolves to men. But this is paradise.'

Norfret's eyes, full of mischief, smiled back. 'I heard about the court,' she murmured. 'The attack on you.'

'Prenhoe has been here?'

She nodded.

'Such things happen, you know.'

'That doesn't really frighten me.'

He seized her by the arms, catching the mischief in her voice. 'What else did Prenhoe tell you?'

'How Maiarch the queen courtesan invited you to her House of Love.'

Amerotke smiled. 'Why go there?' he teased. 'I'm in the Hall of Love.'

Norfret's fingers flew to her lips. 'A messenger brought something!'

She got up, went to a small alcove and brought back a cleverly wrought box of sandalwood. She opened it. Amerotke took out the piece of papyrus, unfolded it and stared down at the carob seedcake it contained.

*   *   *

Pepy, the itinerant scholar and scribe, was full of himself, as well as the beer and wine he had drunk. He lurched along the smelly, fly-ridden street towards his lodgings. He couldn't believe his good fortune. Truly the gods . . . He stopped and smirked. If they existed, truly the gods had smiled on him. He paused outside a small courtyard and blearily gazed at the fountain splashing there. He lurched through the gateway and smiled at the porter, a grizzled old woman, sitting in an alcove. He thrust a coin into her hand and staggered up the steps into the House of Love. Servants appeared with garlands of flowers, a cake of perfume was placed on his head. They looked askance at him, rather disdainful. Pepy grew his own hair, moustache and beard, and his white robe and the gaily coloured cape over his shoulders was badly stained. Nevertheless, they could hear the clink of his purse and noticed the expensive gorget round his throat. They led him into the Hall of Waiting. Girls lounged and lazed on couches there, as graceful as fawns. All were naked except for linen loincloths, and their necks, arms, ankles and feet glittered with ornaments.

Pepy walked round inspecting them; full of his new-found wealth, he felt like the lion of the desert. One girl caught his eye. She was graceful, sinuous, her copper-coloured body shimmering with oil. He took her by the hand and pulled her to her feet. She followed demurely, slightly resistant, but Pepy knew the game. In the entrance to the porchway he agreed a price with the mistress of the house, smiling up at her muscular Kushite slave armed with sword and club.

'You'll not take your pleasure here, lord?' the woman simpered.

Pepy shook his head. 'I'll pay the difference,' he slurred.

Coins exchanged hands and Pepy and his companion walked out into the street. The girl tripped behind. Now and again Pepy would stop to embrace and try to kiss her. The girl's painted, kohl-rimmed eyes fluttered as she resisted. He used the occasion to push her body voluptuously against his. The little bells on her wrists and ankles tinkled in their pretty struggles. A group of soldiers stopped to offer crude advice. The girl whispered in his ear and Pepy hurried on.

Darkness had now fallen, lamps were being lit in windows and doorways. Pepy reached the tavern and went up the outside staircase. He opened the narrow, wooden door and ushered the girl into the room. He didn't notice the bucket of oil just inside the door. The girl wrinkled her nose at the sour smell. Pepy slapped her on the buttocks. She started, a look of petulant anger on her face. Pepy dug into his purse and took out two small cubes of silver.

'One of these is yours,' he said thickly.

He recalled the papyrus he had studied in Memphis, showing erotic love scenes. He'd educate this pretty one in a way she'd least expect. She went across to fill two cups with wine but Pepy seized her by the wrist and dragged her across to the broad couch beneath the window. Again the petulant resistance but Pepy had his way, forcing her down, lying alongside her, running his hand over her body. He was so engrossed he didn't hear the door open. The girl's eyes widened in alarm. Pepy turned round but he had hardly time to raise himself from the couch. He saw the wooden bucket being pulled back then its contents came splashing over him and the concubine. Pepy drunkenly staggered to his feet but, even as he did, the second bucket, placed just within the doorway, was tipped over and a lamp was thrown. The fire spread across the oil, turning the room into a blazing inferno.

Acacia: a tree of ancient Egypt under which the
gods were born.

CHAPTER 6

Amerotke tapped the table with his fingers, trying to curb his impatience. He had arrived at the Temple of Horus just after dawn with Prenhoe and Shufoy. He had been welcomed and feasted, the meeting had begun but two hours had passed with little progress made. Amerotke's mind wandered back to the principal case before him in the Hall of Two Truths. He had ordered it to be put in abeyance. The royal prosecutor was searching for more evidence while Rahmose was placed under house arrest. The carob seedcake, that dire warning from the Amemets, Amerotke ignored. He'd quickly diverted Norfret, teasing her continuously until they retired to their own chamber to eat, drink and relax on their couch on the roof of their house. They'd lain there, bodies entwined, staring up at the night sky

Amerotke sighed and stared round the council chamber. This was an ancient part of the Temple of Horus, a gloomy room with grim, bare walls. Garlands of flowers did little to cheer the place or dispel the rather musty smell. Despite the shafts of sunlight piercing the narrow, high windows, oil lamps and torches had had to be lit. Amerotke and the others were seated on cushions, small tables before them, arranged in an oval. The high priests Isis, Osiris, Anubis, Amun and Hathor were all present. Amerotke didn't know their real names and he didn't care. They all looked the same:

crafty-faced men whose appearance of humility and sanctity hid burning ambition and intense competition. They were dressed alike in white robes of finest linen, adorned with leopard or panther skins.

On Amerotke's left sat Hani, his feet on a small footstool, as if to emphasise his pre-eminence. Beside him was his wife Vechlis, a silver filet round her wig. She had every right to be present as the chief concubine of the god Horus and leading priestess of the temple. Amerotke was more interested in the man opposite: Sengi, chief scribe of the House of Life, a small, plump man with thick lips, podgy cheeks and ears which stuck out like handles on a jug. He caught Amerotke's gaze, smiled and raised his eyes heavenwards as if he, too, was deeply bored. So far they had discussed nothing but protocol and etiquette – who would sit where, who would talk first, what proof should be offered and accepted.

Sengi quietly mouthed words. Amerotke couldn't understand him so the chief scribe picked up his stylus, scribbled on a scrap of parchment and gave it to one of the servants, pointing at Amerotke. The High Priest of Isis was talking about whether the meeting should he moved elsewhere. Amerotke looked at the message placed before him: 'You are Pharaoh's representative. This nonsense must be brought to an end.'

Amerotke smiled and nodded. He moved on the cushions and clapped his hands loudly. The priests gazed at him in astonishment.

'My lord.' Amerotke addressed his words to Hani. 'How long have we been sitting here?'

Vechlis grinned behind her hand.

A servant examined the water clock in the far corner. He came across and whispered in the high priest's ear.

'Over two hours,' Hani replied wearily.

'My lords,' Amerotke spread his hands, 'here we sit battling while more important matters await us. I carry the cartouche of the divine Hatusu.' He picked it up from the

table and showed it to the room. The priests bowed sub-
missively.

'That, indeed, is what we are here to debate,' retorted High
Priest Amun maliciously, hollow eyes blazing with fury, his
slit mouth pursed in angry petulance.

'In any other place,' Amerotke replied, 'my lord, your words
could be construed as treason. Divine Hatusu is Pharaoh and
King of the Two Lands. She has royal blood in her and her
rule has been vindicated by great victories as well as the
acclaim of the people.'

'I do not doubt that,' Amun replied. 'But the high priests of
Egypt have a special responsibility to debate it.'

Amerotke studied his spiteful face. This man had a clear
view of what he regarded as politic: Pharaoh must be a male;
Hatusu should be kept in the House of Seclusion, consort
with the other women of the harem and not hold the flail and
rod. Vechlis was glaring at Amun, her hand on her husband's
wrist as a sign to keep quiet.

'The purpose of this meeting,' Amun continued, hitching
his robe back and looking round at his companions for
support, 'is to discuss matters, not, my Lord Amerotke, to
accept some royal decree that we accept this or that.'

'And then there are the murders,' said Hathor. 'Is the
Temple of Horus a fitting place for our discussions? Have
not its precincts been polluted by violent death?'

'True,' said Amerotke, glad that the discussion had been
diverted to more pressing matters. 'Two members of this
temple have been murdered but that is a matter for
Pharaoh's justice. Indeed, both men, unless I am wrong,
loudly acclaimed Hatusu's accession to the throne and both
have died violent deaths. You say people whisper about
Hatusu's right to rule. They are also gossiping about why
these murders have been committed.'

'Are you implying the assassin is in this room?' Sengi broke
in. 'What proof do you have?'

'We are not criminals on trial,' Isis declared. 'This is not the

Hall of Two Truths. We are not malefactors but high priests of Egypt!'

'I didn't say you were malefactors,' Amerotke responded calmly. 'I was talking about gossip. When Neria and Prem were killed, where were you all?'

His question was greeted by an immediate outcry. Hathor sprang to his feet. A little man with a monkey-like face, he would have thrown the small table across the room if he had not been restrained by Amun sitting next to him. Amerotke picked up the royal cartouche.

'You can jump about like dancing girls,' he mocked, 'or you can answer my questions – here or in the Hall of Two Truths or before Pharaoh herself. Neria and Prem were killed because they supported Pharaoh's accession. Their murders were calculated, malicious and blasphemous.'

The sight of the royal seal quietened their anger. Vechlis whispered to Hani. He nodded and raised his hands for silence.

'My Lord Amerotke speaks the truth. He is Pharaoh's chief judge. Before we continue, each must account for his actions. Neria was killed at the ninth hour. Everyone in this room must give an explanation.' He let out a long sigh. 'And I shall do so first. On the night Neria was killed, I was with my wife in our own chamber.'

'How do we know that?' Amun asked.

'We were together,' Vechlis retorted. 'When the water clock indicated the ninth hour I ordered food to be brought from the temple kitchens. My husband vouches for me, I for him. However,' she spread her hands, 'when divine Father Prem was killed, my husband was in the Holy of Holies before Horus. I cannot remember where I was.'

The other priests took this as their cue. Amerotke realised their rushed explanations would never reveal the truth. Only Sengi remained impassive and silent.

'Where were you, my lord?' Amerotke asked.

The chief scribe lifted his head. 'In truth, and by all

that's holy, I cannot say except on both evenings I was studying.'

'What were you studying?' Amerotke asked.

Sengi shrugged. 'Like all my brothers here, searching the records and archives. The Temple of Horus is ancient, its libraries contain treasures not found elsewhere in Egypt.'

'But what were you looking for?' Amerotke persisted. 'Share your knowledge with us.'

'The history of ancient Egypt,' said Sengi, 'is hundreds of years old, going back to the first Scorpion kings. I, like others here, am intent on discovering if, in our line of ancient rulers, any woman wore the two crowns, held the crook and the flail and sat on the throne of Ra.'

'And have you discovered anything?' Amerotke asked.

Sengi shook his head.

'But what could this evidence be?' Amerotke now had the attention of them all.

Hani was smiling to himself, pleased that at last the real reason for this meeting was now being addressed.

'It could be anything,' Hathor answered. 'A decree, a letter, a fragment . . .'

The discussion was about to continue when there was a loud knocking on the door. A temple guard came in and whispered for some time to Hani, who then snapped his fingers in annoyance and rose to his feet.

'Divine Fathers, it seems that the scribe scholar Pepy has been murdered in his chamber down near the quayside.'

'What happened?' Sengi asked, springing to his feet.

'We have few details,' Hani replied. 'The Maijodou, the city police, are investigating. Our wandering scholar apparently came into some wealth. He ate and drank liberally. Last night he hired a courtesan from a House of Love and went back to his chamber with her. He, his companion and the entire room were consumed by fire.'

'Could it have been an accident?' Isis asked.

'The proprietor who also lost his tavern was quite clear on

this,' Hani replied. 'Pepy's room had scarcely enough oil for lamps, let alone a conflagration like that. The corpses were nothing but blackened ash.'

Amerotke gazed round at the priests. It would be useless to ask where they were last night. He would be given another farrago of babbled explanations.

'It's the same way Neria died.' Amerotke rose to his feet. 'I don't want to hear nonsense about the displeasure of the gods. My lords, this is murder.'

'The library!' Sengi exclaimed, fingers going to his lips.

'What about it?' Amerotke asked.

'It's two days since Pepy was here.' Sengi looked nervous.

'Get out!' Vechlis spoke to the guard.

The man hurriedly withdrew. Everyone sat down again. Sengi was now rubbing his cheeks.

'Share your troubles with us, brother,' Amerotke said softly.

'Pepy was brilliant but poor. Everyone here knows that. He was always begging for this or that. Suddenly he moves out of the temple. He hires a chamber, fills his belly with all that's good and has the wealth to hire a courtesan . . .'

'He could have stolen something,' Amerotke finished for him.

Sengi nodded. 'I hired him to help us but he was of little use. He may have—'

'Ridiculous!' Hani snapped. 'Our library is well guarded. Pepy was watched and searched.'

Amerotke got to his feet again. 'I think we should investigate.'

No one objected. They left the council chamber. Prenhoe and Shufoy were sitting in an alcove, a bunch of grapes between them. They sprang to their feet as Amerotke strode away from the rest.

'Prenhoe, you carry my seal.'

'Yes, my lord.'

'Go back to the Temple of Ma'at. Collect Asural and some of

the temple guards. Go down to the quayside, make inquiries about a man called Pepy who, together with a concubine, was burnt to death in a chamber. You won't have to search for long. You know how gossip spreads.'

Amerotke rejoined the others. Hani hurried ahead along a colonnaded walk and out across the gardens, a cool, beautiful place with luxuriant vines, their large purple grapes hanging from trellises attached to stone walls. They passed the Pool of Purity surrounded by palm trees, fish ponds, arbours and orchards of fig trees where temple servants were using trained monkeys to bring the fruit down from lofty branches. Now and again the garden would give way to small parklands where deer and sheep grazed. They passed other buildings, storehouses, granaries, the School of Life and slaughter sheds.

Amerotke looked up at the high garden tower which soared above everything, its crenellated top stark against the blue sky. Its stone wall was sheer, difficult for anyone to climb, and once again he wondered how the old priest Prem had been so cruelly killed.

On the far side of the temple gardens, surrounded by a stone wall, were double-barred gates guarded by sentries of the library, a spacious, two-storeyed building of white limestone. The lintels and pillars of the great cedar door were covered in gloriously coloured hieroglyphics and paintings depicting scribes and scholars reading, writing, discussing or sitting at the feet of their teacher. Inside, the small hallway was cool, the floor of Lebanese wood. Its lamps were specially protected by capped alabaster jars. Sentries and servants stood to attention at the arrival of such august visitors.

The main library was on the second floor, a long rectangular room. Its sycamore shutters were thrown open but the windows were barred and narrow to deter thieves. The walls of the library were covered with specially carved racks, pigeonholes and shelves which held books, manuscripts and papyrus rolls. Down the centre of the room ran a line of tables with cushions before them for use by .the scholars. Each table bore a writing pallet with styli and pots of blue, red and green ink. The place was fragrant with the smell of gum, resin, parchment and ink. A young scribe came out of one of the chambers off the library.

'Divine Father.' He bowed towards Hani.

'The library is empty?' the high priest asked.

'Divine Father, it was your personal wish that, during your important meeting, the library be left for the use of our visitors and, of course, the scholar Pepy.'

'It's about him we've come,' Sengi declared. 'He worked here, did he not?'

'Until two days ago.' The young scribe was now becoming quite flustered.

Amerotke stepped forward. 'And did you expect him to return? I am Amerotke, chief judge in the Hall of Two Truths.'

'Yes, my lord, I know. You gave judgement in favour of my mother, a dispute over a field whose boundary stones had been moved. And yes, we did expect Pepy to return.'

Amerotke walked further along the library, staring up at the stacked shelves and pigeonholes which stretched to the ceiling. He noticed a small frieze along the wall just under the ceiling, depicting monkeys collecting books from trees. Above these was the all-seeing eye of Amun-Ra as well as the Ankh, the symbol of eternal life.

'Pepy is dead,' Amerotke declared quietly. 'Murdered down near the quayside. According to rumour, our noble Pepy seems to have become a rich man.'

'That wasn't the case when he was here,' the library scribe stammered. 'He couldn't even afford a proper pen. He was always begging this and borrowing that.' The scribe blanched and his fingers went to his lips. 'Oh dear!'

'Which manuscripts was he studying?' Amerotke asked.

The librarian looked at Hani.

'Lord Amerotke has jurisdiction in these matters,' the high priest said.

The scribe hurried further down the library, to chests and coffers fashioned out of oak and bound with bronze clasps. He opened one of them and brought out a box of polished sycamore. He placed it on the table, undid the clasps and opened it, his visitors crowding round. Hani lifted out some glazed papyrus sheets between which lay inscribed fragments.

'What are these?' Amerotke asked. He recognised the writing was ancient, hieroglyphics and symbols he had studied as a student in the House of Life.

'They are manuscript fragments,' Sengi answered. 'Some of them are hundreds of years old.'

Amerotke took out another piece of manuscript about a hand-span in length and the same in width. The colour was faded. It showed a priest before an altar and, beneath, what looked like a blessing or curse. He put it back.

'Is there anything missing?'

The scribe took out everything, counted the papyrus sheets then consulted the makeshift index written out and gummed to the lid of the box. Concerned, breathing sharply, he began to count again, a fine sheen of sweat breaking out on his forehead.

'What is the matter?' Sengi demanded.

'There should be eleven pieces here. There are only ten.'

'What's missing?' Amerotke asked.

'A piece of parchment about two hand-spans long and half that in width. It's an extract from a chronicle, an ancient book about thirteen hundred years old.'

Amerotke whistled under his breath, ignoring the consternation breaking out behind him.

'It was a painting,' the scribe stammered. 'A depiction of the first Pharaoh of the Scorpion dynasty.'

'Menes?' Amerotke asked.

The scribe nodded and put his face in his hands.

'Would it fetch a high price?'

'Of course.' Sengi was now sifting through the manuscripts. 'Yes, yes, it's gone.' He glared at the library scribe. 'And this is what Pepy was working on?'

The young scribe nodded, his fear apparent. Theft of such an ancient manuscript from a temple library could mean disgrace, imprisonment, even death. 'But it's impossible!' he exclaimed. 'When Pepy came here . . . Wait here, my lords, please wait.'

The scribe hurried out of the door. He came back with two guards, burly fellows, dressed in the same fashion as the Nakhtu-aa, the 'strong-arm' boys of the infantry: leather kilts and sandals with war belts across their sweaty, muscular torsos. Each wore a stiffened red and white head-dress which fell down to the nape of the neck.

'These guards were here,' the scribe said.

'Did you watch the scholar, Pepy?' Amerotke asked.

'Of course,' the taller, more grizzled one, replied. He pointed down the library. 'He sat at a table and we sat opposite. Why, is something wrong?' His eyes rounded in alarm. 'I never liked him,' he continued hurriedly. 'We never left him alone and every time he left we searched him.'

'Did he carry a bag?' Amerotke asked.

'Bag?' the soldier sneered. 'He couldn't afford one. We even shared our rations with him.'

'And we always gave him a good search,' the other one added. 'From head to toe. My lord,' he bowed, hands extended, 'Pepy meant nothing to us. We regarded him as a smelly scholar.' He ignored Sengi's quick intake of breath. 'Shifty-eyed and light-fingered. Our allegiance is to Horus not to him.'

'Could he have concealed a manuscript?' Amerotke asked.

'That's the problem,' the library scribe broke in. 'If he had, the papyrus was so old it would have crinkled and cracked.'

'Did he seem particularly interested in this missing manuscript?' Amerotke demanded.

The librarian shrugged. 'My lord, he asked for this and that, but yes, he spent more time on this file than any other.'

The guards concurred with this.

Amerotke sat down on a stool and stared at the sycamore box. 'What did the manuscript actually say?'

'I don't really know. The picture had hieroglyphics beneath it. It was nothing remarkable.'

'But it would still fetch a good price?'

'Oh yes, at least three to four ounces of pure gold.'

'Sengi,' Amerotke smiled thinly at the chief scribe, 'you hired this man—'

'I know nothing!' Sengi was agitated. 'Pepy didn't care about who sat on the imperial throne. He said he'd search for evidence of a female Pharaoh then tell me. In the end,' Sengi licked his lips, 'he told me nothing.'

'But you asked him?'

'Of course. He replied he'd tell me only when he was finished.'

'Well, he is now!' Vechlis scoffed.

Amerotke lifted his hand for silence and chewed the corner of his lip. Thebes was full of wealthy merchants. Collectors of artefacts, valuable relics from Egypt's past. If Pepy had stolen then sold the manuscript, it could be anywhere. He dismissed the guards and asked the others to sit round the table. They did so hurriedly; the apparent theft of the manuscript made them respect Amerotke's authority. In theory, all temples and their contents were the property of Pharaoh. Hatusu would not be pleased. Amerotke gestured at the young librarian to join them.

'This is a mystery,' he began. 'If Pepy had tried to steal that manuscript, the guards would have found it. Yet it's gone, and Pepy, before he was killed, became a wealthy man.' He looked round the library. 'Neria was the principal keeper, wasn't he?'

The librarian's face softened, eyes brimming with tears. 'He was a good master, my lord, a true scholar.'

'Do you know why anyone would want to kill him?'
Amerotke asked.

'Neria was a gentle soul, my lord. This was his world, books
and manuscripts. Time and again I would find him here late
at night, poring over some manuscript, talking to himself.'

'And the days before he died?'

'Neria was a scholar, my Lord Amerotke, a bachelor. He
claimed these manuscripts were his wives and children. He
was very excited about the council of the high priests at the
temple and what evidence might be found.'

'Did he tell you anything?'

'No.' The librarian shook his head. 'He did not. Neria could
be very secretive. He certainly resented Pepy. Once, I heard
harsh words exchanged between the two but about what I
don't know.'

Vechlis tapped the table top with her purple-painted
fingernails. 'Neria was much beloved but when it came
to knowledge he was a miser. He would dig out nuggets,
precious items, but keep them to himself.'

'Neria, too, was involved in the search for evidence to
either confirm or question the divine Hatusu's right to rule,
wasn't he?'

'You are correct,' Lord Hani conceded.

'I cannot speak for Pepy but Neria was very busy,' Vechlis
put in. 'I often saw him writing here, filling up a roll of
papyrus. One day I asked him about it. He looked up at me,
his eyes bright with excitement then smiled and shook his
head. Before you ask, my Lord Amerotke, the evening he was
killed, my husband had Neria's chamber carefully searched.
That roll of papyrus had disappeared and the fruits of Neria's
research with it.'

'I sifted through all his possessions carefully,' Hani confirmed. 'As did Sengi here. Nothing was found.'

'And now?' Amerotke asked.

'I have begun again,' the librarian said, 'but I am not a
scholar like my Lord Neria.'

'Have you discovered anything?' Amerotke asked.

The librarian looked at Hani; the high priest gestured with his hand.

'I have found nothing,' the librarian mumbled.

'Oh, come.' Amun leaned forward. He pointed at the young librarian. 'You mean you have found nothing to prove that a woman has ever held the crook and flail and been Pharaoh of Egypt. That is because you never will!'

'Don't be presumptuous!' Vechlis exclaimed. 'This matter is not yet resolved.'

They would have returned to their altercation in the council chamber but Amerotke gestured for silence.

'My Lord Hani, you should use your temple treasure to discover if this manuscript was sold by Pepy.' He smiled. 'You must have informants along the quayside. The sale of such a manuscript would cause some excitement among the collectors and buyers of precious things. One question I do have: on the day Neria was killed, Divine Pharaoh graciously visited this temple to offer sacrifice. She then left. Where, during all this, was Neria?'

'A feast was later held,' Hani replied quickly. 'A banquet for my brothers here and their retinues. Neria should have attended but did not. He went down to the secret caverns and passageways beneath the temple to visit the tomb of Menes.'

'Why should he do that?' Amerotke asked.

Hani just gazed back.

'What is down there?' Amerotke insisted.

'Directly beneath the shrine,' Vechlis answered, 'lies the royal mausoleum of Menes, the first Pharaoh of Egypt, founder of the Scorpion dynasty. That is his burial place. When the Hyksos invaded Egypt in the Season of the Hyena, when they laid waste with fire and sword and turned the Nile red with their blood offerings, the priests of Horus abandoned their temple. They hid in those passageways.' She gestured round the library. 'The Hyksos seized all this.

However, in the secret galleries beneath the ground, a few priests survived. One of them thought that the light of Egypt would go out for ever. He therefore covered the walls of the chamber, which holds Menes's tomb, with frescoes which chronicled the history of Egypt so that future generations would at least recognise the glory that Egypt had had before the barbarians came.'

'Neria liked going there.' The librarian smiled and pulled the sycamore box across. 'He said it was quiet a place to think.'

'So it was common knowledge that Neria could be found down there,' Amerotke commented.

'Of course.' Vechlis half laughed. 'If you were searching for him you'd look either here or in Menes's chamber. In fact, he made himself custodian of the shrine, although he was not a high priest.'

'I went down there once,' Sengi declared. 'The torches and lamps had been lit. I tiptoed round the passageways. Neria was sitting before the tomb, talking to it like you would to an old friend.'

'He did say something.' The young librarian stared up at the ceiling. 'I asked him about the divine Hatusu,' he bowed his head, 'and the meeting that was to be held here, the great council of high priests.' He paused.

Amerotke realised how still the library had become. The silence was broken only by the buzzing of bees which had slipped through the barred windows, drawn by the fragrance of the flowers and the sweet-smelling wood.

'What did he say?' Amerotke asked.

'I-I'm trying to remember, my lord. I asked him for his opinion. Neria replied: "In the beginning, all there was was the divine Mother. All things in the beginning are female."'

Vechlis clapped her hands in excitement. 'See!'

'But we all accept that,' Hathor said. 'The theologians argue that before the land was formed, the boiling seas contained, and the darkness divided from the light, one being existed: Nut the Sky Goddess.'

'I think Neria meant more than that,' the librarian mumbled. He saw the look of annoyance on Hathor's face. 'But I am no theologian,' he added hastily.

'Are there to be more questions?' Osiris, a lean, sardonic-faced man got to his feet. 'The time of purification is on us. We must pray and rest from the heat of the day.'

The others agreed. Amerotke beat his hands on the table. 'You talk of rites and purification, food and drink, lying in the shade of the sycamore tree. Will Neria ever feel the sun on his face? Or divine Father Prem gaze into the starlit sky? We talk of murder. Seth the God of the Red Lands, the creator of chaos and division, is in this temple. Filling our bellies with honey cakes and swilling the sweetest wine and finest ales will not drive him away. Can't you see, divine Fathers?' he asked angrily. 'Any one of us here could be marked by the Angel of Death!'

Ba: an ancient Egyptian word for the psychic
force.

CHAPTER 7

Amerotke's words quelled their arrogance. Sengi was nodding wisely. Vechlis put her hands together in silent applause. Hani smiled.

'You have spoken the truth, my Lord Amerotke,' he said. 'Your bluntness is well known.'

'I didn't mean to be blunt,' said Amerotke, 'just truthful. Look around this temple. Oh, the gardens are spacious and sun-filled, the roses and lilies and lotuses perfume the air. The grapes hang fat and purple. The colonnades are cool but there are dark places, narrow galleries, shadow-filled recesses. At night the darkness sweeps in and who will be safe, eh? We can sit and chatter but remember why I am here. Two priests, scholars, scribes, high-ranking members of the Temple of Horus, have been brutally killed. These deaths did not begin until this council meeting was convoked. It is my belief, and I do not wish to frighten you, that the killer is here among us.' Amerotke sighed. 'After we finish here, I wish to visit the vaults and galleries beneath the temple. And remember that I, too, am stalked by danger.'

'I will have the lamps and torches lit,' Hani murmured. 'You do speak the truth, my lord. We should all walk wary of Seth's red shadow.'

The other priests concurred reluctantly, a twist to the lips showed their truculence. Nevertheless, Amun, Osiris,

Hathor, Anubis and Isis all agreed. Amerotke still found it hard to warm to them: tough, wiry men, their souls full of ambition. Hatusu's accession had created an opportunity for them to clack and preach and they would not give that up lightly. He expected them to object, see through the cunning of his advice: the Temple of Horus was a dangerous place, the speedier they finished their business, the sooner they'd get away.

'Have you other questions?' Osiris demanded.

Amerotke nodded. 'Divine Father Prem's death is a true mystery. He was studying the stars, he left the roof of the garden tower and went back down into his own chamber. He was then brutally killed but when the door was forced, the murderer had fled. How? The assassin couldn't have escaped through a window. A rope ladder would have been needed, the mud beneath was undisturbed and the murderer would have needed more time to escape.'

'It is a mystery,' Sengi agreed.

'In reality there are two mysteries,' Amerotke said. 'First, how did the assassin kill the divine Father then escape? Secondly, why go to such lengths?'

'In what way?' Hathor asked.

Amerotke spread his hands. 'The divine Father often walked in the gardens or rested beneath a tree. He ate and drank. An arrow or a cup of poison could have despatched him just as effectively as a blow to the head in his own chamber.'

Silence greeted his words.

'One thing is clear,' said the young library scribe. He licked his lips, glancing nervously at his high priest. 'Divine Father Prem died as if he had been killed by the blow of a panther.' He gestured to the racks of manuscripts behind him. 'The ancient chronicles are full of the cruelty of the Hyksos. They used wild cats, panthers and leopards, to hunt and to kill their enemies. The Hyksos warriors also carried a bronze club with the stiffened claw of a panther on the end.'

'And do such clubs still exist?' Amerotke asked.

'We have artefacts from the time of the Hyksos. They can be found in the House of War.' He was referring to the temple armoury. 'They can be fashioned or bought in the marketplace.'

'But why not just use a simple club or a dagger?' Amerotke asked.

All eyes turned to the young librarian who blushed at such attention from his superiors.

'The garden tower is very ancient,' he replied. 'They say it was built by the Hyksos themselves, who used slaves to build and dress the stone. When divine Pharaoh's grandfather attacked the Hyksos, the barbarians often used such citadels as a centre of resistance.'

'What has this got to do with Father Prem's death?' Osiris snapped.

Amerotke made a sign with his hand for the librarian to continue.

'Rumour has it that the Hyksos mixed human blood with the lime and water for the bricks and they buried prisoners alive beneath the foundations as an offering to their war god. The tower has a reputation for being haunted by these miserable unfortunates and the Hyksos who died there.' The librarian paused. 'One possible theory is that the assassin wished to provoke unrest and disquiet among our temple family. There's nothing like the story of ghostly murder and brutal death, by forces unseen, to unsettle the minds and souls of our community.'

Amerotke studied the librarian closely: smooth, thin-faced with shaven head, his narrow nose crooked, as if it had been broken. He was slightly foppish; one gold ring hung from the lobe of his right ear. Amerotke admired his scholarly astuteness.

'What is your name?'

'Khaliv, my lord.'

'And you reasoned this out yourself?'

The young man, lips compressed, nodded.

'Then you have done very well. My Lord Hani,' Amerotke turned to the high priest, 'the Temple of Ma'at would dearly love such a scribe as our librarian.'

'There is more,' Khaliv continued. 'The Hyksos were a warlike race. They treated their women, even their own, as mere animals. There was no female aspect of their god.'

'Ah.' Amerotke leaned forward. 'So you are saying that divine Father Prem's murder in the garden tower was deliberately planned and carried out to unsettle the temple community at a time when the high priests from all over Thebes are discussing the divine Hatusu's accession to the Throne of Eternity?'

'Yes, my lord.'

'I think you've spoken the truth.' Amerotke shook a warning finger at the assembled priests. 'In normal circumstances we would discuss the accession of Pharaoh in an atmosphere of scholarly serenity. Now we have bloody chaos, secret threats, mysterious murder.'

'But it won't shake us,' Amun spoke up. 'From the matter in hand, the will of the gods must be proclaimed.'

Amerotke could tell by the stubborn cast on Amun's face that this high priest had already made up his mind. But was it as a matter of principle or had Hatusu slighted him? Or, worse, refused to bribe him? Amerotke dismissed his sense of unease. He now realised why Hatusu had been insistent he come here. If high priests like Amun had their way, Hatusu's reign would be constantly undermined by silent animosity and whispered gossip from the priestly aristocracy of Thebes.

'I understand why Neria was killed,' he said abruptly. 'But Prem?'

'He was a scholar,' Hani replied. 'He, too, was interested in the question of the succession of a woman to the throne of Egypt.'

'Was there a close relationship between Prem and Neria?' Amerotke asked.

'They were friendly enough,' Vechlis supplied. 'But they were not scholarly colleagues. Their relationship was more on a spiritual level – Neria regarded Prem as his confessor.'

'He would go to him for counsel and advice?'

'Every priest in this temple chooses such a man,' Hani explained.

'So it's possible that Neria discovered or saw something which he told Prem. Therefore both had to die. But what it was, why they had to be murdered and by whom remain a mystery.'

'It also means,' said Vechlis, 'that the assassin must have known this secret.'

'Yes, yes, quite,' Amerotke replied. 'So we must also pose the question: who else in the temple would Neria and Prem talk to?'

All eyes looked at Hani. He blanched and dabbed at his mouth with the tail of his linen belt. 'I know nothing,' he said tersely. 'Nothing at all. My Lord Amerotke, have you finished?'

'For the moment.'

Amerotke sat while the rest filed out. Only Khaliv the librarian remained.

'Do you need anything, my lord?'

'Will they be searched?' Amerotke nodded towards the door.

'No, my lord, only if they'd asked to study a manuscript. I would then summon the guards and the usual routine would be followed.'

Amerotke thanked him and the librarian went into a small chamber leading off the library. The chief judge sat staring along the shelves and pigeonholes. He listened intently. Nothing disturbed the harmony of this beautiful, fragrant-smelling chamber. He tried to impose some order on the thoughts and images teeming in his brain. The case of the young woman, Dalifa, in love with her new husband. He recalled Antef's arrogant face, the look of hate in his eyes.

Well, he could do nothing about that for the moment. And Rahmose, now under house arrest on suspicion of murder? Amerotke knew he would have to go out to the Hall of the Underworld, he would have to see the labyrinth for himself. To do that he would need a military escort. The oasis of Amarna was a dangerous place, not only because of man-eating lions; sand-wanderers, desert dwellers and marauding Nubians were always on the prowl looking for easy pickings. Indeed, the more Amerotke thought about the case, the more suspicious he became.

Rahmose had either acted very stupidly or very maliciously. Why had he taken the horses? What had happened to those two young men, trained soldiers? Surely they couldn't disappear off the face of the earth? But when could he go there? And this business? Neria had been killed in a barbaric fashion. Prem's murder was truly mysterious. And what was the connection between the two? Neria was the source. He'd worked here in the library but he'd also visited the vaults beneath the temple where he had been killed.

Amerotke's eyes grew heavy. The door to the library was flung open and Vechlis came in, a handmaid trailing behind her.

'You should relax.' The chief concubine smiled. She had changed her clothes; a white robe of pure wool hung over her shoulders, bound round the middle by a silver embossed belt. She had removed her wig. Amerotke realised how much younger she looked, a thin, sinewy woman but graceful and majestic.

'I'm going for a swim,' she said.

'Not in the Nile!' Amerotke joked.

She glanced over her shoulder at the handmaid still in the doorway. 'I am sure some of my husband's colleagues would love that! The stretch of river alongside our temple is infested with crocodiles but perhaps they would ignore me. I am not the tender morsel I once was.'

'You are still beautiful,' Amerotke responded. 'When I came to the House of Life here—'

'Hush! Hush!' Vechlis raised her hand and shuffled her feet. 'Sweet memories make me sad. The others are now feasting in the gardens. You should join them, Amerotke. Even if they resent your company.'

'Resent?'

'They fear you. You always were one for questions. That sharp, clipped voice, those hooded eyes! No wonder the criminals in Thebes quake at your name.'

'Now you flatter,' Amerotke joked.

Vechlis laughed and left the chamber. Amerotke sighed and got to his feet. He felt hungry, a little tired but he had said he would visit the vaults and passageways, the tomb of Menes the Scorpion Pharaoh.

He left the library and, taking directions from a servant, walked along the deserted galleries and passageways. In some parts the temple was golden and and spacious, the light reflected in the brilliant paintings on the white limestone walls, the marble floors and porticoes, and pots of expensive perfumes. He could hear laughter from the garden and chanting from one of the chapels. A group of hesets, dancing girls, were rehearsing their steps in a sun-washed courtyard. They danced, their naked, voluptuous bodies covered by the flimsiest gauze robes, their heads covered in beautiful wigs, faces rouged, lips painted carmine, eyes ringed with black and green paint. They moved as one, sinuously, slowly, in an eye-catching, heart-tingling rhythm. The sistra they carried rattled like the beat of a drum while the bracelets of bells on their ankles and wrists clinked and tinkled. As Amerotke passed he caught the drift of their song:

> I have danced for you, my God,
> By the river and in green fields.
> I have opened my body to you,
> I have accepted your sweet strength within me.

119

The chanting was low but carrying. One of the girls caught his eye and smiled but their teacher rapped her cane on the paved floor. Amerotke smiled apologetically and walked on. He passed through a gateway, across an open courtyard enclosed by colonnades which provided a margin of shade. The walls were carved with scenes of gods and kings painted in brilliant colours. Eventually these gave way to darker, narrower places where the sunlight only filtered through. To his right and left opened darkened recesses and passageways from which black granite statues of gods and exotic animals leered down at him. It was colder, the limestone smelt damp and sour. This was in an ancient part of the temple. Beyond its gloomy walls and gateways sounds from the gardens echoed faintly: laughter, the tinkling of a harp and the bubble of water.

A guard gave him fresh directions and eventually Amerotke reached the gloomy shaft leading down to the vaults. The door at the bottom, reinforced with copper studs and brass clasps, was open. Hani had been true to his word: torches had been lit, oil lamps placed in niches in the walls. Amerotke went down the steps, along the grim galleries into a cavernous chamber full of dancing shadows. In the centre soared the great sarcophagus emblazoned with strange hieroglyphics and symbols.

The black marble of the tomb felt ice-cold. Amerotke walked slowly round it and repressed a shiver when he saw the eyes painted above the red doorway. Did Menes, the old Scorpion Pharaoh, still gaze out? Did his Ka wander here from the Fields of Eternity? Amerotke recalled Neria and went back along the galleries to the steps. The odour of burning oil and human flesh had gone, the steps carefully scrubbed and sanded, but he could still see the stain and the burn marks on the wall.

He returned to the sarcophagus chamber and walked round the walls. The frescoes and paintings had been hurriedly done, the paintwork crude, yet they had a vigour and

120

life of their own. They showed the history of Egypt: the creation of cities, the building of the pyramids at Sakarra, the attack of the shepherd kings and the invasion of the Hyksos. The latter were depicted as terrible warriors, their horses, demons from the underworld, had fiery eyes and flailing hooves. The artist had filled every scene with detail as if desperate not to omit anything of the glory that was Egypt. Amerotke took a pitch torch out of its niche to examine the frescoes more carefully. Each wall was covered in different scenes; it would take weeks to study all of them in detail. So what had Neria hoped to see here that he could not find in the ancient manuscripts? Some of the paintings were faded. In other places the plaster had fallen off and decayed.

Amerotke walked to where this chronicle began. He recognised the symbols of the sea and sand, the cartouche, or seal, of the Scorpion kings. Each of these monarchs was depicted enthroned in splendour. Amerotke peered at Menes, the first Pharaoh of the Scorpion dynasty: smooth-faced, sloe-eyed with a distinctive head-dress and jewelled necklace. Part of the painting had faded away, the wall was scratched. Amerotke was about to continue when he heard a voice, deep and rather hollow, call his name.

'My Lord Amerotke!'

'Yes, what is it?' He was shielded from the doorway by the huge sarcophagus. He was about to go round it when he stopped. How many people knew he was down here? If this was a servant or messenger why not just come running in?

Amerotke quietly cursed. He was totally unarmed, not even a dagger in his belt. He peered round the sarcophagus and, as he did so, an arrow came flitting through the air, smacking the wall behind him. He hid behind Menes's tomb and glanced quickly round it. He glimpsed a dark shape, at a half crouch, the horn bow already coming up. Again an arrow whipped through the air, cracking the plaster behind him. Amerotke pressed his hot, sweaty back against the cold marble and edged round. What could he do? It would take time for an archer to draw another arrow but if he began to run, he might mistime it, and the torchlight made him an ideal target. He crouched behind the tomb; this was his only protection. Another arrow whirred through the air. He looked round. The chamber was empty. Had the secret, silent archer retreated? Or was he still here in the crypt on the other side of the sarcophagus?

Amerotke forced himself to relax, using techniques taught in the House of Life: deep, long breaths, allowing his shoulders to sag, his arms to hang loose by his side. He listened. If the archer was moving there'd be a rasp of breath. There was nothing but silence. Amerotke wetted his lips and crept along the side of the sarcophagus. The chamber was empty. He bounded along the passageways. Nothing but a deep silence. He went up the steps, opened the door and stared around. The assailant wouldn't wait here, surely. He walked along the colonnade, trying to control his fury. He heard a sound, stopped, pressing his back against the wall. He heard gasps, squeals of delight and peered round. High Priest Amun was there pushing one of the dancing girls against the wall. He had pulled her up, her thighs were round him, his hands were squeezing her buttocks. He was having rough, crude intercourse with her, moving backwards and forwards as if he was some common sailor taking a whore against a beer shop wall in a stinking alleyway of the city. The girl didn't object, the bangles on her wrists and ankles tinkled as Amun thrust time and again. The girl's face was contorted with pleasure.

Amerotke smiled and quietly walked past the recess. The sight of the high priest, his backside bare, taking one of the temple girls so roughly made him forget the immediate terror of the crypt. He would return, perhaps investigate the passages leading off, but next time he'd be armed and have Shufoy or Prenhoe with him.

At last Amerotke reached the garden. He wondered if he should check on where everyone else had been but that would take hours. The midday heat was now receding, white puffs of cloud dotted the blue sky. He went and sat beneath the tree, letting the birdsong calm his mind. He thought of Amun, his rough taking of that girl, and wondered if the deaths of Neria and Prem really were related to the council meeting or just casualties of temple politics and intrigue. Looking up, he glimpsed the crenellations of the garden tower above the trees and decided to go there.

He got up and walked across the grass. The gardens of Horus were beautiful, full of flowerbeds, irrigation canals, water tanks, and trees of every description: figs, palms, sycamores, persea. The air was sweet with the smells from the various workshops and storehouses, busy preparing offerings for the morning service: bread, cakes, beer, wine, vegetables and fruit. Amerotke realised how hungry he was and recalled that tonight there was going to be a great banquet.

At last he reached the garden tower. Steps led up to a wooden door. First he walked round it. Oval-shaped, it rose sheer against the sky. The stone was smooth, though here and there the masons had inserted pointed bricks as if to discourage any climber. The windows were large and square and, despite the pleasant surroundings, Amerotke could appreciate how, in a siege, a small force could shelter here and withstand a series of attacks.

He walked up the steps and opened the door. The walls of the tower were at least an arm's span thick. It would take catapaults and battering rams to make any impression on such fastness. The inside smelt sweet from the cut flowers strewn on the floor. He grasped the rope rail and climbed the steps. On every stairwell stood a chamber. In the main, the tower was used as a storehouse, the dry, cavernous rooms being full of baskets, boxes, barrels, nets, everything the temple wished to keep dry and well away from vermin. He climbed further and reached the top. A door opened and a servant waddled out. He was stout and corpulent, dressed in a kilt knotted with a girdle. The upper part of his torso was damp with sweat. He carried a watercolour palette of boxwood. He stopped and gaped at Amerotke, eyes unblinking.

'What are you doing here, sir?'

Amerotke introduced himself and the fellow became unctuous and servile.

'My name is Sato,' he explained. 'Once servant to the divine Father Prem. I have heard of you, my Lord Amerotke. You are a child of the cap.' This was a reference to Amerotke's days as a page in the royal palace. 'You are visiting here, aren't you?' he burbled on. 'You've been asking questions. All the temple knows about it.'

'Do they now?' Amerotke smiled. He pointed to the door. 'This was divine Father Prem's chamber?'

'Oh yes. I'm just collecting his . . .' Sato's eyes filled with tears. 'I am collecting his possessions. His body is with the embalmers. Soon he will be taken across the river. The temple has its own tombs over there.' Sato smiled. 'I've been promised a chamber, a little recess near my master.'

'And well deserved too,' Amerotke replied.

He moved past Sato and walked into the chamber. It was box-like, the walls lime-washed and gleaming white. Very little remained in it except the reed bed, some stools, a chair and cushions. The shelves were empty except for a few pots and a cracked water basin.

'Where did divine Father keep his manuscripts?'

'Oh, sir, he had very little. What he wanted he took from the library. Or the manuscript room in the House of Life.'

'But the night he died he had charts of the skies, didn't he?'

'Oh yes, sir, but they have been collected, taken away.'

'Anything else?' Amerotke asked.

Sato blinked, fingers going to his lips. He really didn't like this sharp-eyed judge who came gliding up the stairs like a hunting cat. It brought back bad memories. He wanted to forget that dreadful evening, that's why he was so busy cleaning the room. Divine Prem had gone on, travelled into the West. It was best if things were kept silent, calm and peaceful.

'I asked you a question,' Amerotke prompted.

Sato sighed and sat on the edge of the bed. 'Holy Father Hani asked me the same, and do you know, sir, my master did have . . .' He coughed. 'Well, before his death, he carried a papyrus roll, tied with a piece of red cord. He took it everywhere with him. I remember that. He came up here and would lock his chamber. When I brought him some food or drink he'd always be kind. "Come in, Sato," he'd say. Yet I'd notice he'd cover the manuscript with his arm, as if he didn't want me to read or see something.'

'And did you?' Amerotke took the purse from the small pocket in his robe. He opened it and shook out a silver disc.

Sato smiled. He'd need money, particularly in the days ahead. After all, what was he but a middle-aged temple servant who liked his beer?

'Two days ago,' Sato replied, 'I brought in his evening meal. Divine Father as usual put his arm across the parchment but then he thought the cup was going to slip so he moved his hand.'

'And what did you see?'

'I am not sure.' Sato glimpsed Amerotke's annoyance. 'I think it was a beetle, a drawing of a beetle.'

'A beetle?'

'Or it might have been a scorpion. Yes, I think it was a scorpion.'

Amerotke held on to the piece of silver. 'Tell the truth.'

Sato closed his eyes. 'I-I'm sure it was a scorpion, a crude drawing of one.'

'Very good.' Amerotke pressed the piece of silver into the fleshy palm of Sato's hand then he gripped the man's thumb and squeezed it. 'And where is that drawing now?'

'I really don't know, sir. When we broke into divine

Father's room, I must admit I was curious. I looked around but I could see no trace of it.'

'And you found nothing suspicious?' Amerotke asked.

Sato shook his head.

'In the days before your master died, were he and the librarian Neria often closeted together?'

'No, no, they weren't.'

'Did Neria come here?'

Sato shook his head.

'Well,' Amerotke said exasperatedly, 'did divine Father go and visit the librarian?'

'No, sir, but,' Sato looked towards the door, 'I do think their deaths are connected.'

Sato didn't look so simple now. Amerotke glimpsed the cunning in his eyes.

'Come, Sato,' he murmured. 'Tell me what you know.'

Door: in ancient Egypt a symbol for both defence
and entry.

CHAPTER 8

In the death house of the Temple of Horus, the killer sat and watched the doctors and embalmers prepare the corpse of divine Father Prem for his final journey into the West. On a slab at the far side of the room lay the blackened remains of the archivist Neria, wrapped in white bandages. The embalmers had tried their best but what could they do with flesh charred to the bone, eyeballs turned to water, tongue and other organs shrivelled and blackened? Would Osiris, the Father of the Westerners, understand? Would Neria's Ka be allowed to travel on to the Fields of the Blessed? Neria had been a good man. When his soul was weighed in the Halls of the Dead, he might be protected from the Devourers, those evil demons who crouched beneath the scales of justice waiting for souls rejected by the gods. The killer felt no qualms. What had to be done was done. How could a woman, a pathetic creature like Hatusu, dare to wear the sacred double crown and holy coat, and perch her pretty feet on the ancient footstool of Pharaoh?

The killer had ostensibly come to pay the final respect due to a dead priest but also to ensure nothing untoward was discovered. Thankfully, the light was poor. The embalmers and purifiers were more concerned to perform the sacred rite in accordance with the ritual as laid down by the Book of the Dead.

Prem's body lay stretched out, naked, clothed only by the darkness of this underground chamber. The light of the red mortuary candles, set in silver filigree sticks, outlined the podgy contours of his corpse. The master of ceremonies now leaned over the cadaver and, with bronze hooks, completed the drawing out of the brain through the nostrils. This was gathered up and placed in a gold bowl. A priest chanted a prayer while a scribe drew a line of red ink, four inches long, on the left side of the corpse, exactly where Horus had opened the body of the divine Osiris. A deep, broad cut was made along the line with a knife of Ethiopian obsidian. An embalmer put his hands in and, murmuring a prayer, drew out the intestines, heart, lungs and liver. These, too, were placed in bowls while others washed the cavity with spiced palm wine. They withdrew. The corpse was lifted by servants and dipped in a great barrel of liquid natron. It would lie there for seventy days before they returned to stuff the corpse's belly with fine linen, sawdust and scented wool.

The killer turned and glanced across the chamber. Already the other burial items were being prepared: precious wrappings, a silver mask, a pectoral of gold symbolising Prem's Ka, his soul, soaring into the beyond. Collars and rings for the legs and toes, a precious casket on a pillow over the Book of the Dead. Canopic jars, ornamented with the heads of men, hawks, jackals and baboons, stood ready to receive the entrails and brain.

The killer watched the body sink into its huge bath of natron salt and murmured a prayer. All had gone well. Nothing had been noticed. The doctors, the physicians and embalmers were more concerned with preparing the corpse than discovering the cause of death. The killer relaxed. True, Amerotke had escaped and, because of his sharp eyes and probing mind, would have to be silenced but there was time, no need to rush. The murmuring had already begun. The whispers and gossip had spread to the bazaars and marketplaces. It would creep along the quayside, be

130

repeated in the wine shops and beer booths. Should Hatusu be Pharaoh? Could a woman, whatever her supporters might say, whatever great signs she wrought, be lord and ruler over the people of the Nine Bows?

In the garden tower Sato, helped by a jug of beer, was becoming more loquacious. He was flattered by this chief judge who had gone down the steps and brought back an earthenware jug and two cups. He was also feeling rather sorry for himself and indulged in a outpouring of woes about what might happen to him now that divine Father Prem was dead. Amerotke sipped the beer and watched. He recalled Shufoy's maxim: 'Wine and beer fill the belly and loosen the tongue.'

'Did divine Father Prem always study here?' Amerotke asked, bringing the conversation back to the matter in hand.

'Oh yes. The tower is deserted. The other chambers are used as storerooms. My master was an astronomer. In his prime he was consulted by divine Pharaoh himself.'

'But he was in no danger surely. So why were you on guard?'

'I always was,' Sato answered defensively. 'Divine Father could be absent-minded. He'd forget this or forget that. He'd go to sleep and not blow out the wick. He'd leave oil lamps near his parchments or, in the early hours, demand something to eat or drink.'

'And the night he died?'

'It was no different.' Sato pushed his lower lip out. 'I was tired.' He smiled lewdly. 'A dancing girl had deigned to notice me. I had spent the afternoon with her and a jug of beer.'

'Very nice,' Amerotke replied. 'And so you were late coming to the tower. You were, weren't you? Don't worry, I won't tell the others that.'

'I was late,' Sato confessed, 'when I came here.'

'There's something else, isn't there?' Amerotke pressed. 'Tell me the truth now.'

131

'I came here, my lord, but I had forgotten to bring some provisions, so I hurried back to the kitchen, then I returned. I climbed the steps. I noticed nothing untoward. Divine Father's chamber was closed and locked.'

'Was it always like that?'

'Sometimes.'

'But you said he was forgetful.'

'Not about his chamber, he wasn't. Anyway, I thought he might be in the tower, either studying or praying. He didn't like to be disturbed. I went up and peered out.'

'What was he doing?'

'Kneeling. He had a shawl over his shoulders and his favourite straw hat on.'

'At night?'

'It kept his head warm against the cold night breezes.'

'And then?'

'I came back down here and waited.'

'Then divine Father Prem joined you?'

'He came down the steps, I heard him wheezing. He wore a ring on his finger, a silver one. It fell off. I went to retrieve it. When I came back, divine Father was in his chamber at his desk. I placed the ring there.' He pointed to a small, polished table, inlaid with lapis lazuli, just within the doorway. 'Divine Father then closed the door and bolted it. A short while later came that terrible screaming.' Sato pulled a face, the tears rolling down his plump cheeks. 'The rest you know.'

'No, I don't.' Amerotke smiled. 'Tell me.'

'I fled down the steps, out of the tower. I began to scream. Guards and servants appeared. Then all the other priests.'

'Who, precisely?'

'Oh, all of them.'

'And?'

'Well, the door was forced, divine Father's corpse was found lying on the bed, his head smashed in, his face scarred.'

'But no sign of the club?'

'Now that is something new.' Sato drank noisily from his cup.

'What is?' Amerotke asked.

'I didn't tell holy Father Hani but divine Father Prem had a club with a panther's paw on the end.'

'I beg your pardon?'

'I . . . I only remembered it just now,' Sato stammered. 'Divine Father used to laugh about it. He said it was a reminder of the Season of the Hyena, the time of famine and sword.'

'And, of course, the club's gone?'

'Yes, my lord, it has.'

Amerotke got up and went to the window. Everything made sense until it came to the escape of the killer. He looked over his shoulder. The door to the chamber had not been repaired and he could see where it had been forced. But how did the murderer escape? He peered down over the sill. It would take even a skilled soldier some time to fasten a rope and clamber down; even then his knees and arms would be bruised by those sharp stones.

'Let me see the top of the tower.'

Sato put his beer cup down and led him up the steps. The door at the top was open, allowing in a cool breeze. Amerotke walked out. The top of the tower was square, its curtain wall high and crenellated with narrow slits for archers and defenders. There was a small table in the centre, weather-stained and cracked. Sato explained that Prem used it for his maps and charts. Amerotke walked to the wall and stared out. The afternoon was drawing on, the light breeze was cool and refreshing. Below him he could see people walking; he caught various smells from the kitchens and vine groves. The tower also provided a breathtaking view of Thebes. He glimpsed the soaring pylons of the House of a Million Years, the gold-tipped obelisks, the Avenue of Sphinxes, the great red flagpoles of the temples. He leaned over, a dizzying drop. The tower was clear on all sides except

133

on one, where a cluster of rose bushes and other plants grew. Amerotke walked carefully round the tower. It was strewn with pebbled sand to ensure people kept their footing. He could see no mark of violence. He paused and crouched down and picked up a knotted piece of twine. It was like horsehair but tougher and greased with oil. He took it over to Sato.

'Strands from a rope, aren't they?'

'Divine Father didn't keep one here,' said Sato, 'He only brought out food, parchment, his box of styli, pens and ink.'

Amerotke sat down with his back to the wall. He twirled the piece of twine between his fingers. 'Very clever,' he murmured. 'I wonder if my theory is built on sand or rock.' He got to his feet. 'Sato, I thank you.'

'My lord?'

Amerotke clapped him on the shoulder. 'You've been of more help than you think.'

Sato opened the door and listened as the chief judge went down the stairs. Sato followed him slowly and stood in the doorway, just as he had the night divine Father Prem had been killed. Hadn't he seen something then? Something untoward? What was it? The chief judge had been very generous; with the silver piece he had given him he might be able to buy the charms of that dancing girl who was now so elusive. She hadn't been so cold when they had lain together and she had writhed beneath him. Sato sighed and sat down. He tried to recall what he had seen that night. He licked his lips. That girl, so young and lithe, he'd seek her out.

Amerotke left the tower and walked round the rose bushes he'd glimpsed. Their stems were thick with sharp thorns. He moved carefully and then he saw the broken stems, the tendrils of twine. He closed his eyes and murmured a prayer.

'You have shown your face to me, Divine One, and you have smiled on me.'

'I didn't know you were interested in roses.'

Amerotke spun round. Shufoy was watching him, staff in

134

one hand, leather bag in the other. On either side of him stood Prenhoe and Asural, both looking rather woebegone and dusty.

'We've been looking for you everywhere.' The chief of temple police mopped his brow. 'My lord, I am tired, I am hungry.' Asural rubbed the tip of his podgy nose.

'Well,' Amerotke replied, 'if you insist on walking around armed to the teeth and dressed in that leather corselet, no wonder. But come.'

He led them through the temple grounds past the vineyard into the shade of acacia trees where butterflies flitted among the flowers and the perfumed air made the bees buzz in frenzied haste. In the far distance the divine lake shimmered in the weakening sun. Amerotke made them sit down. He stretched out and stared up into the trees, watching a black-tipped hoppoe bird swaying on a branch as if it, too, was savouring the afternoon breeze.

'Don't go to sleep.' Shufoy edged over and pushed his grotesque face close to his master's. 'We have things to tell you.'

'And I have a great deal to tell you.'

Amerotke helped Asural take off his leather corselet. He gave Shufoy his ring and sent him off to the temple kitchens. Soon Shufoy returned with servants bearing platters of freshly baked bread, roast goose, bowls of fruit. These were laid out on the grass before them.

'They are preparing a feast,' Shufoy beamed. 'The Lady Vechlis says we are all to attend.'

Amerotke smiled and let them slake their thirst.

'Now,' he said, 'tell me about Pepy.'

'There's very little to say,' Asural grumbled, 'because there's very little of him left. The Maijodou are in charge of the investigation so I couldn't discover much. Pepy may have been a brilliant scholar but he was a scrounger, begging food and wine. Then he suddenly hired that chamber and carried more silver and gold than a rich merchant.'

'And the fire?' Amerotke asked.

'Both his chamber and the tavern beneath were gutted from floor to ceiling. All we saw of Pepy and his courtesan were their skulls and some blackened bones.'

'So, everything there has been destroyed?'

Asural dabbed at the sweat on his neck. 'All gone,' he breathed.

'The sages remark,' said Shufoy mournfully, 'that a silly woman acts on impulse, is foolish and knows nothing. To this fool she says, "Stolen waters are sweet and bread tastes better when eaten in secret."'

'What are you prattling about, Shufoy?'

'The courtesan,' Shufoy retorted. 'In Pepy's case, her secret bread led to death.'

'What was the source of his sudden wealth?' Amerotke asked, ignoring his enigmatic servant.

Asural shook his head. 'No one knows.'

'Was there talk of manuscripts for sale by Pepy?'

'No. Why, did he steal one from here?'

'He may have done,' Amerotke murmured.

'The wages of sin are death,' Shufoy intoned. 'Can a man carry fire inside his shirt without setting his clothes alight? Can he walk on red-hot coals without burning his feet?'

'We are truly in perilous times.' Prenhoe now decided to show his knowledge. 'I had a dream last night, master. I was sitting by the banks of the Nile and this woman, like a crocodile, came out to copulate with me.'

'That's enough,' Amerotke snapped. 'Let me tell you what I've found here.'

'One moment, master.' Asural shifted on the grass. 'Do you remember Nehemu?'

'How can I forget him?'

'And his threats?'

Asural searched Amerotke's face. 'You've had a warning, haven't you?'

'Yes.' Amerotke sighed. 'A carob seedcake was delivered

to my house wrapped in linen and placed in a sycamore box.'

'What?' Shufoy bawled.

'Well,' Asural replied, ignoring the dwarf, 'you can forget the Amemets.'

'I beg your pardon?'

'The Guild of Assassins disappeared in the Season of Planting. They followed their master north and haven't been seen since.'

Amerotke closed his eyes. In a trice he was back in those secret passageways beneath the Great Pyramid: the roof was falling in, crushing those black-garbed killers.

'Master?'

Amerotke opened his eyes.

'I heard rumours,' Shufoy said, 'that they'd re-organised with new members.'

'Oh, there was a remnant left in Thebes,' Asural declared. 'Nothing but pebbles rattling in an empty jar. Master, I want to take you across the Nile to meet Lehket, a member of the Society of the Undead.'

Amerotke ignored Prenhoe's swift hiss of disapproval.

'The undead!' Shufoy exclaimed, mouth full of meat. He swallowed hard. 'What would a group of lepers have to do with the Amemets?'

'Lohket was one of them,' Asural explained, 'before the contagion struck. I've been to see him, master. He will speak to you. Anyway, you were going to tell us what's happening here.'

Amerotke hid his unease. What could Lehket tell him? Was it a trap? Some wily ruse to lure him into an ambush?

'He's safe, master,' Asural added softly as if he could read Amerotke's thoughts. 'He'll do you no harm but, like his kind, he must be paid in gold.'

'How did you find him?'

Asural grinned. 'You have your laws, I have my spies. Lehket will see us tomorrow after dawn.'

'And the other business?' Amerotke asked. 'The young woman married to two men?'

'I have it in hand,' Shufoy declared sententiously. 'But what has been happening at the Temple of Horus?' Although he had been filling his belly with bread and roast goose, he had been studying Amerotke closely. He sensed something was dreadfully wrong. His master was nervous, irritable. He'd hardly touched the food but he'd drunk his beer rather quickly.

'I was attacked,' Amerotke replied.

'That was foolish,' Shufoy snapped. He waved a finger in Amerotke's face. 'You went somewhere by yourself, didn't you? I have warned you before about that! If the Lady Norfret got to know!'

Amerotke seized Shufoy's fingers and squeezed. 'Well, she won't, will she? But, more importantly, I know how divine Father Prem was killed. He was in his garden tower and the killer called on him. It must have been someone Prem trusted and liked. They probably had a drink of wine or beer. Only what Prem drank had a potion in it which made him sleepy. His killer seized Prem's Hyksos war club and struck him on the temple. Prem's old head would have split like a soft-shelled egg. The killer then turned to the real reason for his visit, the roll of papyrus Prem carried everywhere. Only he misjudged the time. That drunken guard Sato turned up. The killer hid Prem's corpse beneath the bed, took his shawl and straw hat and went up onto the roof.' Amerotke paused. 'Or perhaps the killer was more cunning. Maybe Sato didn't surprise him. Whatever, the important thing was that the killer had to leave the tower unnoticed.' He scratched the side of his head. 'Some details are not clear yet. Anyway, the killer takes Prem's straw hat, his shawl and, yes, his ring, then goes up onto the tower.'

'Of course!' Prenhoe interrupted. 'And he pretends to be divine Father!'

'Precisely. In the gathering darkness, the back of one

138

shaved head looks like any other, particularly if it's covered by a straw hat and the shoulders by a shawl. Sato, being deferential as always, would think it was his master and return to his guard post. Eventually the killer came down the steps. He had the key to divine Father's room but he had to distract Sato long enough to get inside.'

'So he drops the ring?'

'Yes. Sato, being the faithful guard and servant he is, trots down after it. The killer then unlocks the door and goes into the chamber. It is shadowy and he keeps his back to the door. Sato places the ring on the table. The door is then locked and barred.' Amerotke paused. He gazed up to where he could see the garden tower soaring above the trees.

"This is where the killer showed great cunning. He emits a terrible scream as if Prem's being slain. Of course, he is simply playing a trick. He has taken Prem's corpse from beneath the bed and placed it on the top. Perhaps it was then that he actually killed the old man, striking his forehead with that club.'

'But how did he get out?' Asural demanded.

Amerotke grinned. 'When we think of an escape from a chamber high in a tower, we naturally think of someone going down to get away. Prem's killer was more cunning. Before he left the top of the tower, he slung a small rope ladder over the battlments down to the window of Prem's chamber.'

Shufoy clapped his hands, his little, ugly face chortling with glee. 'He left the chamber and climbed back up, kicking the shutters closed as he went.'

Amerotke nodded. 'Once he was on the top, he unhooked the rope ladder and threw it into the rose bushes below. Then he had two choices. He could either wait on the top of the tower until the door was forced, then slip in among the rest. Alternatively, he could follow Sato down the steps, stay in one of the chambers below and then join the others when they came to break down the door.'

'But why such subtlety?' Asural asked. 'Why not just poison divine Father Prem or put an arrow in his throat? Wasn't the killer taking a risk?'

'Yes, I thought of that myself,' Amerotke replied. He paused, listening to a peacock shriek from the gardens on the far side of the trees. 'I have a number of explanations for that. First, Prem had to be separated from his roll of papyrus. The divine Father had to be killed and his precious manuscript filched. That would take some planning and some plotting. The killer would have to be assured that, when he struck, the manuscript was at hand.'

'Yes.' Asural filled his beer cup. 'An old priest like Prem would probably keep such a papyrus well hidden. Maybe his killer expressed an interest and Prem decided to share his knowledge.'

'Secondly,' Amerotke continued, plucking at the grass, 'Prem was a man of certain habits. From what I gather, he was usually either in the library or the garden tower. When he was in the latter, Sato was always somewhere around, hence the clever preparations. The rope ladder was probably taken there in advance and left in the shadows at the top of the tower. Finally,' Amerotke wafted away a fly, 'the killer is deliberately creating an atmosphere of unease and terror. Neria's death was sudden and brutal. He was probably coming up the steps from the vaults when he was covered in oil and turned into a living torch. I suspect the same thing happened to our wandering scholar with his concubine friend. Brutal, mysterious death unnerves a priestly community unused to violence.'

'And the papyrus scroll? The Hyksos war club? The rope ladder?' Prenhoe asked.

'I'd wager the papyrus roll has been destroyed. The club and rope ladder were thrown into the rose bushes and later retrieved. I agree, Asural, the killer took a chance but, in the end, he was very successful. The only time he was ever in danger was climbing from Prem's chamber to the top of the tower, but bearing in mind darkness had fallen and it would only take a very short while, the gamble was worth it. Everything else could be explained.'

'And the motive?' Asural asked.

'It is something to do with the council meeting and divine Hatusu's accession.' Amerotke abruptly stopped. 'What is the killer really trying to do?' he whispered to himself. 'Werc Neria and Prem truly friends of the divine Hatusu and her court?' he asked aloud. 'Oh, Ma'at, be my witness!' he exclaimed.

'What's the matter?' Shufoy asked sharply. 'You rebuke me for quoting proverbs and being mysterious!'

'Can't you see?' Amerotke smiled. 'Either way, the killer cannot lose. Here we have two faithful temple servants killed at a time when the priests are debating divine Hatusu's accession. Some people will think they were murdered because they found something which would prove a woman cannot sit on the throne of Egypt. And our wandering scribe Pepy's cynicism was famous.'

'So all three deaths,' said Asural, 'could be portrayed as divine Pharaoh's attempt to stifle debate.'

'Yes, they could,' Amerotke replied. 'On the other hand, when the divine Hatusu learns that the murdered men found important evidence to support her and were brutally slain for it and the evidence stolen, her rage will know no bounds. What was Neria carrying when he died? What did Pepy steal and sell from the library? What was in divine Father's secret roll of papyrus? I know the divine Hatusu, she will lash out and, in doing so, will provoke even greater enmity among the priestly caste. Moreover, the killer has soured the council meeting. He has created an atmosphere of terror. So we must regard our killer as a hunter who is trying to corner the divine Hatusu.'

'And what do you think the conclusion will be?' Shufoy demanded.

'If I had to give a decision in the Hall of Two Truths,'

141

Amerotke declared, 'it would be that this council meeting will lead to nothing. Neither side will have their way. The doubts and uncertainties will flourish and, one way or another, divine Hatusu, Senenmut, even myself, will take the blame for these murders.'

'And you have a solution?' Shufoy was now alarmed by what his master was involved in.

'There are two solutions, my dear Shufoy. First, we must find evidence that a woman can be Pharaoh. Secondly, we must unmask the killer.'

Geb: an Egyptian Earth God, often depicted as a
crocodile.

CHAPTER 9

The great double doors of Lebanese cedar had been closed.
The light from the torches, candles and cressets glittered in
the mirror-like bronze sheets on the door. Amerotke studied
the shimmering glare. It reminded him of sunlight on water.
He made himself comfortable on the cushions and pushed
away the small table in front of him covered in gold plates,
cups and silver bowls. The banqueting hall of the Temple of
Horus was a splendid chamber with red and gold pillars and
walls covered in glorious paintings depicting scenes from
the life of the gods. The motif of the Golden Hawk was
everywhere. On the pillars inscriptions had been carved.
Amerotke smiled as he read one:

> Beer and wine tear the soul to pieces.
> A man who gives himself up to drink is
>   a camel without a goad.
> A house without bread, its walls are holed
>   and tottering and the door is about to fall.

A group of dwarfs, one of whom looked remarkably like
Shufoy, led splendid dogs on silver leashes: bassets, grey-
hounds, jackals dressed in scarlet jackets shot through with
threads of gold and emerald.

Hani and his wife sat at the top table. Slaves of many

nationalities, dressed in white kilts, served platters of red cabbage, sesame seed, aniseed and cumin. These were the hors d'oeuvres to dry the throat and make the belly crave for the ice-cold beer which was served. Amerotke had wisely decided to ignore this.

A hushed silence fell as Hani staggered to his feet, a golden goblet in his hand. He raised the goblet and all heads turned to the far end of the hall where the huge, limestone statue of Horus stood, its hawk's head plated with gold. Hani intoned the prayer:

> Turn your face to us, oh Golden Hawk,
> Whose wings span both worlds.
> Oh Bird of Light who drives the darkness
> beneath him.

A murmur of approbation greeted his words then the main courses were brought in – roast geese and quail, legs of small calves adorned with ham frills. In the far corner the music women of the temple struck up a tune with double flute, lyre and harp, echoed by the muted singing of a choir who clapped their hands, giving the music a rhythmic trance-like cadence. Pages moved round the different tables. On each they placed a small wooden mummy in a miniature coffin. As they did so, the pages murmured: 'Look at this then drink and make merry for, after death, you will end like this.'

Shufoy immediately pocketed his and returned to his conversation with Prenhoe. Amerotke leaned closer to listen in. Shufoy was determined to make himself a well-known seller of cures and potions in the markets and bazaars of Thebes and he was doing his loquacious best to persuade Prenhoe to support him.

'I tell you,' Shufoy murmured, 'if you take a woman's urine and mix wheat in it, you can determine if she'll have a boy. Mix barley and you'll discover whether it is going to be a girl.'

146

Amerotke bit his lip and did his best to control his laughter.

'Master, do you think this is funny?'

'Well, if a woman's pregnant,' Amerotke replied, 'it is bound to be either a boy or a girl.'

'Yes, but by the different samples you can predict which the child is going to be.'

'How?' Amerotke asked curiously.

'By the discolouration that takes place.' Shufoy gestured round the hall. 'I could do so much business here, master.' He pointed to the different wigs worn by the priests and their wives; these were all now drenched in the beautiful cakes of perfume given to them as they had come in. Amerotke had refused his. 'Most of them now feel good, perfumed and relaxed under their wigs. Afterwards they will suffer from indigestion. They will need greyhound's foot, date seed mixed with ass's milk and served in olive oil. Or couch grass and powdered . . .'

Amerotke laughed and turned away. He was about to pick up his wine cup when he was distracted by a scream from the other side of the hall. High Priest Hathor had sprung to his feet, one hand round his throat, the other clutching his belly. The pretty young concubine sitting next to him was staring up in horror. Hathor lurched forward, hand lashing out. He overturned the table, spilling cups and dishes to the floor. His face had turned puce, his eyes were bulging, a white froth had appeared on his lips. Amerotke watched appalled as the high priest staggered towards him. Was he having a fit? The music died. Servants hurried up but Hathor gestured with his hand. He fell to his knees, mouth opening and shutting, and then crashed to the floor, arms stretched out, legs twitching. Amerotke recovered his wits and sprang up. He turned the body over, ignoring the pool of urine staining the man's kilt. He seized Hathor's chin and put two fingers down his mouth – perhaps something was stuck. But he could feel nothing. He knew the priest was dying. His skin was clammy and cold, the pulse in his neck faint. His jagged teeth scored Amerotke's fingers as he withdrew his hand. Others gathered round. A temple physician was sent for but Hathor was beyond help. He gave one spasmodic jerk, legs thrashing, then his head rolled to one side.

'He has gone,' Amerotke murmured.

'Clear the hall! Clear the hall!' Hani shouted.

Temple guards appeared carrying calfskin shields and spears. Retainers, servants, the dancing girls, concubines and musicians were summarily driven out. Hathor's corpse was lifted and placed on a makeshift couch of cushions. The temple physician came and crouched beside him, prodding his stomach, listening to his chest, pulling back the lids of the staring eyes. Like Amerotke he was concerned at how cold the corpse was.

'What was he eating and drinking?'

High Priest Amun hurried across. He picked up a tray left by one of the servants and collected the platters and cups from Hathor's table. The physician examined them carefully and shook his head.

'What is it?' Hani asked.

'Holy Father,' the physician replied, 'I cannot be certain but High Priest Hathor, his death is . . .'

'Poison?' Osiris intervened. 'He has been poisoned, hasn't he?'

The physician nodded.

'With what?' Amerotke asked.

The physician shook his head. 'My lord, I don't know but it is easy enough to buy powders to kill a man in a few heartbeats in the bazaars of Thebes.'

The remaining priests were staring accusingly at Hani.

'We thought we were safe here,' Amun declared. 'But now it seems that in the Temple of Horus no man is protected.'

The other four, clustering around him, agreed.

'We should leave,' Isis stated. 'The council meeting should be brought to an end.'

His words were greeted by a chorous of assent.

'That can't happen,' Amerotke put in since Hani seemed too fuddled in his wits to respond. Vechlis was no help either. She was staring open-mouthed at the corpse, one purple-nailed hand raised, as if she couldn't really believe he was dead.

'Why not?' Osiris demanded. 'Your own physician has said Hathor has been poisoned. How high must the tally of corpses rise? Until all of us are dead? Is that why we are here? Will Her Majesty then appoint men more to her liking?'

'If you repeat such a remark outside this hall,' said Amerotke sternly, 'you could face a charge of treason!'

Osiris's face paled; he blinked and muttered something under his breath.

Amerotke grasped Hani's hand. 'Holy Father, we have only this physician's word that Hathor was poisoned. He may not have been.' He sounded more confident than he really was. 'But if murder has taken place then it's wrong to apportion guilt without a proper inquiry.' He jabbed a finger in the direction of Osiris. 'What makes you suspect either your host or divine Pharaoh had a hand in this man's death? We should be careful of what we say.' He glanced over his shoulder to where Shufoy and Prenhoe stood watching from the shadows of a pillar.

'My Lord Amerotke is right,' Hani declared, recovering his wits. 'I will summon others to examine the corpse.'

And, spinning on his heel, led them out of the banqueting hall. They went down a passageway into a small chamber, used as a waiting room for guests or special visitors to the temple. A seating ledge had been built into the wall. The high priests, together with Vechlis and Amerotke, sat in silence while Hani barred the door, then leaned against it, his head back. Amerotke could see he was trembling; whatever the truth, Hani would bear some responsibility for these terrible murders. After all, he was the host, responsible for their lives and safety.

'I am sorry.' Hani stumbled over his words. He took the gorgeous pendant from round his neck and almost threw it on the floor. He then unclasped his ceremonial bracelets and handed then to his wife. He lowered himself to the floor, sitting with his back to the door, his head going backwards and forwards as if lost in a trance.

'We should not make accusations,' Vechlis declared. She went and crouched by her husband, taking a cushion to make him more comfortable.

'What do you suggest, my Lord Amerotke?' asked Isis.

'We are here on divine Pharaoh's orders. You all know what you are here to debate. If we leave, nothing is resolved. Divine Pharaoh will simply order us to continue our debate in another place at another time.' Amerotke paused. Aye, he reflected, and by then the damage would be done.

His words were greeted with protests and exclamations. Amun jumped to his feet and walked to the door, beating against it with his fists.

'I came here to talk, not to die!' he exclaimed.

Hani, helped by his wife, got to his feet and rubbed his face in his hands.

'No one is going to die,' he said slowly. 'Lord Amerotke is correct. We have important matters to discuss.'

There was a knock on the door. Amerotke went and opened it. Asural, who had not attended the feast, stood there, grim-faced.

'I heard what happened, my lord,' he whispered. 'Another physician has examined the corpse, as has Shufoy, who has some knowledge of poisons. Holy Father Hathor was murdered.'

'You'd best come in.' Amerotke led him into the chamber and closed the door. 'Our worst fears are realised,' he said. 'The captain of my temple guard assures me that Hathor was poisoned.'

'How?' Amun asked.

'I don't know, my lord,' Asural replied quickly. 'Both physicians, as well as my Lord Amerotke's manservant, say the venom was quick-acting.'

'So it must have been administered at the feast,' said Hani.

'Yes, my lord.'

'In which case,' Amerotke concluded, 'it must have been during the first course. But the food was served on platters. Hathor was given what we all ate.'

'And the same is true of the beer,' added Hani.

'But all our beer cups were on the table,' Isis pointed out.

'What are you saying?' Vechlis demanded.

'We all came into the chamber,' Amerotke replied slowly. 'We each took our seat. On the table before us was nothing except plates, platters and a beer cup. The first course was served, both food and drink, and then the plates and cups were cleared away. So the poison must already have been in Hathor's beer cup, put there before the banquet began. The hot food was served and Hathor, like the rest of us, would have drunk his beer quickly.'

'Is that possible?' Hani asked.

'Why not?' said Amun. 'How many of us remember looking into our beer cups before we were served? It would be easy to put in a touch of powder which dissolved when the beer was poured. If Hathor tasted anything untoward he would, like the rest of us, think it was the spices, not realising until it was too late.'

'And,' said Amerotke, 'it would be futile to question those who came in and out of the banqueting hall before we took our seats. The list would be endless – servants, musicians. It could be done in the blink of an eye.'

'What are you going to do, Amerotke?' Osiris asked. 'Set up a court of inquiry?'

'It may come to that,' the chief judge replied. 'However,

my Lord Hani, tomorrow morning I must leave here. I have business in the Necropolis.'

'Fashioning out your tomb?' Isis taunted.

'My life rests in the palm of my god,' Amerotke snapped. He turned to Hani, unwilling to be drawn into personal invective with these spiteful priests. 'My Lord Hani, the matter is urgent.'

'So you will need the temple barge?' Hani asked.

Amerotke nodded. 'My scribe Prenhoe will stay here. I shall leave in the morning but be back by midday. For the rest,' Amerotke got to his feet, 'there is little more to be said or done but I urge you all to take care.' He bowed towards Hani, the others he ignored and walked out of the chamber.

He returned to his quarters. He told Shufoy what had happened and made his excuses for the night.

'I have my own chamber,' Shufoy declared. He hitched his robe round his shoulders. 'As befits a practitioner of medicine.'

Amerotke slouched in a chair and smiled at this most irrepressible servant and friend.

'Are you really a practitioner, Shufoy?'

'By the time I'm finished, master, I'll know more than the quacks and hucksters who give themselves the title of physician. I will specialise.' Shufoy's lower lip came up, a sign that he was determined on a course of action. 'I'll become a guardian of the anus, skilled in healing diseases of the bowel.'

'That,' Amerotke murmured, 'is perhaps a fitting statement to end a day like this.'

He took off his bracelets and rings, the pectoral and his white robe. He tightened his loincloth about him and lay down on the bed. Shufoy came over and pulled the linen sheets up over his shoulders.

'Search the chamber,' Amerotke murmured sleepily.

'I already have, master. No asp, scorpion or venomous snake will dare come in here. I have taken the fat of a mongoose and rubbed it on the walls.'

Amerotke smiled and fell asleep, his curiosity satisfied about the rather peculiar smell in this once pleasant and fragrant chamber.

He slept late, Shufoy had to shake him awake. He still felt heavy-headed. He went out onto the balcony which faced north, from where the breath of Amun came. He knelt, forehead to the ground, and prayed for himself and his family. IIe then swam in the sacred lake and allowed Shufoy to massage oil into his legs and arms. He shaved while Shufoy held the mirror, chattering all the time. The little man was full of his new remedies and potions. Amerotke dressed. He agreed to take his war belt and Shufoy insisted on collecting his little horn bow and quiver of arrows. They ate breakfast with the others out on the grass which was still slightly damp from the morning dew. They could hear the hymns of the priests in the temple as they celebrated the first service of the day.

The sun was rising strong and hot, dispelling the mists, as they made their way down to the small quayside. Amerotke clasped Prenhoe's hand, told him to be careful and then walked along the red-brick paved way to the quayside steps and the waiting barge.

It was a long, rakish craft, called *Glory of Horus*, made out of strengthened reeds tightly woven together. It had one mast, its sail already loosened, and the high poop was carved in the shape of a hawk's head. In the elaborate raised stern sat the principal boatman, hand on the tiller. Amidships, on either side, were two rowers. Above the wooden partitions leading down to the hold a small awning had been erected against the sun, with cushions and blankets beneath it. Amerotke, Asural and Shufoy took their seats. The tillerman shouted out an order and the boat pushed away from the quayside, going along the Nile before it turned through the swirling river mist across to the Necropolis.

The quayside and banks were now busy; the crew stopped to watch priests and priestesses from a minor temple come out along the river to practise their joyous rites in a cacophony of castanets, flutes, cow horns, cymbals and tambourines. Men and women swayed to the sound of these instruments, dancing round the sacred statues they carried. The rhythm increased and the worshippers waved their arms and kicked up their legs at a pace bordering on frenzy. Danga dwarfs with huge straw 'Pharaoh crowns' on their heads turned somersaults and rent their clothes.

'We should join in,' one of the oarsmen bellowed.

This was greeted by raucous obscenities from the other sailors. Shufoy waved his hand deprecatingly. Asural, more sententious, declared they were drunk and should be careful not to fall into the river. 'There are crocodile pools here,' he warned.

Amerotke glanced above the trees and glimpsed the terraces, temples and mansions of Thebes. He wondered what Norfret and the two boys were doing. The tillerman shouted an order, the boat turned, the oars rising and dipping. The sail, bearing the arms of Horus, billowed out; the sailors pulled at the ropes, turning and twisting the sail so it caught the morning breeze. There was a thud and clatter from the hold. Amerotke, alarmed, looked at one of the rowers.

'It's only the water jars.' The man smiled in a show of jagged teeth. 'I just hope the fools sealed them properly. Our food and clothes are down there also.'

Amerotke relaxed. The boat picked up speed. The oarsmen rested on their oars as the breeze caught their craft and sent it faster. They would only bend their backs and lift the oars if the breeze failed.

It did. The sail hung flat and loose. The tillerman shouted; one of the rowers began to sing: 'My girl has breasts, soft and juicy, more fertile than any tree.' The refrain was taken up by his companions. The boat creaked, the splashing oars creating their own rhythm.

Amerotke glanced over his shoulder and glimpsed the scaly green head and neck of a crocodile, eyes just above the water, swimming directly towards them. Not an uncommon sight. It was still early morning. Crocodiles usually absorbed the heat of the sun before they became frenzied hunters.

Asural had followed his glance. He grasped Amerotke's arm. 'Look, master, behind us!'

Other crocodiles had appeared. Five, six, seven. More were grouping on the port side. The tillerman had also noticed them and was standing up, a worried expression on his face.

'What is the matter?' he shouted.

As if in answer, the craft shuddered as though it had hit a rock. There was banging along the starboard side, followed by other crashes and blows.

'They're attacking!' one of the oarsmen screamed, letting go of his oar. He sprang to his feet and stared over the side.

Shufoy swiftly notched an arrow to his bow. Asural and Amerotke drew their swords. The boat swayed and tipped. No doubt about it now. The crocodiles were closing in, submerging, and hitting the boat beneath the waterline with their hard, scaly snouts.

'It's impossible!' The oarsman turned.

Amerotke gazed in horror. A huge crocodile lurched out of the water, head and jaws swinging, a terrible sight. Its sharp-teethed snout caught the oarsman on the side of the neck. Amerotke sprang forward but the man went overboard. Shufoy loosed an arrow but it was futile. The man came up, mouth screaming. Other crocodiles converged, turning and twisting in the water, tearing at the man. One huge beast seized him, cruel jaws clasping him round the waist, thrashing the water which bubbled and frothed, red with blood. The tillerman was shouting out orders, trying to impose discipline.

'What has attracted them?' Asural gasped.

Amerotke pushed the cushions aside, drew back the cover over the hold and went down the small set of wooden steps. Two or three jars had overturned. The drinking water lapped around his sandals. There was something else, a smell which reminded Amerotke of the temple slaughter yards. Again there was a crash against the side. He could see water trickling in as the hard casing began to split. He leaned down, scooped up the water and sniffed. He ran back up the steps.

'It's blood!' he yelled. 'The jars below are full of blood!'

Asural, Shufoy and the others gaped at him. They realised the terrible danger they were in. A barge like this should never carry blood or flesh of any kind, particularly in a stretch of the river notorious for its crocodile pools.

'The beasts smelt it,' Asural gasped. He steadied himself as the boat again juddered and jarred. All kept well away from the side. Amerotke pushed the men back to the rowing benches and, sitting down, seized the dead man's oar.

'Come on!' he yelled. 'Pull! Pull or we'll sink!'

The oarsmen obeyed. The tillerman grasped the great arm of the rudder. Amerotke leaned over the oar. Asural stood on guard one side, Shufoy on the other. Amerotke felt the sweat break out and shooting pains in his back and arms but at last they established a rhythm. He tried to concentrate on rowing, ignoring the shouts of Shufoy. They were moving too sluggishly, the rents and tears in the hull were growing larger, the water pouring in. Already they were lower in the water than they had been. Shufoy kept releasing arrows. Crocodiles in a frenzy would turn on anything including their own but the dwarf's arrows made little impact on the hard, scaly armour of the huge river beasts.

The barge was moving slowly. A breeze sprang up but they hadn't time to unfurl and manage the sail. All Amerotke could think of were those shattering blows. Now and again a crocodile would lurch out of the water with a snap of jaws. One of the rowers panicked but Asural, with the tip of his sword, forced him back to his post. The look-out on the poop had now taken his handbell and was ringing it over the river, the accepted signal of a boat in distress. Water, tinged with red, began to bubble up from the hold.

Amerotke closed his eyes and prayed to Ma'at. If the barge foundered, there would be little they could do. The crocodiles would swarm in. Accidents like this happened on the Nile – young men, drunk, impervious to the danger of these river monsters, were not infrequent victims. The crocodiles had acquired a taste for human flesh, savaging the corpses of the drowned, attacking the unwary along the mudflats.

Abruptly, as if in answer to his prayer, Amerotke heard the sound of another bell. Looking to his left he saw a huge red and green barge break out of the mist. Its high poop, carved like a lotus, was moving swiftly towards them. Amerotke tried to keep the rowers at their posts but one sprang up and hurried to the side, shouting and waving. A crocodile, swifter than the rest, closed in, like a cat leaping for a bird. It took the man under the arm, sweeping him off his feet into the water.

'Stay still!' Amerotke shouted. 'Pull in your oars!'

The men did so. The approaching barge was now closer. Its rowers were half-naked women and Amerotke realised this must be some wedding party or celebration. The tillerman had the sense to bring his boat alongside and the two boats jarred together. Amerotke was fearful theirs would tip over but it stayed steady.

There was shouting. Rope ladders were lowered. Amerotke helped Shufoy onto one of them, then Asural. The rest of the crew clambered up and Amerotke followed. He was aware of faces, hands stretching out, and then he was pulled over the side and just lay in a heap on the deck.

He was aware of soft hands touching his face, of being moved, half carried, to the great awning under the sail near the mast. He smelt rich perfumes, glimpsed gaily-coloured cloths, red, yellow, blue and green. Soft cushions. A cup of chilled wine was pushed into his hands. He sipped it but felt sick and just sat, head down. His whole body throbbed with pain. He sipped again and then glanced up at his saviours. The barge was almost as long as a war galley. It was decorated with countless bouquets of flowers, coloured streamers, small tables filled with food and cups. A young man, a flower garland round his neck, crouched down before him.

'You were not invited to our wedding,' he smiled. 'But you are most welcome.'

Amerotke clasped him round the shoulder. 'I promise you,' he gasped, 'I will hire a chantry priest to sing your praises to the gods!'

He glanced round. Shufoy and Asural were in no better state than he was. One of the sailors had fainted. The others were sobbing in a mixture of grief and relief at what had happened. Amerotke staggered to his feet and, holding his wine cup, walked along the deck to the foot of the raised poop. The barge was turning. He looked down. The temple barge lay low in the water. All around it the scaly backs of the crocodiles were wrenching at the hard reed hull, eager to get at the blood still drawing them in with its iron-tang smell.

'To do green things': an ancient Egyptian phrase
meaning to do good things.

CHAPTER 10

Sato, the temple servant, dispiritedly climbed the stairs and went into his chamber above the storerooms in the Temple of Horus. It was a rather mean-smelling place with a box-like window and a few simple sticks of furniture. Sato put his face in his hands and rubbed away the sweat. He fought back tears of self-pity. Last night he had tried to search out the girl who had entertained him so generously only a few days before. He'd shown her the silver Amerotke had given him but she would have nothing to do with him.

'Go away!' she cried and flounced off, hips swaying, bracelets clicking. Sato couldn't understand it. He wanted to talk to her, explain what he knew.

He'd searched the temple for Chief Judge Amerotke, asking this person and that. All had shaken their heads. 'Oh, he's gone away,' one of the temple guards told him. 'Crossed the river to the Necropolis.'

Sato had then been given a number of tasks. He'd grumbled loudly; as Father Prem's former servant he was in mourning and this should be respected. Sato had also listened to the gossip. The temple had been shocked by the sudden death of High Priest Hathor. Sato, eager to show his knowledge, had, once again, told all who would listen about the death of his own master. No one was really interested. Perhaps he should leave here.

He stared across at the small statue of Isis standing on a wooden plinth in the corner of the room. She was Sato's favourite deity, yet all the statue did was provoke memories of that pleasure-house girl. Well, perhaps he should make his presence felt. The only person who'd treated him kindly had been Chief Judge Amerotke. Sato had said as much to the other servants. Perhaps if he could rack his brains and recall what he had seen more precisely, Amerotke might reward him again, even find him more fitting employment away from this place of sudden and brutal death. Sato lifted his head and, for the first time, noticed a flask of wine on the table. He sprang up and walked across. The wine flagon was beautiful, glazed pottery with pictures of storks, geese and other birds. Its cover of stiffened papyrus tied round the rim with twine was also clean and new. Sato seized a cup. No doubt a present from the generous Amerotke.

Sato undid the twine, poured out the wine and drained the cup in one gulp. He was on the second cup when the pain struck, turning like a knife in his belly. Sato staggered to his feet. This was no present. He tried to make himself sick but it was impossible. He gagged and choked; flailing about, he knocked the wine over. It seeped out of the flask like blood. Sato remembered what he'd seen and, dipping his hands into the wine, he staggered to the white wall. Time and again he forced his imprint against it, until the pain became too much and he sank to the floor unconscious.

Amerotke, Shufoy and Asural sat beneath a palm tree near a beer shop on the quayside of the Necropolis. Amerotke had insisted on buying them strips of well-cooked gazelle meat grilled over charcoal and heavily spiced, a basket of freshly baked bread and jugs of light beer. At first they sat in silence. Now and again Asural got up to walk and stretch. Shufoy said that the policeman looked so pale he was sure he had been sick.

Amerotke forced himself to relax, drawing in deep breaths,

allowing his entire body to sag. He tried to think of nothing, concentrating on the pungent, salty smells drifting down from the 'corpse shops', as Shufoy called them – the houses and workplaces of the embalmers and mummifiers. The Necropolis was devoted to one task, preparing the dead for their journey into the West. Further down the quayside rose the great carved figure of Osiris, God of the Underworld, foremost of the Westerners. The wharves were busy with coffins and caskets being brought ashore. Some were carried by the family. The rich, of course, were more ostentatious. One cart had been gilded with silver to carry the gold-plated coffin within. It was drawn by four white bulls, garlands between their horns, surrounded by priests and singers scattering scented water and milk to lay the dust before them.

'Have you gone dumb, master?'

Amerotke glanced at Shufoy. The dwarf was still beside himself with rage at their narrow escape. Since coming ashore he had spent most of his time muttering curses under his breath.

'At least you're, alive,' Asural, more composed, retorted.

The dwarf pounded the table with his fist, his sallow face flushed with anger. 'I lost my bag, the bastards!' he roared. 'The wisdom of Egypt was in it, medicines any priest would give his eye teeth for. When I catch them, master . . .'

Amerotke burst out laughing, so loud, a group of professional mourners stopped and looked in disdain at them.

'Where are the boatmen?' Asural asked. 'I'd like to question them.'

'I've done that already,' Amerotke told him. 'I've paid them and told them to make application to the Temple of Ma'at for compensation.'

'They were cowards,' Asural snarled.

'They were very frightened men,' Amerotke replied. 'And so was I.'

'It was murder, wasn't it?' Asural asked.

'Yes, it was murder. Two men died but the plan was that

all of us should perish. The news will be all over Thebes by nightfall.'

'Why didn't they check the hold?' Shufoy snapped.

'They did, oh most brilliant of physicians,' Amerotke said. 'They opened the hatch, the water jars were there. They are filled from a well in the temple. The captain of the barge, the tillerman, was told last night to prepare the barge for our journey across the Nile which involved him in little except assembling his crew.'

'And then the assassin made his move,' Asural said.

'Yes, during the night someone went down to the Sanctuary of Boats. The barge is unguarded and why shouldn't it be? It was so easily done. Two or three of the jars of water were emptied and filled with a gazelle-skin full of rich ox blood from the slaughterhouse. The stoppers were put back in but not firmly, the slats securing the jars were loosened.' Amerotke paused and wafted at the flies thronging round his beer mug. 'The boat left the quayside rocking and turning. We heard the jars fall over and the blood gushed out.'

'Very clever,' said Shufoy. 'If we hadn't been on the river, we would have caught the smell ourselves.'

'Crocodiles are like these flies, one becomes excited and attracts the others in. Those sailors weren't cowards, Shufoy, they kept that barge afloat longer than was intended. If it hadn't been for that wedding party . . .' He let his words hang in the air.

Asural turned paler still and even Shufoy was silent as he thought of the horror of what could have happened. A terrible grinding death, bodies being twisted under the water as the crocodiles shredded them. A blasphemous, sacrilegious end, no funeral rites, no embalming, none of the prayers to assist them over the Far Horizon.

'I tell you this,' Amerotke said grimly. 'I swear by Ma'at I am going to trap this killer. I want to see him die.'

He drained his beer cup and got up. His kirtle was soiled, one thong on his sandal was broken, and he had lost his war belt, sword and dagger in the mad flight from the barge.

'We certainly look as if we've had a rough ride,' he commented wryly.

'And you've lost your money as well as everything else,' Shufoy said, a glint in his eye.

Amerotke leaned down, picked up the dwarf and shook him, then grinned at the clinking sound from the dwarf's voluminous robes.

'Put me down, master!' Shufoy shouted.

'Would you lend me money if I asked?'

'With interest,' Shufoy retorted.

The three of them walked through the streets of the City of the Dead. The roads were broad thoroughfares, busy with funeral parties or people visiting the Houses of Eternity where their beloveds slept. Some were even out for a day's shopping, to choose caskets, coffins, funeral furniture as well as to seek the advice of masons and sculptors about how their tombs should be hollowed out and prepared. Apprentices, with trays slung round their necks, cried out for custom, offering miniature samples of what their masters' workshops produced.

Amerotke and his companions crossed the city, past the countless statues to Osiris, the dwarf god Bes and innumerable other deities who would help the dead. They passed the embalmers' workshop where salty smoke curled out to sting their nostrils and eyes. Inside it looked like a butcher's stall with corpses laid out, and some, blue and black, hung on hooks above cauldrons of bubbling natron salt. They went further up, climbing towards the line of bright yellow cliffs into the poor quarter where the shops and booths catered for those less fortunate. The air was thick with smoke, soot from fires floated like flies. The houses rose in terraces on either side. The streets beneath were clogged with piles of ordure and waste. Flies massed, black and buzzing. Dogs and cats fought over refuse, beggars whined for alms; hucksters and traders tried to pluck at their wrists. Asural stopped at a corner. He stared about him, grunted and led them up a narrow, winding alleyway. They stopped at a house. A man emerged from the doorway. He was dressed like a sand-dweller, dirty white bandages from head to toe. His eyes gleamed but Amerotke could see the pitted marks above his brows, the hideous red lacerations of leprosy. Asural told him to keep his distance.

'We've come to see Lehket,' Asural said to him.

The man went up a set of wooden external steps, whispering and gesturing at them to follow. The flat roof of the house was newly swept and surprisingly clean. Bowls of flowers stood near the wall. In the far corner on cushions sat a man dressed similarly to their guide. He was sipping carefully from a bowl. They paused as their guide went ahead.

'Are you Lehket?' Asural called out.

'I am Lehket. Come closer.' He gestured at them to sit at the far side of the table. He, too, was covered in bandages but the eyes which peered out were sharp and bright, the voice low and cultured. 'I understand you wish to speak to me, Lord Amerotke. Asural I know, so this must be Shufoy your dwarf servant.'

'And one of the best physicians in Thebes!' The little man wouldn't be put down.

'So, you have a cure for leprosy, Shufoy?' The eyes behind the mask twinkled with amusement, the voice filled with laughter. Amerotke warmed to him. Leprosy was a foul disease but Lehket seemed philosophical, assuming a calm dignity in the face of this living death.

'You have news of the Amemets?' Amerotke asked.

'Why, my lord judge,' the voice was still full of laughter, 'they are dead and you know that.'

'But we have heard rumours.'

'Oh, Thebes always has its assassins. Undoubtedly, as time passes, a new guild will be formed but there will be a great blood-letting before that happens.' Lehket held up a bandaged hand before Amerotke could speak. 'I know of your problems, judge. Rumour is like the breeze, it goes where it wishes. But I tell you this, Nehemu was not an Amemet. He did not take the oath to Mafdet, their terrible cat goddess. He was a braggart and a drunkard; his death didn't come soon enough.'

'How do you know all this?' Shufoy demanded.

'Little man, in my youth I was an Amemet. For a while I led them, then the gods struck back. I took life, they took mine. So I wandered out into the Red Lands. I've come back to atone. I work for the dead. I embalm the corpses of the poor and ask for no wealth, nothing but wine and food for myself and my servants. I know the Amemets. Nehemu was not one of them.'

'But I received a carob seedcake,' Amerotke declared.

'So, you received a carob seedcake.'

'But isn't that the Amemets' sign?'

'Tell me how it came.'

'In a sandalwood box wrapped in papyrus.'

Lehket laughed. 'If the Amemets were about their bloody business, they would not waste good money on such a box. They can send anything, a cake, a curse, but it is always delivered personally, hand to hand. Whoever sent that seedcake, my lord judge, was no more a member of the Amemets than Asural your chief of temple police. The Guild of Assassins has disbanded. Their bloody work is halted. Look among your enemies, Chief Judge. There you will find your sender and, perhaps, your killer. I have already heard about your journey across the Nile.'

Amerotke thanked him and made to rise.

'Oh, and one other thing.'

Amerotke looked down.

'The Hall of the Underworld, the Hyksos maze out in the Red Lands? Omendap's son is charged with the murder of two of his companions, yes?'

Amerotke nodded.

'When I was an Amemet, and the gods know the blood is still on my soul, we took a merchant out there, a man who hired us but wouldn't pay. We pushed him into the labyrinth.'

'And?' Shufoy demanded.

'He never came out.'

'What happened?'

'I don't know, my Lord Amerotke. But we waited three days. If he had come out, our debt would have been settled. We sent a runner along the top of the maze but we couldn't find him. I swear no wild animal went in and certainly no one ever came out.'

Amerotke and his companions returned to the Temple of Horus. As soon as they landed on the enclosed quayside, High Priest Hani and the Lady Vechlis hastened down to meet them in the Hall of Welcome. They both looked flustered and drawn, as did Prenhoe who stood in the doorway shuffling from foot to foot, eager to hear what had happened. Vechlis seized Amerotke's hand, her eyes searching his face.

'We heard the news from one of the boatmen. May the gods be thanked for your safe deliverance.'

'Aye, and thanks again.' High Priest Amun, followed by Isis, Osiris and Anubis, appeared in the doorway. They pushed Prenhoe aside and strode across, their eyes bright with the prospect of further debate and discussion. 'You remember your words last night.' Amun couldn't hide the spite in his voice. 'You know, my Lord Amerotke, such a barge should never carry blood. It was put there deliberately, you were meant to die a blasphemous death.'

'Do you still counsel that we stay here?' Osiris asked.

'I cannot help what happened,' Hani broke in. He glared at this fellow high priests. 'Anyone could have entered that boat and put blood in the jars.'

Amerotke stepped back and studied the high priests, their shaven heads and narrow faces. Apart from Hani, they looked like brothers, united in their malice and distaste. He wondered if they were all involved in these deaths, each covering for the other, causing as much mischief as possible and spreading the fear, letting it seep out into the many rivers of gossip which ran through Thebes. He could tell from their faces that they would be delighted if the council broke up in such an atmosphere; they could then return to their temples, plot to their hearts' content and leave poor Hani to take the blame.

'You have made careful search?' Amerotke looked at Hani.

The high priest shook his head. 'The Sanctuary of Boats is open to anyone. After darkness it's a lonely, desolate spot. The sailors prepare their barge, make sure it's ready for the morning and then go about their own business.'

Vechlis again seized Amerotke's hand and squeezed it. 'We are truly sorry,' she murmured, her eyes filled with tears. 'Must divine Hatusu know?'

'She probably knew before we did,' Amun mocked.

'Truly a place of death.' Isis shook his head. 'My Lord Hani, I understand one of the temple servants has also died.'

'Of apoplexy,' Hani retorted quickly. 'A well-known drinker.'

'Who?' Amerotke asked, though he knew before the answer came.

'Sato,' Vechlis told him. 'My Lord Amerotke, he was found dead in his chamber, just before noon. His corpse has been removed to the embalmers. As for the chamber, my husband has decided it would be best if you inspected it. Do you wish to bathe, purify yourself?'

Amerotke nodded. He felt tired and oppressed by these priests clustered about him. He wanted to be away. Above all, he wanted to visit Sato's chamber. He had no illusions that the podgy manservant's death was any more an accident than what had happened to him on the Nile. He bowed, thanked them for their concern and walked through the Hall of Welcome into the gardens beyond.

'I had a dream last night, master.' Prenhoe, all agitation, came running up.

'If you don't leave me alone,' Amerotke retorted through clenched teeth, 'it will be the last dream you have!' He stopped so abruptly, Prenhoe collided with him. 'What other news?'

'Messages from the court,' Prenhoe replied. 'The eyes and ears of Pharaoh insists that he be allowed to lay his case against young Rahmose. He apologises but says, like you, he must respond to pressure.'

'Aye, I'm sure he does.' Amerotke wiped a sweaty hand on his robes. 'And what else?'

'Omendap.'

Amerotke closed his eyes. Omendap, the commander-in-chief of Pharaoh's army, was in turn putting pressure on him to dismiss the charges. He opened his eyes.

'And what did the General's messenger have to say?'

'That the days slip by and he is eager to proclaim his son's innocence to all of Thebes.'

'He will have to wait,' Amerotke snapped. 'Shufoy, find a servant! I want to inspect Sato's chamber.'

When they arrived there, the chamber was empty, desolate. Gazing round, Amerotke realised the other temple servants had been eager to help themselves, However, probably on Hani's orders, the cup and overturned flask of wine had not been removed, and the table had not been cleaned; the spilt wine still lay in a crimson pool, above which flies buzzed.

'Who said it was a seizure?' Amerotek asked, walking to the window and staring out.

'The temple physicians. They came and carefully examined the corpse. It was common knowledge,' Prenhoe continued, 'that Sato was fat and drank too much. But I've been busy on your behalf, my lord.'

Amerotke turned and sat on the windowsill. 'How busy, Prenhoe?'

'Sato went out this morning, they say he was looking for a girl, a courtesan who'd favoured him.'

'Yes, yes, he mentioned her. Does anyone know who she is?'

Prenhoe shook his head.

'When he came back . . .' The scribe paused as he heard snoring and looked over his shoulder. Asural was on guard outside but Shufoy had made himself comfortable in the corner and promptly fallen asleep.

'The little man's tired,' Amerotke said softly, 'and disconsolate at the loss of all his potions and remedies. He fought like a true warrior this morning. I am so tired and weary I haven't even thanked him, or Asural, properly. Continue, Prenhoe.'

'Sato came back to the temple. He had apparently been drinking and, according to the servants, was looking for you. Said he had something to tell you. You know the way servants have when they have important news to relate.'

Prenhoe followed Amerotke's gaze. The chief judge was staring at the wall. He went across and examined the imprints carefully.

'They are freshly made,' Amerotke murmured. 'Five, six or seven of them. Look, Prenhoe, Sato appears to have dipped his hand in wine and slapped the wall.'

'The physician said that may have been done during his death throes.'

'Where was the corpse found?'

Prenhoe pointed to the foot of the wall.

'Sprawled there in a half-crouch. His hands were sticky with wine.'

Amerotke had seen men die of apoplexy. Such deaths were sudden. He looked back at the table, at the fallen cup and wine jug. Sato would have been sitting there; he got up and moved across to the wall. Amerotke looked again at the purple stains.

'Has the wine been checked?'

'I came here when the physicians were examining the

corpse,' Prenhoe replied. 'They sniffed at the wine, the cup and the flask. They even tasted the wine. It's pure, unsullied.'

Amerotke went across to the table and stared down. The wine was thick and rich. He noticed how busy the flies were, none of them had suffered any ill effects. Tainted wine left in a cup was often used by the maids in his own household to trap and kill flies and other insects. He sat on a stool and studied the table carefully.

'Is anything wrong, master?'

As if in answer Shufoy gave a loud snore and smacked his lips, muttering to himself.

'Yes, there is, Prenhoe. Look.' Amerotke waved him to the other side of the table. 'What do you see that's wrong?'

Prenhoe picked up the flask, the piece of twine and the papyrus covering. 'Would Sato have been able to afford such wine?' he asked.

'Good,' Amerotke murmured. 'But the flask is cheap.' He dipped a finger in the wine and smelt it. 'Look at the stain.'

Prenhoe stared closer. 'There are two stains!' he exclaimed. He pointed to the more faded patch. 'Maybe Sato spilled wine before.'

'I don't think so. I think the murderer spilled wine afterwards. Do you know what I believe happened, Prenhoe? Sato went around this morning saying that he wished to see me. The murderer learnt about that. Perhaps he had already marked Sato down for death just in case he had noticed something untoward. So a flask of poisoned wine is left in his room. Sato comes back, weary and disgruntled. A heavy drinker, he can barely believe his luck. Some friends have left him a flask of wine. Perhaps he thought it was from me or a present from that prostitute he lusted after. A man like Sato doesn't ask questions. He has something on his mind. He fills the cup and drinks it quickly. He fills another but the poison's in his belly, threading through his body. He knocks the flask over, drops the cup. Sato is aware of two things: that he is dying and that he has been poisoned, probably

172

because of what he wanted to tell me. He goes over to the wall.' Amerotke looked over his shoulder at the stains, now just dull purple patches but he could make out the palm and the shape of the splayed fingers. 'I wonder what he was trying to say.' He sat and shook his head. 'Poor Sato dies. The poison stops the heart. It has all the marks of a seizure. I doubt if my Lord Hani probed too far; the last thing our high priest wants are more cries of murder.'

'Is he concealing something?' Prenhoe asked.

'He could be.' Amerotke got up and walked back to the window. 'But, there again, the simplest explanation is the most likely. Hani doesn't want Sato's death to be regarded as suspicous. I am sure the physicians won't examine too closely and there are powders and potions which cannot be traced.' He shrugged. 'And who'll care? Fat Sato, a temple servant? They might even say he died of grief though of course people will gossip and murmur.'

'But this wine isn't tainted.'

'No, it isn't. The assassin probably watched Sato return here. It's a lonely, neglected part of the temple. The killer would wait. He'd come upstairs. If Sato was alive he'd probably help him drink the wine, but of course his victim was dead. The murderer carried a bag, a wine flask and a piece of cloth. The tainted flask is removed, the poisoned wine cleaned up and the cup washed.'

'And another flask of wine poured out on the table?' Prenhoe concluded.

'Very good, my learned scribe. So we have a corpse and untainted wine. Sato is quickly removed without anyone crying murder.'

'When will this end?' Prenhoe asked wearily.

'Very soon,' Amerotke replied. 'The answer lies with Neria; he was the first to die. If we find out why, then we'll discover who.'

Selket: an ancient Egyptian goddess, often
worshipped in the form of a scorpion.

CHAPTER 11

Amerotke picked Shufoy up, left the chamber and walked across the gardens to his own quarters. The little man still slept soundly, snoring like a pig. Amerotke made him comfortable, pulling across the gauze veil, protection against flies and mosquitoes.

'Right, Asural, you stay here and guard Shufoy.' Then he looked at Prenhoe from head to toe and walked slowly round him. 'You don't mind getting wet?'

'Master?'

'What was your dream last night?'

'I . . . I was swimming in the Nile with two naked girls beside me. I stopped in the water, my feet could touch the bottom. One stood in front of me, the other behind, their breasts pushing into me.'

'I do wish I had dreams like yours,' Asural sighed.

'Enough said,' Amerotke declared. 'Part of your dream is going to come true. I want you to fetch a bucket of water and meet me at the statue of Horus, you know the one, surrounded by the cedars of Lebanon.'

'A bucket of water, master?'

'Do as I say.'

Prenhoe hurried off. Amerotke told Asural to be vigilant then also left. The day was drawing on. The gardens were peaceful and sun-washed, the air thick with the scent of full-blowm roses and the fragrance of hyacinth and lilies. Priests were filing towards the sanctuary for the afternoon sacrifice where they would open the doors of the Naos to clothe and feed their god. The sound of music drifted out of the temple precincts: the clash of cymbals, the clatter of sistra and the refrain of the choirs:

To you, oh Horus, Golden Hawk,
All praise,
Whose wings stretch out from one end of heaven to
    another,
Lord of Life.

Amerotke walked on. Such a restful, soothing atmosphere yet he had to be watchful; no doubt the person who had tried to kill him on the Nile had also brought about Sato's death. Amerotke knew little of the soul, the workings of the human mind, except what he had learnt in dispensing Pharaoh's justice. Most of the crimes he dealt with were those of passion, of lust, of desire gone wrong, men and women losing their tempers, or being negligent. Occasionally, however, he had come across souls cloaked in eternal night, seething with malice, intent on wreaking death. He always wondered whether such individuals were sane, or possessed by the red-haired god Seth. These slayings in the Temple of Horus were of that ilk, carried out by someone seething with malice and determined to have their way whatever the cost to others.

Amerotke reached the grove of Lebanon cedars and paused beneath their shade. But why? The murders had begun when the council of high priests had assembled to discuss the divine Hatusu's accession. Amerotke recalled Amun taking that temple girl up against the wall. Was that his true attitude towards women? Slaves, playthings? Temple possessions? Did Amun and others fiercely resent a woman sitting on Pharaoh's throne and wearing the double crown? Particularly a woman young enough to be their daughter, even grand-daughter? Amerotke had met such prejudice before. The priestly caste were, in the main, men. True, people like Vechlis could reach high office but it was only a subordinate one. Was male hatred and resentment the root of these killings?

Amerotke crouched down and watched a butterfly hovering over flowers, wings beating against the afternoon breeze. Hatusu was a young woman who made no attempt to conceal her dislike of convention and ritual. Amerotke worshipped the goddess Truth. He found he could reconcile himself with that but he had deep misgivings about other aspects of temple religion. Priests who worshipped baboons, cats, even crocodiles! Did Hatusu believe the same? Sometimes during the most solemn occasions he'd see her smile to herself, eyes full of mischief. Had the high priests sensed her mockery of their rituals? Moreover, Hatusu had lived in the shadow of her father Tuthmosis I and then as the faithful, subservient wife of her half-brother Tuthmosis II. The priests and nobles of Thebes had grown accustomed to her, dismissing her as no more than a handmaid of noble birth, of negligible importance. Hatusu, however, had sprung like a panther out of the darkness. She had marched north and inflicted a crushing defeat on Egypt's enemies. She had then returned to Thebes to purge the royal circle and, together with Senenmut, a more commoner, appointed her own nominees to the House of War, the House of Silver. Such actions only stoked the fury in the hearts of men like Amun. A mere girl had no right to manifest such power, to wear the imperial regalia and watch them nose the ground before her. So, could all these slayings be the work of Amun and his coterie?

'My lord?'

Amerotke started and looked up. Prenhoe was standing beside him, bucket in hand.

'Good.' The chief judge got to his feet. 'Follow me.'

He led Prenhoe across the temple grounds to the dark, gloomy shaft leading down to the vault. At the top of the steps outside the door, Amerotke told Prenhoe to stand aside. He knelt down and soon found what he was searching for: a dark stain on the white limestone floor in the corner. He touched it with his fingers.

'Not water,' Amerotke murmured. 'Probably oil. Pure oil.'

'Is that where Neria's assassin placed the oil?' Prenhoe asked.

'Yes, he did. He placed the bucket there.' Amerotke took a pitch torch from its niche in the wall. He opened the door and thrust the torch into Prenhoe's hand. 'Go down the steps.'

Prenhoe swallowed hard. The vault was cold and gloomy; even from where he stood he could see the marks of fire on the steps, the scorch marks on the wall.

'I want you to go right to the bottom and come back up, Prenhoe. Try and act as normally as possible.'

Prenhoe obeyed. He heard the door close behind him and walked slowly down the steps. At the bottom he stopped and turned. He tried not to look at the shadows which sprang to life in the dancing torch flames. He took a deep breath and began his climb. He almost knew what would happen.

On the other side of the door Amerotke smiled. The steps to the vault created an echo. He could quite clearly hear Prenhoe's footfalls. He waited, measuring the distance, then he threw open the door, picked up the bucket and, although Prenhoe flinched, managed to soak him with its contents. Amerotke threw down the empty leather bucket, pretending that it was an oil lamp or torch. Prenhoe came out of the vaults drenched from head to toe.

'I am sorry I had to soak you,' Amerotke smiled, clasping his hand. 'But now I see how quickly Neria died. Instead of water and a leather bucket being thrown at him, it was oil and a torch or lamp. The same thing happens in sieges. Oil burns easily; a mere lick of flame and a human being is turned into a living torch.' Amerotke paused and used his robe to dry Prenhoe's face. 'The assassin saw Neria go down to the vaults and decided to kill him. He waited here, a lonely, desolate part of the temple. Remember, the rest were well away feasting after Pharaoh's visit.'

'But why?' Prenhoe asked. 'Why not send Neria a poisoned flask of wine? A knife in the dark? Or an arrow flying out from behind one of these buttresses?'

'The assassin was angry with Neria, he wanted to deny him life and honourable burial. But, I agree, the poor librarian could have been slain in many other ways, so why this?'

'And Pepy the scholar, did he die the same way?'

'Ah, that was different.' Amerotke walked up the steps, gesturing at Prenhoe to follow him. 'In my view the killer wanted to slay our wandering scholar and destroy everything he had in that room. You see, Prenhoe, this killer not only wanted to kill these men but remove anything they may have possessed: writings, notes, what they may have copied down in that library.'

'Or what Pepy stole?' Prenhoe queried.

'If he did steal something,' Amerotke answered, 'he'd already sold it, which explains our wandering scholar's sudden wealth.' He paused. 'But perhaps that's not true.'

'What, master?'

'Nothing, Prenhoe.' Amerotke put an arm round his kinsman's shoulder. 'I am sorry for soaking you.'

They returned to their quarters. Shufoy was awake, lecturing Asural about certain ailments which could be spread by touch of hand or even foul breath. The chief of temple police seemed deeply interested; he was on the point of asking Shufoy for some of his magic ointment when Amerotke and Prenhoe entered. Shufoy looked indignantly at his master and mumbled something about 'not being trusted to help'.

'You were fast asleep!' Amerotke retorted. 'Snoring like a little pig.' He crouched down by the dwarf. 'Or a warrior tired after his battle.' He glanced up. 'Asural, I know you have been wandering the markets. You have your eye on a Hittite scabbard. When this is over, that scabbard is yours.

And for you, oh keeper of the breath and guardian of the anus, a proper medical chest made out of purest oak with its own special lock and a new leather bag to hitch over your shoulder. You will be able to sell your potions and philtres from one end of Thebes to the other. Now, I wish to study in the library.'

Amerotke ordered them to stay in their quarters. He took off his dirty, dishevelled robe. Dressed only in his loincloth, he went down into the garden where he swam in one of the sacred pools specially built and filled with water from the Nile. The water was warm, fragrant with the scent of the lilies and lotuses floating on its surface. In the small temple shrine beside the lake, he purified his mouth and hands with natron salt, sprinkled himself with holy water from the stoup, said a quick prayer and returned to his chamber where Shufoy had laid out a fresh linen robe, brocaded belt and new sandals. The manservant also insisted that Amerotke carry a dagger. Shufoy stood and watched as Amerotke rubbed oil into his face and ringed his eyes with black kohl.

'You be careful, master,' he murmured.

'Like a cat in an alleyway,' Amerotke replied. 'And the same goes for you. Eat or drink nothing brought to you. Fetch your own food from the kitchens.'

Amerotke left and went to the library. The young archivist Khaliv was preparing to close the room but cheerfully agreed to stay. He followed as the chief judge surveyed the shelves and small booths crammed with manuscripts and papyrus.

'What are you looking for, my lord?'

Amerotke patted Khaliv on the shoulder. 'I am sorry to take up your time and that of the guards.'

'Oh, it's been quiet enough,' the librarian replied. 'These hideous murders have cast a pall over the temple. People are frightened. Our visitors tend to cluster together.'

'Yes, I am sure they do,' Amerotke said drily. 'Who has keys to this room?'

'Only myself and High Priest Hani. No, no.' The librarian

pressed the heel of his hand against his forehead. 'An extra one was given to our visitors. I think it's held by Amun.'

'So, someone could steal in here when the guards have left.'

'No. A guard stays at night. The boxes and chests are securely locked.'

Amerotke sat down on a stool and gestured at the librarian to sit on a bench opposite. 'I trust you, Khaliv. I want to ask you questions. Neria was the first to die. Did you ever discover what he was reading or studying?'

The librarian shook his head. 'Neria was a scholar. He came in here like a butterfly, moving from one manuscript to another. I let him have what he wanted. After all, he was Master of the Archives and Keeper of the Scrolls.'

'Did he ever talk to divine Father Prem?'

'Of course, but nothing significant, though divine Father Prem was his confessor.'

Amerotke hid his disappointment. 'And the scholar Pepy?'

'Neria kept well away from him. He truly disliked him, he called him crude and vulgar, as did we all.'

Amerotke glanced quickly at the doorway. Sengi the chief scribe had slipped into the chamber. Ah yes, Amerotke thought, and I must not forget you, gliding like a shadow around this temple.

'Can I help you?' Sengi, uninvited, sat down at a nearby table.

'Yes, you can, both of you,' Amerotke replied. 'Let us say you have stolen a manuscript from this temple. Where would you sell it?'

Sengi glanced at Khaliv. 'Not here.'

'You mean in the temple?'

'No, I mean in Thebes.'

'Yes, that's what I thought,' Amerotke replied. 'Pepy's research here wouldn't have taxed him too much, would it?'

Sengi looked puzzled. 'I'm not sure I follow you, my lord.'

'Pepy was insolent, a man who considered he was doing

you a favour if he raised his hand in salutation. I wasn't even too sure how studious and erudite he was. Always chasing the girls and drinking more than was good for him.'

'But he never said he had discovered something?'

'No,' Sengi replied. 'But eventually I would have asked him for a report.'

'Ah.' Amerotke smiled. 'I follow the drift of your argument. Pepy really wouldn't have had to work hard, would he? He was hostile to the idea of Divine Pharaoh being a woman. He could sit on his haunches, pick his teeth and say; "I have studied this and studied that. I have discovered nothing to justify Hatusu's accession."'

Sengi was now plainly discomfited.

'You play a dangerous game, sir,' Amerotke said, his voice hardening. 'Divine Hatusu will not be amused by those who frustrate her will and that of the gods.'

'We are scholars,' Sengi retorted. 'The council meeting was held at divine Hatusu's request. We cannot pluck proof out of thin air.'

'But what happens if it isn't thin air?' Amerotke asked. 'What happens if Neria and divine Father Prem did discover something that might raise eyebrows, make people reflect?'

'Such as what?' Sengi sneered. 'I am an historian, my Lord Amerotke. I can confidently assure you no woman has ever sat on the throne of Egypt. True,' he added hastily, 'there have been female regents, queen mothers—'

'And that's what you and the others want, isn't it?' Amerotke interrupted. 'Divine Hatusu to be some sort of guardian. For how long? Are you married, Sengi?'

The chief scribe shook his head. Amerotke felt a spurt of anger; someone like Sengi was responsible for these murders and the merciless attacks on himself.

'Where should Hatusu really be?' Amerotke hissed. 'In the House of Seclusion with the other women of the harem?

184

Wearing lotus flowers, a cake of perfume on her wig, one hand holding a cup, the other a sistra?'

Sengi swallowed hard. 'I . . . I only did what was asked,' he stammered.

'How friendly are you with the other priests, Isis, Osiris, Amun, Anubis and the now dead Hathor?'

The young librarian was staring open-mouthed. Sengi had blushed deeply.

'I wonder.' Amerotke leaned back. 'Are you in their pay? Did they bribe you as the chief scribe of the House of Life in the Temple of Horus to assert, with the great scholar Pepy standing beside you, that you and they had discovered nothing?'

'I don't have to listen to this.' Sengi sprang to his feet. 'My Lord Amerotke, this is not the Hall of Two Truths.'

'No, but it might be.' Amerotke grinned at him. 'As my manservant Shufoy says, every day is a new life and chance is a fickle wheel.' He gestured with his hand and Sengi sat down. 'You are stupid. Can't you see how the eyes and ears of Pharaoh will twist all this? Divine Hatusu wants her accession to be acclaimed by all but there is dissension and opposition among the high priests of Thebes. Divine Hatusu decided to have the issue debated here in the Temple of Horus. Personally, I think she made a mistake. The priests gathered. Divine Pharaoh has asked them a question and they'll give the answer they want. They'll demonstrate there is no precedent. Oh, true, High Priest Hani and his wife Vechlis are sympathetic but the rest aren't, are they? I suspect that many of them, probably all of them, you included, were supporters of Rahimere, the former Grand Vizier who opposed Hatusu.'

Sengi was becoming agitated.

'I begin to think that this council meeting is a complete waste of time. People pretending to debate when they've already made their decision.'

'But that doesn't make me a murderer!' Sengi rose to his

feet again. 'I am a priest and a scholar. I have served the Divine House well.' And, not waiting for an answer, he strode down the library and out of the door.

'Do you want me to go after him, my lord?'

'He didn't tell us why he came here,' Amerotke murmured.

'He was probably surprised to see you,' Khaliv replied. 'He often comes over here. Did you mean what you said, my lord, that the high priests, apart from Hani, have already decided?'

'Of course.'

'So why the killings?'

'Because Neria may have discovered something extraordinary. I believe he found it here.'

'But he never told anyone.'

'I know, I know.' Amerotke rapped his fingers on the table. 'And that makes me go round and round, which brings me to a question Sengi never answered, or rather he did, but we didn't pursue it to its logical conclusion. Pepy is now regarded as a thief. He allegedly stole a priceless mansucript from here. He was cunning enough to smuggle it past the guards but stupid enough to try and sell it to some merchant in Thebes.'

Khaliv was looking puzzled.

'There's only one conclusion,' Amerotke said. 'I don't think Pepy stole any manuscripts. Someone gave him money, made it look as if he had stolen a manuscript. Which means the missing manuscript that Pepy was studying must still be here.'

Khaliv scratched the side of his head. 'My lord, I am sure it is. Our precautions against theft make it almost impossible for anything to be stolen.'

'But something could be displaced,' Amerotke smiled. 'Where is the best place to lose a book or manuscript, my learned Khaliv, but among other books and manuscripts.' Amerotke got to his feet and moved across to the shelves, staring up. 'When this is all over, Khaliv, divine Hatusu will make her displeasure felt. Her word will go out, her opponents will feel her foot on the nape of their necks.' He looked over his shoulder. 'But her friends, those who upheld the truth, will be lavishly rewarded.'

Khaliv was sitting, eyes bright, mouth half open. 'I will search for Pepy's manuscript, my lord. I will find it.'

'Good.' Amerotke walked back and sat on the stool. 'As I have said, I trust you, Khaliv.'

'You don't think I could be the killer?'

Amerotke shook his head. 'No. You are too young and too innocent. Whoever plotted these murders was old in their cunning. If only I knew more about Neria. Did he like women?'

'Oh yes, but he was very discreet.'

'How discreet?'

'The temple is a village, my lord, as you know. People fall in love, become infatuated.' Khaliv half smiled. 'At night the corridors are full of slipping shadows and the patter of feet.'

'Tell me something.' Amerotke steepled his fingers. 'Did you ever see Neria with a woman?'

'No, my lord, but, well, in the temple or the sanctuary, like any man, his eyes would drift.'

'And, before he died, did he do anything untoward? Anything at all?'

Khaliv shook his head.

'You are sure?'

'My lord, if he did, I would tell you.'

Amerotke closed his eyes. He thought of that silent, cold vault, the steps leading down, the frescoes along the walls. 'Do you have anything here that explains the paintings in the vault?'

'We have a chronicle,' Khaliv replied. 'When the Hyksos invaded Egypt, some of these manuscripts were hidden, others dispersed. The library itself was burnt but when divine Hatusu's father drove the Hyksos out, temple life was restored. An old priest chronicled the times.'

Khaliv got to his feet and walked along the shelves. He found the chronicle, a yellowing papyrus roll which had been specially treated, glazed like a piece of pottery, because of its age. He brought it to the table. Amerotke thanked him and undid the scarlet cord. The chronicle was written in a mixture of styles, some crudely drawn pictures, hieroglyphics, the hieratic writing of the priests. It included prayers and vocations to Pharaoh. There was short biography of the writer and then the old scribe had settled down to recount the terrible events of the Hyksos invasion: their cruelty, human sacrifices, the devastation of cities. How altars were overturned, sanctuaries burnt, priests either killed or driven into exile. The writer proudly recounted how the priests of Horus had remained loyal to Egypt and its gods, and how they had sheltered in the catacombs. Amerotke became engrossed and started when Khaliv touched him on the shoulder.

'Do you wish me to go?' the chief judge asked. He stared round; Khaliv had already begun his search for the missing manuscript.

'No, no, my lord, and nor have I found anything but I have remembered something about Neria.'

Amerotke pushed the papyrus roll away as Khaliv sat on the bench opposite.

'As you know, my lord, certain priests have tattoos on their bodies. It can be the head of Horus or a scarab, some sign to ward off ill luck.'

'And Neria had one of these?'

'No – well, yes,' Khaliv stammered. 'It was two or three days before he died. He came into the library and was limping slightly. I asked him if all was well. "Of course, my boy," he replied. That was what he always called me. "You've fallen?" I asked. Neria replied he had simply been to a tattooist in the city. I teased him. Was it the name of some woman? "No, no," he replied. "Only an image of Selket."'

'The Scorpion Goddess,' Amerotke murmured. 'She's a manifestation of the scorching heat of the sun. Did he have a special devotion to her?'

Khaliv pulled a face. 'I don't know.'

'But you said he limped. Which means he must have had the tattoo on his thigh.'

'I presume so, my lord. It is usually the thigh, stomach, chest or shoulder.'

Amerotke thanked him and Khaliv walked away. Why would a priest do that, Amerotke wondered, a scribe, a librarian? Amerotke clicked his tongue. Was there some connection between Selket and the ancient Pharaohs who ruled Egypt? After all, Neria had been killed in the vaults near Menes's tomb. The pictures on the wall in the burial vault mentioned the Scorpion dynasty that had once ruled Egypt. Amerotke shook his head and went back to his reading.

The light began to fade. Amerotke kept to his task; the chronicle was fascinating. Some of the history he knew but the chronicler was a man who had witnessed these bloody deeds and wrote with a passion which came from the heart. Amerotke made himself comfortable, aware of Khaliv moving around, muttering to himself, emptying shelves. Amerotke admired his enthusiasm for this enormous task. The guards knocked on the door and Khaliv told them to wait.

Amerotke reached a section which quickened his interest. The writer was now describing the depredations of the Hyksos princes in the Red Lands outside Thebes. He described in considerable detail the cruel labyrinth they set up, now known as the Hall of the Underworld. Amerotke paused at one sentence.

'Isn't it strange, Khaliv?'

'My lord?'

'You go looking for one truth and you stumble on another.'

Amerotke read on quickly. He put aside all thoughts about Neria and the murders in the temple. He closed his eyes and said a quick prayer of thanks to Ma'at.

'Khaliv, quickly! Send one of the guards to my chambers. Ask them to bring Asural, Prenhoe and Shufoy here immediately!'

Amerotke checked the papyrus roll then rolled it up. He gave it to Khaliv and tapped him on the shoulder.

'I'll be leaving the temple tomorrow for a short while.' He lifted a finger in warning. 'Continue your searches but do so secretly. If the assassin finds out what you are doing, I assure you, you'll be dead before I return!'

Aker: an Egyptian god with two lion heads – the
Guardian of the Underworld.

CHAPTER 12

The four war chariots thundered across the green and yellow chessboard of fertile fields and irrigation canals which stretched to the east of the Nile. Above them the blue sky had acquired a pinkish haze as the sun dipped. The chariots veered slightly, following the dusty track, leaving behind the mountainous Valley of the Kings and heading into the dangerous Red Lands to the east of Thebes. The rocky ground sped beneath the jolting wheels and drumming hooves. The fading sunlight glinted on the bronze rails and blue electrum of the wickerwork carriages. The great wheels spun, the drivers dexterously managing the reins; their horses were black as the night, the fastest from the imperial stables.

Each chariot carried a driver and his guard. The leading one, in which Amerotke stood, sprouted the silver standard of the Horus regiment. The chariots themselves were emblazoned with the insignia of wild storks, a unit of that brigade, manned by the Maryannou, Braves of the King. These were soldiers who had fought in battle and been personally rewarded by divine Pharaoh with the gold of valour.

Amertoke spread his feet slightly and clutched the rail. The hot desert air whipped his face. He glanced sideways at his driver, slightly crouched, reins round his hands. The man's face was creased in tension though he was thoroughly enjoying himself, glad to be free of the narrow streets and busy thoroughfares. The horses, well fed and rested, strained at the reins, the red war plumes between their ears rising and falling. Amerotke looked down at the arms each chariot carried: two long horn bows, a quiver of arrows, three throwing spears in a sheath and, by his knee, a shield to be used in battle. Not that they expected to meet any foe, although the young officer in charge had been rather cautious. On receiving orders that he was to take Amerotke out to the oasis of Amarna and camp near the House of the Underworld, he'd pulled a face.

'You are not frightened of the legends?' Amerotke had teased.

'No, my lord, but I wouldn't go there by choice. We've heard rumours that some of the desert-wanderers have united and are raiding caravans and one or two of our outposts.' He shrugged. 'But that's a seasonal occurrence.'

Amerotke had spent most of the day making his preparations. He'd sent urgent messages to Valu and Omendap saying that the mysterious disappearance of the two young officers could only be resolved by a thorough investigation of the labyrinth itself. Omendap, of course, had reacted immediately and an entire chariot squadron had been put at Amerotke's disposal. The chief judge had demanded more. He wanted royal hunting dogs trained to sniff out game and trackers from the royal hunting lodges. Omendap sent a message back that this would take time to organise so Amerotke had decided to lead an advance party out and wait for the arrival of the others the following morning.

I might be wrong, he thought, but at least I can return to my court and say I have visited the scene of the crime.

All four chariots clustered together, only a spear length separating them. The horses had been given their heads and seemed to be racing the day as well as the distance. Amerotke looked ahead. In the distance, ash-coloured cliffs rose from sand tawny as a lion's pelt, their rocks turning a strange greyish-mauve against the setting sun. A herd of wild gazelle raced across their path and, on the evening breeze, came the yip of jackals and the mourning laugh of hyenas. The creatures of the desert were preparing for their nightly hunt.

The drivers halted the horses for a while to share out water and continued their journey. Amerotke was fascinated by the desert. The Red Lands consisted of rocky wastes and sandy ridges, broken up by twisting gulleys and narrow gorges. Only the tough gorse and weeds of the desert thrived here. Occasionally they passed a small oasis but now they were on the border of the true desert which stretched to the great river sea in the east. The air began to cool, the sky turning a darker blue as they reached Amarna, where they intended to spend the night. One chariot thundered in, ahead of the rest, to scout that all was well. Its driver came back to report that the oasis was deserted but there were signs that desert-wanderers had recently camped there. The rest of the unit drove in.

Amerotke got down from the chariot. He helped the driver unhitch the harness, release the horses and walk them up and down to cool off before they were allowed to lap the water. The chariots were formed into a protective wall facing out across the desert. Supplies were opened, nothing more than war rations: dry quail meat heavily salted and spiced; unleavened bread; and some rather bruised grapes. Dried dung was collected and a small fire built. Amerotke thanked the men for their speed and, refusing the captain's offer of company, left the oasis and walked towards the grim blocks of granite, that terrible maze known as the Hall of the Underworld.

Amerotke recalled the chronicle he had studied in the House of Life. The maze must stretch at least a mile in either direction. It reminded him of children's blocks scattered on the ground. A cold wind had risen with the sinking sun. Amerotke pulled up his riding cloak to cover mouth and nose and trudged on. The entrance to the maze was most sinister, yawning open like the mouth of a dark cave. Amerotke felt afraid. This was an evil place. Behind him he could hear the whinny of the horses, the shouts and laughter of the charioteers.

At the entrance to the maze Amerotke took from his war belt a small roll of red twine. He let this fall and, as he walked into the maze, reeled it out. The macabre darkness closed about him. He stopped and stared up at the sky. On either side of him rose grim rocks of granite; beneath his feet he felt the dusty, hard gravel path. In the poor light the maze played tricks. Amerotke thought he was walking into solid rock only to find that it turned, sometimes into one passageway, other times two forking off in different directions. The huge slabs of granite had been placed on top of each other to at least twice a man's height. He patted their surfaces; they were smooth, very difficult to obtain a grip or foothold. Anyone who became lost and wished to climb to find a way out or call for help would find it impossible. Sometimes the path narrowed until Amerotke almost had to hunch his shoulders to thread his way through. At other times he could stretch out his arms on either side and touch the granite.

His unease deepened. Were the shadows and shapes the shades of those who had died? He heard noises, like voices whispering or wailing, but it was only the wind blowing through the cracks. On one occasion he stumbled across human remains, a pile of bones and a cracked skull, lying in a pathetic heap. He paused and listened. He could faintly hear the sounds of the night. He reckoned he must have been in the maze only a short while but already his peace of mind was shattered, his nerves on edge. A truly dreadful place. What must it have been like for prisoners herded in here and made to find their own way out? Or for those hunted by wild animals mad with hunger as well as fury at being trapped between these soaring black slabs of granite? Now and again Amerotke paused to examine the ground. Sometimes he felt sand, other times granite rock or the foundations of the old castle which had once stood here. In some places there were gaps, as if the ground had given way, and Amerotke recalled how this place had been shaken by an earthquake.

He found the atmosphere stifling as if the maze was closing in on him. He turned and, following the line of red cord, made his way back to the entrance. He couldn't return fast enough. Was there something following him? Some evil lurching out of the darkness about to spring? By the time he reached the entrance he was gasping, his skin soaked in sweat. The officer standing at the entrance holding a pitch torch was also relieved. He hastened forward.

'My lord, I wish you hadn't done that.' He grasped Amerotke's arm, almost pulling him out of the maze. 'I would be grateful, sir, if you would stay with us. General Omendap would have my head if anything happened to you.'

'I know, I know,' Amerotke apologised. He gazed back down the dark passageway. 'Believe me, if I have any influence at court, I will ask the divine Hatusu one favour: this place should be destroyed. It is well-named the Hall of the Underworld.'

They walked back to the oasis.

'Your concern is laudable, mind you, Captain.'

Darkness had now fallen, abruptly, like some great bird sweeping down from the sky. Amerotke was always amazed how in the desert day and night met so quickly.

The officer hastened him on. 'My lord, I think there may be trouble.'

'What sort of trouble?'

The rest of the unit were gathered round the fire. A look-out was standing near one of the unharnessed chariots staring out into the night.

'I'm not too sure, my lord,' the officer replied. 'But as we were setting up camp one of the men noticed five or six desert-wanderers appear on the ridge.'

'But they won't attack us,' Amerotke replied. 'We are well armed and desert-wanderers move in small groups.'

'I told you, my lord, now and again the tribes gather together. They must have seen us coming. There are only eight of us and the sand-dwellers would love our horses, not to mention the arms and jewellery we carry. Still,' the officer shrugged, 'there's little we can do except wait.'

They sat in the night air and listened to the sounds of hunting animals. The desert became a threatening place. The soldiers whispered about the Shah, that malevolent animal sent by Seth whose gaze would turn men to stone. Or the Saga, a dreadful thing from the abyss with a hawk's head and a tail which ended in a poisoned lotus.

Amerotke took his turn on guard and was back asleep beneath the palm trees when the attack came. Dark shapes hurried across the sand, sending their arrows whistling in. They had little effect. The camp was roused. Every man was armed with a bow and quiver of arrows. They loosed back but their arrows, too, seemed to make little impact. Amerotke took his cloak, drenched it in some oil, set it burning and threw it out onto the sand. It afforded a little light, breaking up the darkness, allowing the archers to find their mark. Screams rent the night air.

The sand-dwellers circled round the wall of chariots but their attack was haphazard. Amerotke and the rest met them just inside the oasis, using the shields to protect themselves. There was clash of sword against dagger, shield against club. Two sand-dwellers fell. One of the Egyptians staggered back, a wound to his arm.

At last the attackers retreated into the night, unwilling to continue fighting. Amerotke and the officer waited for a while, standing near the chariot line, peering into the darkness, listening. Satisfied that the sand-dwellers had withdrawn, they returned to organise the removal of any dead attackers. The bodies were simply taken out and pitched into the sand. One of the charioteers went to see if there were any wounded but the attackers had taken them with them.

'They won't be back,' the officer declared. 'They found us tougher than they thought and they've lost any hope of easy plunder.'

Amerotke agreed and went back to his makeshift bed. For a while he just lay staring up at the sky, wondering about Norfret and the boys, hoping that Shufoy and Prenhoe were keeping an eye on matters in the Temple of Horus. He felt as if he was dreaming: the wild chariot ride, those hideous moments in the Hall of the Underworld, the attack of the sand-dwellers, dark shapes dressed like Lehket from head to toe in rags. Some of their corpses were now stiffening out under the cold eye of the moon. He recalled what Lehket had told him about the labyrinth. The two missing officers were still in the maze and, before he fell asleep, Amerotke prayed that Ma'at would lead him to them.

The camp roused just before dawn. Amerotke woke cold and stiff. The sky was riven by shafts of light, bathing the desert in a myriad of colours. Apart from some cuts and bruises, arrows embedded in tree trunks, and the pathetic bundles of rags lying out in the sand, there was little sign of the previous night's attack. The soldiers were in good heart, eager to break their fast.

They had scarcely finished eating when the look-out reported chariots in sight. The heat was already distorting the landscape. Amerotke shaded his eyes and caught the flash of gold and silver, a shimmer of colour. Soon an entire squadron could be seen, moving slowly because of the party of foot soldiers behind them, their red striped head-dresses clearly visible. On the early morning breeze came the sound of yapping hunting dogs. Soon the oasis was turned into a hive of activity as the chariots arrived, followed by the infantry and the huntsmen Amerotke had specially demanded.

Valu clambered down from his chariot, his fat face wreathed in smiles. He waddled over and clasped Amerotke's hand. 'So, my lord judge, quite a change from the Hall of Two Truths.' He pointed over his shoulder at Rahmose: the young man was unbound but guarded carefully by two officers. 'His father and that of the two missing men wanted to be present.' The royal prosecutor shook his head and mopped his sweating, bald pate. 'But I told them to stay in Thebes.'

He snapped his fingers and a servant ran up with a waterskin. Valu held it up, splashing water over his mouth and his face.

'I can't stand the heat', he said, 'and I don't like the desert.' He pushed by Amerotke and walked to the edge of the oasis, staring out at the maze. 'I came here as a boy, you know. Never came back, the place terrified me. I felt as if I had been touched by a wing of the Angel of Death.' He looked back at Amerotke. 'So you think the young men are still in there?'

'I do,' Amerotke replied, joining him.

Valu stepped out of the shade of the trees, roaring at a pageboy to bring his parasol.

'Come, my lord.' He took Amerotke's elbow. 'Let me re-visit my nightmares.'

They walked across the sand and shale, Valu ordering the others to stay back.

'Couldn't you wait for my return?' Amerotke teased.

Valu shifted the parasol to his other hand to give Amertoke the benefit.

'I heard about the business in the Temple of Horus.'

'Naturally. You are the eyes and ears of Pharaoh.'

'And divine Pharaoh is not pleased. Those murders, you've heard the rumour?' Valu's sharp eyes searched Amerotke's face. 'Oh dear, it appears you haven't. Hatusu and Senenmut are going down to the Temple of Horus. They wish to join the council meeting.'

'That's a mistake.' Amerotke glanced away in annoyance.

'I believe that's what Lord Senenmut said but her Imperial Majesty has little patience with priests, especially when it's rumoured her hand is behind these murders.' Valu stared out over the desert. 'These are not the Red Lands proper, are they?'

'No, they are not.' Amerotke replied. He was still surprised at Valu's news. He suspected Hatusu was coming to the temple not just to overawe the council and flush out her enemies but to demand an account from him.

'Ah well.' Valu peered up at the circling vultures. 'Pharaoh's hens, the troops call them.' He turned to Amerotke. 'I understand you were attacked last night.' Valu kicked the dust with a sandalled foot. 'If this is a waste of time, my lord, Rahmose will take the blame.'

They had now reached the entrance to the maze. Despite the morning sun, the power of Egypt, behind him, Amerotke felt a deep unease. Valu, however, walked into the narrow entranceway and stopped.

'Have you seen the carving here?'

Amerotke followed him. Valu was studying two huge scorpions which had been etched into the granite. The artist had filled their outlines with paint. The two scorpions were facing each other, locked together as if in battle.

'What is it?' Amerotke asked.

'They are mating,' Valu replied. 'Haven't you watched two scorpions at intercourse? They lock and sway together as if dancing. The male eventually impregnates his mate. And if he is stupid enough to stay around, she kills and eats him.' The royal prosecutor grinned. 'A bit like our Pharaoh,' he whispered. Valu raised his thin eyebrows. 'Of course I'm talking of a similarity in power and speed rather than malice.'

'Of course,' Amerotke smiled back. He peered closer at the drawing. It brought back memories of the Scorpion drawings in the vault beneath the Temple of Horus. 'Which is the male?'

'I can't say.' Valu turned away. 'Only an expert eye can tell the difference. But come, my lord judge, we are here in the Hall of the Underworld where terrible crimes have taken place. The power of Egypt is at your command.' He touched Amerotke's hand lightly with the fan he had drawn from beneath his robe. 'But why exactly are we here?'

'I talked to a man called Lehket,' Amerotke replied. 'He claimed men had come in here, or at least one man did. There were no beasts. Lehket and others guarded all the entrances but the man never came out and there was no sign of him when they sent a runner along the top.'

'Fairy stories,' Valu jibed.

'I don't think so. Lehket is not a liar, and I read a chronicle in the Temple of Horus which said the same thing.' He faced the prosecutor squarely. 'It talked of this labyrinth, this place of death, actually eating people, swallowing them up.'

'It's gruesome and it's sombre,' Valu retorted, 'but in the end it's only rock and sand. A good place for murder, my Lord Amerotke.'

'You brought hunting dogs?' Amerotke asked.

'The best from the royal kennels.'

'Good.' Amerotke rubbed his hands. 'Then let us begin.'

He walked back towards the oasis and gestured with his hand. The officer led across the huntsmen with their great, shaggy-haired mastiffs.

'You will be divided up,' Amerotke told them. He saw the look of concern on some of their faces. 'Don't worry. You are not to enter the maze but go above it. The dogs will enter the maze. You will lead them on long leashes. Let them search. It will take some time.'

'What are we looking for?' one of them called out.

'You will know when you have found it,' Amerotke replied. He squinted up at the sky. 'I understand that there are about thirty of you. Try and ensure that every block of granite is walked over. Keep the dogs below. On no account climb down. The heat will grow strong so put paint round your eyes and protect yourselves against the glare. Wear a head-dress. You must not return until you have finished. Drink as much water as you need before you start and piss where you like.'

There was a murmur of laughter.

'The same with the dogs. Don't let them be distracted by anything – skeletons, human remains.' He studied their footwear, good marching boots. 'Your feet will sweat but your boots will protect you as it grows hot. If you find anything untoward, stay where you are and call out.'

The huntsmen chattered among themselves, mystified by Amerotke's instructions.

'They cannot follow a scent,' Valu whispered. 'Any traces of the missing men will be long gone.'

'We will know when we know,' Amerotke responded. He shaded his eyes against the strengthening sun. 'And if we become more knowledgeable by midday, all the better.'

Officers led some of the huntsmen away to the other entrances. A pack pony bearing ladders was brought across. The ladders were lashed together and Amerotke climbed up onto a granite block and gestured at the chief huntsman to join him. The fellow did so, feeding out the long leash and, under Amerotke's instructions, began to walk along the top of the maze. Amerotke watched him go. He walked slowly. Below him, in the narrow passage between the blocks, the dog trotted warily. Now and again it would stop and gaze mournfully up at its master. The huntsman whispered encouragement, clicked his tongue and walked slowly on. Amerotke gazed out over the top of the maze. He felt unreal, strange. He could see how the blocks twisted and turned. At a different part of the maze other huntsmen were climbing up. Behind them a soldier carried a writing pallet to mark and stain each of the walls they passed along. The heat was already harsh. Amerotke felt a little unsteady but stayed where he was. Figures were now appearing on all sides. Some of the dogs whined, frightened of the maze. They protested and two actually pulled their masters in. Another bolted, running out of the maze back towards the oasis. At last the dogs settled to their tasks, breaking the air with their barks and snarls. Amerotke climbed down and sheltered in the shade, quietly praying that this hunt would not be a fruitless exercise.

Time and again he was summoned by different huntsmen and had to walk along the blocks to see what had been discovered. Valu refused to join him. In the main the dogs came across scraps of clothing or the yellowing bones of earlier victims. The sun grew stronger, the heat from the granite became unbearable. Amerotke changed his mind and ordered soldiers up with waterskins. He was about to return to the oasis when he heard a terrible howling as if one of the dogs had been savagely wounded. This was followed by the shouts of huntsmen. Amerotke clambered up on the blocks. All the huntsmen had stopped. One, however, was waving frantically. Amerotke and some of the scouts made their way forward almost to the centre of the maze. The huntsman was straining at the leash, his hands bloody. He was screaming at Amerotke and the others to help him. Amerotke reached him and stared down. The dog below was floundering. It had sunk into the sand; only its head and shoulders were visible. One of the soldiers made to jump down but Amerotke seized him by the arm.

'Don't be stupid!' he roared. 'That pit will suck you in as well!'

They tried to pull the dog forward but it became apparent that the pit was much broader than they thought. Other ropes were thrown down and, cursing and sweating, they managed to extricate the poor animal and lift it out of the pit and up to the top of the block. The dog was wild with fear, its coat was cut and bloodied where the ropes had scored it. Amerotke told them to take it to the oasis, shouting at the other huntsmen to withdraw. Spears were brought to test the ground. The narrow passageway looked no different from the others. Further out it was rocky and hard then it turned to sand, firm enough, but near the centre the spears simply slipped through the sand.

'It could go down for ever,' a soldier whispered.

'I don't think so,' Amerotke replied. 'The desert has sand traps but these are simply gullies filled with loose shale. The Hall of the Underworld was once a frontier post. What we are looking at is perhaps a cellar or a dungeon which has either filled with sand naturally or, more probably, was turned into a deadly trap by the Hyksos. No wonder few people ever came out. If they kept their nerve, didn't faint and weren't overcome by exhaustion, they would eventually reach here.' He pointed back across the granite blocks 'Have you noticed all the passageways and tunnels lead to here? You would only escape it by mere chance.'

He heard his name called. Valu was gingerly making his way towards them, parasol in one hand, the other stretched out to balance himself. He reminded Amerotke of an old woman tottering round the market booths.

'I heard what happened.' The royal prosecutor glared angrily at the grinning soldiers and pushed his parasol into one of their hands. He crouched and stared down at the floor of the maze. 'A trap from the underworld,' he murmured. 'Only the most experienced and keen-eyed would notice any change to the texture of the floor. Even then it might be too late.' He glanced up at Amerotke. 'You think the missing men fell into that?'

'The pit's certainly large and deep enough to swallow two men and their weapons.'

Valu breathed in, cursing the heat. He clambered to his feet. 'It's enough to vindicate Rahmose,' he said. He gestured at Amerotke to follow him. 'You will stay the day? We must search that pit.'

'Have you ever tried to turn back the sea?' Amerotke retorted. Then he shrugged. 'But it might be possible. It depends how deep the pit is. We'll lash spears to poles and thrust them down. If they come back clean, perhaps it's too deep. But if they're stained . . .'

Valu agreed.

The huntsmen and their dogs were withdrawn. Spears were prepared and scouts began to thrust the long poles into the sand, sinking them time and again. The heat had grown oppressive so Valu called out that everyone should rest in the shade of the oasis.

They'd returned to their labours for a short while when shouts were raised. Something had been found. A makeshift pulley was set up. An engineer, who had accompanied the chariot squadron, now took over. He reported back that the pit, probably a wine store, did indeed contain something. The sand was drawn out and late in the afternoon the first corpse was removed, eyes, nose and mouth choked with sand. Rahmose demanded to see it then knelt, face in hands, to the north. Valu tapped him on the shoulder.

'The other corpse will be found. All charges against you will be withdrawn and your innocence proclaimed. No murder was committed.'

'I disagree.' Amerotke looked down at the corpse twisted in the grotesque contortions of a horrible death. 'In the end,' he declared, 'they were murdered. The Hall of the Underworld claimed them as it did others.' He bowed to Valu. 'The matter is now in your hands. As you know, I have other business in Thebes.'

Sa: an ancient Egyptian symbol for magical protection.

CHAPTER 13

Shufoy and Prenhoe were thoroughly enjoying themselves. The large drinking house cum brothel near the quayside was thronged with customers. The low life, the outcasts, the pedlars, soothsayers, quacks and conjurors all mingled here. They had enough sense not to try and sell each other their goods. Shufoy and Prenhoe, sitting in a corner, watched round-eyed. Girls of every nationality were there: Nubians, Libyians, Caananites, Kushites, even fair-skinned girls from the islands beyond the great Delta. They catered for every taste, or so the inscription on the wall boasted.

'Every villain along the Nile eventually visits here,' Shufoy murmured wistfully. He pointed to a Phoenician sailor. 'He's been to places we can only dream about. He claims to have sailed across the great green to lands where forests are thick as the quills on a porcupine and the mountains are snow-capped. He can tell stories to give you nightmares for weeks.'

'But are they true?' Prenhoe asked anxiously.

'Who cares!' Shufoy rubbed the place where his nose had been. 'It's not the tale, Prenhoe, but the telling that counts.'

Prenhoe liked being here but he was slightly wary. The room was thick with the fug of oil lamps which stank as much as they provided light. Shadows flittered across porticoes and recesses. Somewhere in the yard outside a knife fight had broken out. A death carrier from the Necropolis went round the tables soliciting customers for a tour out to a cave where he would show them the mummy of a man buried alive.

'Hair the colour of wheat,' he declared. 'And skin as fair as the sand.'

Shufoy made an obscene gesture and the man backed away.

'What are we waiting for?' Prenhoe asked.

'My master gave me a task,' Shufoy declared, 'and I'll complete it.'

A shadow appeared out of the gloom and sat on a stool opposite: thin, wiry, sharp-featured, a nose as pointed as a quill, slanted eyes. The man's skin was burnt by the sun. He grew his own hair and looked as if he hadn't shaved for days. He wore a dirty yellow tunic. Prenhoe noticed that he had only one arm, the other was a stump cauterised by black pitch. He opened his good hand, gesturing with his fingers.

'I found what you wanted.'

'Who are you?' Prenhoe asked.

The man's eyes shifted. 'None of your business. Who's your gawping friend, Shufoy?'

'A good one,' Shufoy replied. 'And a clever scribe.'

'Donkeys fart, scribes write.' The fellow pointed his nose at Prenhoe. 'I have no name. They call me the River Wanderer.'

Shufoy handed across a small wedge of silver. 'If you lie—'

'I won't,' said the River Wanderer quickly. 'But the news isn't all good. The man you call Antef, he did march with the army. He was apparently wounded at the great battle near the Delta.'

'I know the one,' Shufoy said. 'My master was there.'

'Then he appeared in Memphis. He claims he lost his memory, does he?'

The dwarf nodded.

'Well, that's not what I've heard. There are rumours that he deserted, even married again.'

'Who did he marry?' Prenhoe asked.

'Why, scribe, a she-ass of course!' The River Wanderer laughed and picked at his dog-like teeth. 'He fell in love with a trader's daughter who has a booth in one of the temple forecourts at Memphis.'

'And then what happened?'

'I'm not too sure. Some family quarrel, he was thrown out by the father.'

'For what?'

'Stealing.'

'Money, silver?'

'No.' The River Wanderer shook his head. 'Small sandal-wood boxes.'

'Did he now?' Shufoy beamed from ear to ear. 'Can you do me one further favour?' He leaned over and whispered into the River Wanderer's ear.

The fellow pulled a face then nodded. 'It will cost you.'

'I have given you enough,' Shufoy declared. 'But if you do what I ask perhaps I won't tell my friend in the temple police about little artefacts which have disappeared from certain stalls . . .'

The River Wanderer grinned, pushed back his stool and quickly left.

'What's going to happen?' asked Prenhoe. 'I had a dream last night that I was riding a hippopotamus and a girl rode in front of me. I could feel her soft bottom against my penis. What do you think it means, Shufoy? An augury for good fortune?'

'Certainly,' said Shufoy, 'but you've got to find two things. A hippopotamus that will carry you and a girl who will climb up in front.'

'Are you gentlemen at ease?'

Shufoy looked up. Two ladies of the night, identical twins, stood before them, hands joined. They wore oil-drenched wigs, their faces and lips were heavily painted; little bells hung from their nipples, silver cloths covered their groins.

'The beds are soft here.' Both of them spoke as one. 'For a price you can take either, double that and you can have both of us.'

Prenhoe coughed in excitement. Shufoy, whose face was hidden in the shadows, leaned forward. The girls gave a scream and quickly ran away.

'Just as well,' Shufoy declared. 'You wouldn't want to dip your hands in paint, would you?'

'What do you mean?'

'Come, I'll show you. I guess we'll be here for some time.'

Shufoy took Prenhoe across the room, through a portico. The twins, either side of a sailor, were now staggering up the stairs. Prenhoe gazed in astonishment at the wall. It was covered in different handprints, some blue, some purple, red or green.

Shufoy pointed to the bottom of the wall.

Prenhoe stared at the little yellow imprints. 'That's you, isn't it?'

Shufoy nodded proudly. 'A number of years ago now,' he said. 'A big Nubian girl, she was. Hathor be my witness, we bounced so hard the bed broke. If you buy one of the girls, or rather their services, you choose your colour and put your imprint on the wall.'

'Why?' Prenhoe asked.

'The owner of this place is a Kushite. Apparently in his land when you take a temple prostitute that's how you make your offering to the gods. You swear you'll pay, put your hand in red dye and touch the temple wall. The place must be covered in handprints,' Shufoy laughed. 'Anyway, the brothel master introduced the custom here.'

There was a commotion at the top of the stairs. An old man, cursing and muttering, came running down. He turned at the bottom, bent down, picked up his robe and waggled his scrawny arse at the burly guard on the top of the stairs.

'Oh, that's the other reason,' Shufoy grinned. 'The only people allowed upstairs are those with dye on their hands.

It's quite common for a customer, how can I put it, to try and take what he hasn't paid for or watch others who have.'

They returned to their table in the corner. Two bargemen had taken their seats. Shufoy looked threateningly at them, mentioned Amerotke's name and the bargemen disappeared back into the throng. The two friends ordered more cups of beer. Prenhoe felt slightly sick. Those handprints reminded him of what he had seen in Sato's chambers. Why had the dying servant placed his hands in the poisoned wine and pressed them against the wall? What was he trying to say? What message was he leaving? Prenhoe sprang to his feet.

'He learnt it from here!' he exclaimed.

'What's the matter, Prenhoe? Lost your wits?'

'No, no.' Prenhoe shook his head and sat down.

'Not another of your dreams?'

Prenhoe told him about Sato's chamber.

'So, you're claiming there's a connection between Sato's chamber and this brothel?'

'Of course!' Prenhoe exclaimed. 'That's why Sato did it. Perhaps the poisoned wine was brought by one of the girls from here.' He scratched the side of his head. 'I remember my master telling me how Sato had been late the day Divine Prem died because he had been with a whore. On the morning he was killed, he went out into the city to try and buy the services of the same prostitute but came back disgruntled.'

Shufoy clicked his tongue. 'Prenhoe, stay here.'

Shufoy left the table. Prenhoe leaned back and watched a whore accept a bet from a snake charmer that she wasn't frightened of his so-called pet. The snake charmer opened the basket and allowed the snake out onto the table. The girl stretched out her arm. The snake went up slowly, as it would a branch of a tree. Then it moved quickly, coiling round her neck. The girl began to scream, drumming her heels on the floor. The snake charmer laughed. The girl's screams attracted the attention of the oafs who guarded the place. The snake charmer whistled softly and, as he did so, gently undid the snake, releasing the girl. Then he insisted that he had won his wager. The crestfallen girl had no choice but to agree to settle her debt above stairs.

Shufoy came back. 'I asked the brothel master. He knows nothing of Sato and does not recall any man of his appearance setting foot in here recently.'

Prenhoe sighed in disappointment.

The River Wanderer reappeared. He grasped Shufoy's shoulder and whispered, 'He's outside in the yard. I told him that you had good news about his claim in court.'

'Do you carry a knife?' Shufoy asked.

The River Wanderer pulled back his dirty shawl.

'Good. Follow me.'

Antef was standing in the shadows at the mouth of the alleyway which ran down the side of the brothel. Shufoy took him by the arm, drawing him deep into the darkness.

'I am glad you came.'

Antef looked down at Shufoy, then at Prenhoe and the River Wanderer.

'What is this?' He lifted the cudgel he carried. 'I was told you had good news.'

'Oh, for you, my lad, it is. We will give you time to get out of Thebes before my master returns. Otherwise it's a long time in the stone quarries or imprisonment in one of the oases out in the Red Lands.'

Antef's face turned ugly. 'Dalifa is my woman!' he spat out. 'I'll go back to the court and say I was threatened.'

'If you don't lower that cudgel,' Shufoy warned, 'you really will be threatened. Now, listen, Antef. I don't think you got a knock on the head. You deserted from the army and had a merry old time travelling from town to town back down the Nile. Did you pose as the brave soldier? The wounded hero?'

'You have no proof of that!'

'No, but a certain merchant in Memphis has.'

Antef's face became slack, his eyes watchful. He shuffled his feet and looked longingly back up the alleyway.

214

'In Memphis you got married which means you must consider Dalifa divorced. You stole little sandalwood boxes from your second wife's father and when you were thrown out you scuttled back to Thebes where, to your delight, your previous wife had come into a small inheritance. It was time, once again, to act the role of the wounded hero returning to hearth and home. You were so confident. You took your case to the Hall of Two Truths but my Lord Amerotke is a cunning man. He could teach a mongoose a trick or two. Perhaps he recognised you for the villain you are.'

'I don't know what you—'

'Yes you do. You were furious that my Lord Amerotke didn't agree to your claim. You were in the court, you saw that evil bastard Nehemu make his threats and launch his attack. So what do you do? You pretend to be an Amemet and send my master a seedcake in one of your little boxes.'

Antef was clearly agitated,

Shufoy tapped the purse on Antef's belt. 'I'll take that.'

'No you won't!' Antef's hand fell to his dagger.

Prenhoe felt his mouth go dry. The situation was turning ugly.

'I'll take the purse,' Shufoy insisted. 'Then you'll go to a temple, write out a bill of divorce giving up all claims over your wife and her property. By dawn you'll be out of Thebes.'

Antef stood back. 'You think I'll do that, you miserable mannikin? Pile it high on a platter then walk away for others to enjoy?' His face was contorted with rage.

Antef had an ugly soul, thought Prenhoe.

'You'll do it' said Shufoy, 'or it will be the mines or a prison camp for you!'

Antef moved quickly. Drawing his dagger, he lunged at Shufoy but the little man skipped sideways and, as he did so, drove his own knife straight into Antef's stomach. He fell to the ground, blood bubbling on his lips. He lashed out with his legs, coughing and spluttering, his body gave a few jerks then lay still.

'You've killed him!' the River Wanderer yelped.

Prenhoe backed away, licking his lips.

Shufoy was unabashed, eyes gleaming. He confronted them both. 'He was a villain, born and bred. He threatened my master, Chief Judge in the Hall of Two Truths. He was given his chance for life but he chose death. The decision was his. You are my witnesses. It was self-defence, wasn't it?'

Prenhoe nodded. 'But you did that deliberately, didn't you, Shufoy?'

'Perhaps,' Shufoy smiled. 'Antef was a violent, vindictive man. Our master would have had no rest from him. A coward, a deserter, a thug and a thief.' He took the man's purse and tossed it to the River Wanderer. 'Take his body to the Necropolis. Ensure his soul makes the journey to the Far Horizon.'

Amerotke sat cross-legged on the bed in his chamber at the Temple of Horus. He had arrived back late, washed, ate and slept. He smiled at his companions.

'It's like being back in the Hall of Two Truths. I can tell from your faces that you have things to tell me.'

'What happened in the Red Lands?' Shufoy demanded.

Amerotke described what they had found in the Hall of the Underworld.

'So Rahmose is cleared of all charges?' Prenhoe asked.

'Yes and no, my dear kinsman. The two young men entered the maze and were swallowed by the sand. Rahmose is innocent of any malice; the case will not come before me in the Hall of Two Truths. Nevertheless, what that young man did was stupid. If he had gone looking for his friends instead of taking their horses as a joke, there's a remote chance they might have survived. Rahmose will have to live with that for the rest of his life. Nothing in life is clear cut. And what has been happening here?'

Prenhoe told him that the other priests were still in discussion. 'But they've reached no conclusion. I suspect that's how they will leave it: neither yea nor nay.'

Shufoy then recounted what had happened in the brothel the previous evening. Amerotke listened intently.

'It's a fitting end,' he declared then glanced at the dwarf whose eyes were bright and expectant, mouth half open. 'You are no fool, Shufoy. You knew Antef was a brawling man. Still, if the case had come to court, it wouldn't have been exile or imprisonment for him but death. The divine Hatusu and Lord Senenmut have precise ideas about those who threaten royal officials. And you, Prenhoe, must also be thanked. You say Sato never went near that brothel?'

The scribe shook his head. 'Yet it is a mystery, master. Why should a dying man leave such signs on a wall, dipping his hands into poisoned wine?'

'I searched Sato's chamber,' said Asural. He looked discomfited, like a fish out of water. He did not like this temple with its open gardens, surrounded by shadowy recesses and ancient passageways and porticoes.

'And?' Amerotke prompted him.

'Nothing. I also went down to the Sanctuary of Boats. If I'd found the bastard who put that blood on board the barque, I would have done what Shufoy did to Antef!'

'But you found nothing?'

'Nothing, my lord. The boat is moored from sunset till dawn. There's no guard, no reason for one. They've already replaced the lost barge. I went on board, down into the hold. It wouldn't take long for someone to empty a jar and fill it with blood. I also visited the chambers of both Neria and Prem.'

'But everything has gone, I imagine,' Amerotke said.

'Most of their possessions will follow them into the tomb,' Asural replied. 'High Priest Hani said he found nothing untoward.'

'And our wandering scholar, Pepy?'

'Well, according to the servants, he took everything with

him. However, there's something behind the headrest of his bed which I must show you.'

'What?' Amerotke inquired.

Asural laughed. 'I couldn't bring it with me. You'll have to see it to believe it.'

Amerotke dabbed at the sweat on his neck with a damp cloth. 'It stands to reason that the possessions of all the murder victims, particularly those who served in the Temple of Horus, would have been carefully scrutinised by their killer. After Neria died, it wouldn't have taken long for the assassin to rifle through his belongings. We know that happened to Prem's things, while whatever Pepy had was consumed in that terrible conflagration. As for poor Sato,' he pressed the damp cloth against his forehead, 'the assassin had time to change the poisoned wine, never mind search the room.' He moved his legs and sat on the edge of the bed.

'Do you want beer, master?'

'No, Prenhoe, I want the truth. What do we have here? Neria the librarian was a secretive man.'

'I would agree with that,' nodded Asural. 'He kept himself to himself but not like divine Father Prem.'

'What do you mean?'

'Well, Prem was old and venerable. Neria was, according to some people, rather sly.'

'We know that Neria supported the divine Hatusu's accession. He discovered something in that library and the vault. What, we don't know. We suspect that he may have told his confessor Prem about his discovery and thus sealed both their fates.' Amerotke paused and half smiled at the beautiful singing which came from a distant part of the temple.

> How beautiful are your feet, oh Horus!
> Your eye is sharp as an Eagle,
> All Egypt hides under your wing.

'For some reason Neria was killed in a gruesome fashion, not the silent knife or the subtle poison, but turned into a living torch.'

'And so was Pepy,' Prenhoe observed.

'Pepy's different,' Amerotke replied. 'An atheist, a cynic, loud-mouthed and quarrelsome. He was hired to do research but he was a rogue and a charlatan. I wager he did very little, more interested in snooping round the temple than studying manuscripts in the library. Pepy was given comfortable quarters here but then he moved out as a man of wealth and substance. We are led to believe that he stole a manuscript and sold it but Pepy was too clever for that. He didn't steal any manuscript, it's probably been hidden away in the library.'

'So, what do you suspect?' asked Shufoy.

'I am beginning to wonder if Pepy was bought off, given some money to leave. He wouldn't have left a comfortable mooring like the Temple of Horus unless his purse was full of silver. I think the assassin bought him off and then hid the manuscript, thus throwing the suspicion of theft on our wandering scholar. A short while afterwards, the assassin went into Thebes and burnt both Pepy and his chamber, silencing his clacking tongue for ever.'

'So it's possible that Pepy's death may have nothing to do with the others,' said Prenhoe.

'It's possible,' Amerotke conceded. 'Except that Pepy and Neria died in the same horrible fashion.'

'And divine Father Prem?'

'Ah, that's different.' Amerotke picked up a beaker and sipped from it. 'Divine Father Prem's murder was clever but almost bungled. Sato was distracted by a whore. It's well known that he was always looking for some girl but rarely had the wealth to achieve his desire. On the day Prem died, Sato was late. The assassin wanted that to give him time to speak to Prem, find out what he really knew, and search his room. Sato returned before the killer was finished but he had prepared for that eventually and in the end he was successful. Prem, too, was silenced.'

'And High Priest's Hathor's death?'

'I don't know. To cause chaos, I suppose. Or, there again, Hathor may have seen or learnt something. However, we mustn't forget that no one knew at which table the visitors were going to sit. Hathor's murder may have been a mere whim.'

'But why?' Prenhoe insisted.

'The killer is bitterly opposed to divine Hatusu's accession. Murder and chaos followed by a conclusion which is neither yea nor nay will do very little for our divine Pharaoh's reputation among the priests.' Amerotke sighed. 'And, finally, we come to Sato. Fat, clumsy, lecherous, ale-swigging Sato, so easily fooled over his master's death. Then he remembered something and he, too, is sent into the Kingdom of the Dead.' Amerotke got up and slipped his feet into his sandals. 'Asural, show me what you found in Pepy's chamber.'

'Do you think you'll ever discover the truth?' Shufoy asked as they made their way to the room Pepy had used.

'I'm beginning to wonder. Maybe our librarian will find something, or the assassin might make a mistake.'

Pepy's chamber was simple and stark. The windows were shuttered, a vase of dead flowers still stood on the sill. Reed matting hung against the walls. There was a stool and a camp chair. The bed was broad with lion-shaped legs and a long, curved side rail. The mattress and sheets had been removed, exposing the cord webbing beneath. At the top of the bed was a headrest of dark purple wood with gold hand-rests carved in the shape of mushrooms. Asural pulled the bed away. Amerotke crouched down. On the wall behind the headrest somebody had scratched an obscene drawing of two people having sex. One was bending over, the other was pulling his partner's buttocks into his groin. The figures were crudely etched with a dagger. The person responsible had clothed both figures in what looked like a spotted leopardskin, the insignia of the high priests. Above them was a drawing of a small hawk.

'Is this Pepy's work?' Amerotke asked.

'According to the servants, yes. He'd done other carvings but they have been painted over. This one was missed. I told the servants it would have to stay until you returned.'

'It looks like two bum boys having sex,' Shufoy remarked. 'That's common enough among temple priests.'

'Oh yes,' Amerotke agreed. 'But it depends which two and, more importantly, is this what Pepy discovered? Some secret, sexual scandal in the Temple of Horus? Knowing what we do of our wandering scholar, I suspect he may have attempted a little blackmail.' He rose and pushed the bed back.

There was a knock at the door. Shufoy pulled it open and Khaliv the librarian came in.

'I've been looking for you, my lord. I think I've found something. Of course, I can't bring it with me but—'

'Is it important?' Amerotke asked.

'I am not too sure, my lord. It's best if you come and see for yourself.'

The tongue: the ancient Egyptian symbol of
the will.

CHAPTER 14

Khaliv laid the piece of weathered papyrus on the table before Amerotke. Its colours had long faded, the golds, reds and blacks merging into a dull greyness. The hieroglyphics beneath were ancient and the passage of time had made them look deformed. Amerotke stared down in disappointment; it was nothing but a picture of a Pharaoh dressed in his crown and regalia and a pious acclamation of praise.

'Is this the manuscript Pepy is supposed to have stolen?'

'Yes, my lord. I have studied it carefully. There is nothing exceptional about it. I don't even know who the Pharaoh is. Some ancient ruler, certainly not of the Scorpion dynasty.'

'So why should it be hidden away, made to look as if Pepy stole it?' Amerotke demanded.

'Oh, it's valuable enough,' Khaliv replied, 'to the collectors of curiosities and ancient things. It would fetch a good price. But the library is full of such manuscripts. However,' Khaliv's face broke into a smile, 'in my searches I also came across two other manuscripts which had been misplaced.'

'Were they used by Neria?' Amerotke asked.

'The fact that they had been removed from their box would indicate that.' The librarian walked to the door to make sure it was closed. 'I don't think we'll be disturbed,' he murmured, coming back. 'But I have found something which will certainly please divine Hatusu. Before I show

you it, my lord, let me give you a short history lecture.'
Khaliv sat on the stool like a teacher about to address his
scholars. 'One thousand five hundred years ago, as you know,
my lord, Egypt was united under the Scorpion dynasty by
King Menes, whose body does not lie in the Necropolis at
Sakkara—'

'But here in the vault beneath the Temple of Horus.'

'Correct, my lord. Now Menes was a prince of southern
Egypt who probably came from the town of Abydos. His
ambition was to unite the north and south of Egypt in one
great kingdom. At that time the north of Egypt was ruled
from the Delta and had its own ancient goddess, Neit, whose
cult centre is at Sais in the western Delta.'

'Neit is the goddess often depicted as a woman who wears
the red crown, the diadem associated with the old northern
kingdom.'

'Correct, my lord. Now Neit was a primeval, bisexual
goddess. According to legend she created the world and was
the virgin mother of a son.' Khaliv stopped and rubbed his
face. 'The Temple of Neit at Sais was called the Mansion of
the Bee, as the bee was one of Neit's symbols. When Menes
married a princess from the north, he was actually marrying
their Pharaoh or King.' He saw the surprise in Amerotke's
eyes. 'In other words, my lord, the first rulers of the northern
kingdom were women. Indeed, they took the name of Neit as
their own. Finally, both Menes and his son Horaha adopted
a title, an archaic Egyptian term, meaning "He who belongs
to the bee" – in other words, Neit.'

'If I follow your argument, learned librarian,' Amerotke
replied. 'Before Menes, Egypt was divided into two. The
north and the south. Menes ruled the south. The north was
ruled by women who took the title of Neit after their mother
goddess whose temple is at Sais. They were the legitimate
wearers of the red diadem.'

'Yes, my lord.'

'But after Menes's marriage to a northern princess,'

Amerotke continued, 'the legitimacy of Pharaoh to rule both kingdoms, to assume the red diadem, depended upon his subservience to both his wife and the goddess she served.'

'More than that, my lord. Menes's dynasty adopted the sign of the scorpion in their royal seal.'

'And the scorpion,' Amerotke interjected, recalling the engraving he had seen in the Hall of the Underworld, 'is a hermaphrodite symbol, both male and female.' He paused. 'How did you discover all this?'

'In an ancient manuscript. A chronicle. I found more.' Khaliv got up, walked to a gable-shaped coffer, undid the locks and pulled out two stiffened pieces of papyrus. He opened the covers. 'This is a picture of Menes, the first in the Scorpion dynasty. Study it carefully.'

Amerotke exclaimed in surprise. Hatusu, when she had acceded to the throne, had deliberately worn the royal regalia of a male Pharaoh, including the ceremonial beard. However, this painting of Menes wearing the double crown showed him doing the opposite. He was depicted as a female rather than a male: slim-necked, enlarged breasts and narrow waist. His shaved face had been painted like that of a woman; his groin was covered in a special cloth priestesses used to cover their private parts; his hands and fingers were thin and slender, the nails vividly painted a light green. All around him were pictures of the bee, the symbol of the divine Neit. His legs, half covered by a cloak, were also those of a woman, while the sandals were the high raised footwear of a noble lady.

'In all things a woman,' Amerotke murmured. 'Menes only became Pharaoh and was allowed to rule both the north and the south by devotion to the mother goddess and by becoming a woman himself. Oh, Khaliv.' He grasped the librarian's wrist. 'Divine Hatusu will sit you at her feet and pour your wine herself.'

Khaliv removed the drawing and put a second in its place. 'This is an inscription, a prayer of praise to Menes.'

Amerotke quickly read the lines. Some of the phrases were conventional, still used in the temples of Thebes, but the thrust of the words was different. Menes was no longer the royal father but 'divine mother,' 'beloved daughter of Neit whose womb was the source of all life'. Amerotke pushed it away.

'Why is this not commonly known? True, it's some one and a half thousand years old. But, if these manuscripts are to be believed, the first Pharaohs of Egypt, those who united the north and the south, were only recognised as legitimate because of their marriage to the princesses of Neit, their devotion to the mother goddess and the taking of female attributes.'

'History is constantly being re-written,' Khaliv replied. 'Think of the consternation these manuscripts would cause in the temples of Thebes. The centuries passed, the male priestly caste in the south reasserted themselves. Little by little the titles and the prayers were changed. The only remnant was the vulture crown, the right of Pharaoh's Queen to be regarded as sacred and divine.'

'And Neria discovered all this?'

'Undoubtedly. He must have been deeply excited which explains why he had the scorpion tattooed on his thigh.'

'And why he would tell divine Father Prem,' Amerotke added. 'The old scholar must have been fascinated. Both men would have taken notes, perhaps a crude drawing, a transcription of the prayer I have just read.' Amerotke slapped his hand on the table. 'It explains why Neria was killed that way. His body had to be burnt, to hide any sign of the scorpion. I suspect, if you found the tattooist, he would tell us the scorpion was clothed in Pharaoh's regalia.' Amerotke paused. 'After killing Neria the assassin went to his victim's chamber and removed and burnt any manuscripts or personal memoranda. Once Neria was dead, it was the turn of divine Father Prem. The killer had to visit him to see how much he knew and then he carried out his dreadful murder. As for the other deaths,' Amerotke shrugged, 'Pepy, I believe, was killed because he was a blackmailer. Sato because he had seen something. Hathor, well, he was an offering to the dark chaos in which the assassin wished to engulf the council meeting.'

'The assassin,' Khaliv went on, 'then came to this library. He'd learnt about these manuscripts. He hid them away, thus depriving supporters of Hatusu any evidence as well as depicting Pepy as a thief.'

'Can you remember who might have borrowed the manuscripts?'

Khaliv pulled a face. 'It would be impossible to list all who come here and what manuscripts they read. It would be so easy to lose a manuscript, move it from one shelf to another.'

Amerotke got to his feet, so excited he walked up and down.

'This still leaves two questions,' he declared. 'Important ones. Who else did Neria tell? And what was so important about the vault? The first I can't answer but the second – do you wish to join me?'

Khaliv nodded.

Amerotke pointed to the manuscripts. 'Put those away, hide them well. When we leave the library, appear calm, tell no one what we have discovered. Do you have a knife?'

'I have more than that, my lord; I have a small horn bow and a quiver of arrows.'

'Bring them with you,' Amerotke ordered.

A short while later Amerotke and Khaliv took a torch and went down the steps into the vault. The librarian quickly lit the lamps and torches. The hollow galleries and cavernous chamber sprang into life. Amerotke walked round the tomb.

'I take your point, Khaliv, about history being re-written. This sarcophagus is relatively new.'

'Of course, my lord. I suspect the old one was covered with the symbols and drawings depicting Pharaoh as a female.

229

The priests of Horus, long before the Hyksos invasions, probably destroyed the tomb and fashioned a new one. However, the wall drawings tell the truth.'

'Why?' Amerotke asked. 'Why don't these paintings continue the lie, perpetuate the myth of Egypt's rulers being only male?'

Khaliv placed the horn bow and arrows down on the floor and patted the walls. 'These drawings were made by priests, scholars who truly believed the Hyksos would bury Egypt under a sea of burning ash.'

'And such a time of threat,' Amerotke answered his own question, 'requires the truth not lies.'

'The artist had seen what we have,' Khaliv nodded. 'Probably other manuscripts which have now been destroyed.' Khaliv looked into the darkness. 'I have studied some of these wall paintings,' he murmured. 'They look faded in places but that was probably deliberate.'

They went into a shadow-filled corner where the paintings depicted the origins of the Scorpion dynasty. Pharaoh, undoubtedly Menes, was sitting in glory, wearing the double crown of Egypt. Khaliv, holding the torch high – it was shaking, he was so excited – pointed out how the painting had been deliberately damaged. A figure that had been seated next to Pharaoh had been washed out. It was made to look as if this was due to the passage of years but Amerotke realised it was deliberate. The same was true of the figure of Pharaoh himself. No sign now of the enlarged breasts; the symbol of the bee and references to Neit had all been carefully scrubbed away. Nevertheless, anybody who had seen the drawing Khaliv had produced in the library would notice the faint outlines which showed the female attributes that Menes, the first ruler of all Egypt, had assumed for himself.

'Once this is known,' said Amerotke, stepping back, 'the council meeting will end. Hatusu will emerge in triumph.' He patted the librarian on the shoulder. 'I am going to protect you. You are not to stay here. No, no,' Amerotke insisted when Khaliv seemed about to protest, 'you must leave for your own safety, at least for a while. Asural will guard you while you write down what you have discovered. I will also send a letter to my Lord Senenmut—'

'Where are you?'

Amerotke started as Shufoy, followed by Prenhoe, came clattering into the chamber.

'How did you know we were here?' Amerotke demanded.

'A guard saw you.' Shufoy glanced suspiciously at Khaliv. 'You shouldn't go wandering around this benighted place by yourself.'

'I have enough friends,' Amerotke replied, 'and Khaliv is one of them. Shufoy, do something useful. Extinguish the lamps. We are leaving here anyway.'

'You've uncovered the assassin?' Shufoy asked excitedly. 'We'll see him hang from the walls?'

'No, we have not.' Amerotke walked back along the galleries. 'But we've found the reason why he kills. Prenhoe, I want you to take Khaliv immediately to Asural. He is to go to the royal palace and be placed under the personal protection of Lord Senenmut. Do it now!' At the top of the stairs Amerotke turned. 'Khaliv, tell no one where you are going. Take nothing with you, just go.' He grasped Shufoy by the hand. 'Most learned of physicians, take a message to Lord Hani, tell him it's imperative I meet him and the council in the banqueting chamber. Oh, and after that, come back and meet me beneath the acacia tree next to the sacred pool. From now, until this business is finished,' he took the bow and arrows from Khaliv and thrust them at Shufoy, 'carry these.'

'Are you going to tell the priests?' the librarian asked.

'I am. It may, at least, prevent further murders.'

A full hour passed before Amerotke, seated on cushions in the banqueting chamber, was joined by the other priests:

Hani and Vechlis, Amun, Osiris, Isis and Anubis. The chief
scribe Sengi arrived last. Of course they all made excuses,
saying how busy they were. Amun even hinted he was on
the point of leaving. Amerotke was about to reveal what he
had discovered when a royal messenger was admitted and
hurried across to whisper in Hani's ear. The high priest,
looking pale and drawn, nodded quickly, dismissing him
with a flick of his fingers.

'I have had a message from the Divine House,' he
announced. 'Tomorrow morning, before the ninth hour,
Her Imperial Majesty, the divine Hatusu, escorted by the
Lord Senenmut, will grace this temple with her presence.'
He glared spitefully at Amun. 'So no one will be leaving.'

His words were greeted by silence. The high priests all
looked distinctly uncomfortable.

'Why is she – I mean, why is Her Imperial Majesty,'
Isis corrected himself, 'deigning to show us her face? Or
is it just the pleasure of seeing us nose the ground before
her?'

'We are scholars,' said Amun. 'We have served Egypt and
its rulers for many years. We are also priests, we cannot be
overawed.'

'You won't be overawed,' Amerotke retorted. 'For I have
something to tell you. It will put an end to your debates and
explain the hideous murders which have taken place.'

Vechlis clapped her hands, her eyes bright, face flushed.
The rest muttered among themselves. Amerotke, choosing
his words carefully, described what Khaliv had found. At
first he was interrupted by snorts of disapproval and cries
that they were not here to be lectured on Egypt's past.
However, as he continued, he noticed a shift in both mood
and expression from incredulity to fear as the priests realised
they had opposed something more ancient and venerable
than themselves.

When Amerotke had finished, no one challenged or criti-
cised him. They sat, faces set, and although he studied each

carefully, Amerotke could detect no guilt or alarm in any of them, no slip of the mask exposing the assassin.

Amun held up a hand, palm forward in a sign of peace. For the first time since they had met he looked at Amerotke with some respect. 'I know you speak the truth, my Lord Amerotke, but you must accept that this is surprising. It . . .' He glanced sideways at his companions. 'It changes many things.'

'And yet at the same time,' Osiris broke in, 'it also confirms what many of us suspected.'

Amerotke glanced down. The priests had read the signs and, like ships waiting for a wind, were changing sail to tack accordingly.

'This council meeting,' he said, 'must be brought to an end. Divine Hatusu asked you one question, or rather Lord Senenmut did: could there be any objection to a woman, divinely conceived and approved by the gods, wearing the two crowns and holding the crook, the flail and the rod over the people of the Nine Bows? How can there be objection,' he asked, 'when the first Pharaoh who united Egypt subscribed to the female more than the male? Indeed, he based the legitimacy of his rule on it.'

'I wish High Priest Hathor was here,' Isis remarked sadly.

'Why is that?' asked Amerotke.

'After we went to the library to make inquiries about what manuscripts the rogue Pepy might have stolen, we went for a walk out into the city. Myself, Lords Hathor, Isis and Anubis.'

'I came too,' Sengi spoke up, eager to be associated with anything which might win approval from the court.

'We sat sheltered under a palm tree,' Isis continued. 'Lord Hathor, as high priest to the goddess of Love, put forward something very similar to what you proposed.'

Very good, Amerotke thought. He hid his contempt of these treacherous, conniving priests who now had no choice but to accept, in its entirety, Hatusu's accession and the gods' approval of it.

'My Lord Amerotke, you seem a little disconcerted,' Hani remarked.

Amerotke gave a deep sigh. 'The divine Hatusu will come here tomorrow, It is good that we will be able to speak with a common voice and lay before her,' he paused, 'the fruits of our research.'

The other priests relaxed, plucking at their robes, smug smiles on their lips. Why make enemies? thought Amerotke. Who knows when, for the good of justice or Egypt, he might need these men? It would be best to present the discoveries of Khaliv as the common cause of them all.

'We must honour our librarian, of course.'

'Of course!' they answered in unison.

'It is only right,' Hani added. 'Khaliv is a remarkable young scholar. He must be presented to Her Imperial Majesty.'

'He already has been,' Amerotke said bluntly. 'We must not forget, my lords, that we have unfinished business. Khaliv has been sent to the House of a Million Years for his own protection. The Lord Senenmut will place his hand on his shoulder.'

'The murders?' Hani asked.

'Yes, my lord, the murders. The gruesome killings. The wicked attempts on my life and those of my companions. These are still to be dealt with.'

'And are you near the truth?' Vechlis asked.

'My lady,' Amerotke smiled, 'I wish I could say I was.' He shrugged. 'Certain things I have discovered.' He gave a pithy account of his conclusions regarding Neria and the deaths of Pepy, Prem, Hathor and Sato.

'This, this . . .' Hani stammered, 'is not what we thought. My lord, I don't know what to say. Neria was a secretive man but this business of the tattoo . . .' He wiped the sweat from his face. 'Yet what you say is logical.'

'Have the drawings in the vault been deliberately vandalised?' Amun asked.

'Oh no.' Amerotke replied. 'They probably faded over the years but I think they had a little help from the priests.'

'But Prem's death,' said Isis. 'Why such subterfuge?'

'And surely Sato's death was accidental?' Vechlis put in. She looked at her husband. 'Didn't the doctors test the wine?'

'It was made to look accidental,' Amerotke said. 'My lords, you now know as much as I do.' He stared at a picture of a brilliantly plumaged bird in flight painted on the far wall. Something significant had been said here. He shook his head. He'd have to recall it later. 'Is there anything you can add to my conclusions?'

'Hathor could have been killed because of his sentiments,' Amun offered.

Amerotke shook his head. 'No. Hathor's death was simply to spread chaos.' He sat tapping his fingers on the table top. He was certain the killer was here, present in this room. But how could he expose him? They were all canny men, tough and wiry, capable enough of climbing a rope ladder, firing an arrow or throwing oil over poor Neria. The question was, which one? Or was there more than one? Were the killers running hand in hand, protecting each other?

'Is there anything else?' Lord Hani asked.

Amerotke shook his head. He got to his feet, absent-mindedly acknowledging their thanks. He walked out and strolled across the garden to where Shufoy waited beneath the acacia tree.

'You've heard the news, my lord? Divine Hatusu will be joining us.' He studied his master closely. 'You are melancholic,' he said. 'I can distil you a concoction: the bone of a mongoose crushed and mixed with deer's foot, pure wax, a touch of the poppy?'

Amerotke shook his head. 'I am trying to uncover a murderer and a very clever one—'

'I spoke to Khaliv,' Shufoy interrupted. 'Neria discovered something, didn't he?'

Amerotke nodded.

Shufoy opened the little pouch he always carried and took out a piece of hardened wax which he used to calculate how much he had earned. Crouching next to his master, he drew a pyramid.

'Neria is the bottom line,' he explained. 'Divine Father Prem is one side.'

'And the third side?'

'He is the killer. We know there's a relationship between Neria and Prem. They both knew the third person, and spoke to him together or singly. Now, if I was gambling, I'd wager on Lord Hani. After all, he knows the Temple of Horus; and Neria and Prem worked with, and for, him. Except for one thing.'

'What's that?'

'Lord Hani has a great fear of heights.'

Amerotke's jaw sagged.

'You see,' Shufoy grinned, patting the side of his head. 'I may be small but I can creep where others can't and I listen to the servants chatter. It's well known that Hani gets dizzy just going up steps.'

'So, he's not the person to be climbing up rope ladders?'

'Well said, my lord.'

Amerotke ignored the sarcasm. 'What else have you discovered?'

'Why, my lord, something you haven't. Neria, Hani, Hathor, Amun, Osiris and Isis all attended the House of Life together. True, Neria was much younger than the others.'

'Which House of Life?' Amerotke asked.

'Why, most learned judge, here in the Temple of Horus. And there's no love lost between them; that's why Neria, if he discovered something, would keep it to himself.'

'But he told divine Father Prem.'

'Ah yes, but Prem, in his middle years, was a teacher and scribe in the House of Life. He was well liked by all of them but Neria was his favourite, which explains why he became his father confessor.'

Amerotke leaned back against the tree and stared up. A brightly coloured singing bird perched on a branch, piping its music. Amerotke had assumed that Neria had told both Prem and the killer what he had discovered but Prem could have been the assassin's sole source of information.

'They also lie in each other's pockets,' Shufoy continued. 'In more ways than one.' He raised one eyebrow archly.

Amerotke laughed. 'Scandal?'

'Yes, my lord, scandal. When they were young.' Shufoy licked his lips. 'You know my weaknesses, master – a bouncing girl, a cup of wine and a soft bed. But, according to chatter, in their younger days these priests loved one another.'

'But you said they disliked each other.'

'That's the source of the dislike. They are worse than silly lovers.'

Amerotke closed his eyes. What Shufoy was saying sounded like the truth. When he had attended the House of Life, homosexuality was rife. Sometimes it was frowned on, sometimes it was encouraged. In most cases, the men were bisexual. They viewed women as a mere appendage to life, hence the priestly attitude towards divine Hatusu. Amerotke opened his eyes and smiled.

'I thank you for what you have told me, Shufoy. Now, leave me alone for a while.' He grasped the dwarf's little hand. 'But don't go too far. Gardens might be beautiful but so is a journey across the Nile.'

Shufoy wandered away.

Amerotke reviewed the murders yet again. He might be able to exclude Hani from the killing of divine Father Prem, yet it was still possible he was involved. A man who was desperate might do anything to achieve his end. And the others? Any one of them could be the assassin. And Pepy's murder? Had he discovered something scandalous? Hence that crude drawing on the wall? Amerotke beat the ground with his fist. He felt like one of his son's pet mice going round and round in its cage. Was there any other path to the truth? Should he try a fresh key to turn the lock? He thought of his meeting with the priests and Osiris's words about poor Hathor.

'Do you want some wine or beer, master?' Shufoy had wandered back.

'No, no, not now.'

From the temple sanctuary Amerotke heard the sound of singing and smelt the fragrance of burning incense. Hani would be opening the doors of the Naos, offering the god his morning meal. Amerotke turned his attention to the attack on himself. Placing the blood in the barque would have been easy; under the cover of night, anyone could slip down to the mooring place. And Sato's murder? Amerotke curbed his impatience. Tomorrow morning divine Hatusu would sweep into the temple. Oh, she'd be pleased at what was said but she'd also demand vengeance for the killings. He wanted the same. He recalled that dark shape on the steps of the vault, the arrows singing through the air. Who could that have been? And where were the rest? Amun was near the vaults, pleasuring that temple girl. Amerotke thought for a while and abruptly went cold. He jumped to his feet so quickly he banged his head on a branch and cursed. Shufoy appeared from behind a bush.

'What is it, master?' He gazed in alarm at the judge standing gaping like a fool.

'Something so small,' he muttered. 'The only one who made . . .'

'My lord?'

Amerotke sat down. 'Come here, Shufoy. I want you to do something for me. Go into the temple. This will take some time but listen.'

Shufoy squatted before him and Amerotke gave strict instructions on what he was to do.

'Where is this leading to, master?'

Amerotke caught the glint in his manservant's eyes. 'Why, Shufoy, the truth which you and I serve. The assassin made one very small mistake. So small I overlooked it. Now I know what it is.'

'Tell me.'

'No, Shufoy, I won't. I know you. You'll take the law into your own hands.'

'And you have proof?' Shufoy demanded.

'No, that's the second problem. Do what I have told you, Shufoy. This murderer is not going to be unmasked but trapped and I intend to do it in the presence of divine Hatusu.'

He paused as the door was pushed open and General Omendap swaggered into the room.

'My Lord Amerotke?'

'Yes?'

'I have come to thank you.' The General's face creased into a smile. 'And to discuss a dead soldier, Antef?'

Uraeus: 'She who rears up.' A striking cobra with
an inflated hood, the emblem in the Pharaoh's
crown.

CHAPTER 15

Under a blazing sun, soldiers, their backs shimmering with sweat, rowed the great royal barge, the *Glory of Amun-Ra*, along the Nile. The divine Hatusu, the Golden Hawk, beloved of the gods, ruler of the people of the Nine Bows, had deigned to show her face to the people by sailing in glorious triumph up the Nile to the Sanctuary of Boats at the Temple of Horus. Along the banks marched battalions of élite foot soldiers and, beyond them, guarding the flanks, squadrons of chariots. The air thrummed with the sound of music and the shouts of the crowds. Fragrant perfumes were wafted by the great ostrich plumes which almost shrouded the divine person.

Hatusu sat on her gold-plated throne, her face set in a look of imperial serenity. Beginning in the early hours the keepers of the perfumes and ointments had washed and oiled her light-coppered body. Dark shades of green had been rubbed into her eyelids, black kohl rings carefully drawn round the beautiful eyes. An oil-drenched wig, its strands plaited with gold and silver, was bound to her head by a silver filet on which the Uraeus, the spitting cobra that defended Egypt, lunged in ferocious display. She wore a white gauffered linen gown under a golden coat encrusted with jewels and fastened by silver hooks and chains.

Beside Hatusu sat the Lord Senenmut, Grand Vizier, mouth of the King, her most chosen friend and, of course,

243

royal bedfellow. Hatusu's hands gripped the arms of her throne. She felt profoundly gratified. She had listened most carefully to the young librarian Khaliv and now she would show those priests! She would make them bend their necks and nose the ground before her. She would permit them to look on her glory and, if appropriate, reward them with a glance. Hatusu's carmined lips opened in a slight smile. She would reward Amerotke. She would also mete out the most terrible punishment for the malefactor who had dared to raise his hand against the servant of the Lord's anointed.

'Enjoy your triumph, Majesty,' Senenmut whispered. 'We rest in the palm of your father's hands, the glorious Amun-Ra.'

Hatusu breathed in. She had prepared this trip, this royal going forth, in great detail. The barque was the finest in the royal fleet. Its silver hull was overlaid with gold, the bow and stern, carved in the shape of rams' heads, glittered with jewels. Between the tall, silver masts with their flying red pennants stood the silver-chased personal tabernacle of the God. A servant girl held up a mirror so Hatusu could bask in her glory. In fact, she felt like giggling. Hatusu insisted on court etiquette and protocol but, sometimes, she felt an urge to throw off the trappings of office and dance like the little girl she had been at her father's court.

Senenmut sensed her excitement and gently coughed. Hatusu studied her reflection. She was like a statue under the huge, gold head-dress with its great white ostrich feathers. She would discard these tonight and dance naked before her lover, the man who had helped bring her to power.

To distract herself Hatusu slightly turned her head. The crowds on the right bank of the Nile saw this and roared in approval. Pharaoh had deigned to look at them! Hatusu, to show favour to all men, now looked to her left. On the near bank, escorting the barge, walked priests chanting hymns, priestesses shaking sistras, castanet players dancing and chanting. She glimpsed the gold-topped obelisks of the city, the pink-coloured temple colonnades, their walls shadowed by the rising sun. From behind her the captain of the imperial guard rapped out an order. The barge changed direction and headed towards the mooring place. Further orders were shouted; the oars came up and the barge glided in.

A royal palanquin was waiting. Hatusu glimpsed the assembled priests. She glanced at them coldly. Amerotke was there. She smiled at him, raising her hand slightly, then she stepped into the palanquin. It was gently lifted and she was borne along the royal way into the temple. Great clouds of incense billowed up to greet her, flower petals, drenched in perfume, were strewn before her. Choirs, assembled on the steps, chanted a divine psalm.

> How beautiful are you, how beautiful are you,
> Oh Egypt's glory.
> Manifestation of the divine will, turn and smile at us.
> Our hearts will rejoice,
> Our bodies thrill,
> As if we had drunk the sweetest wine.

Hatusu let herself relax. The palanquin was put down. She stepped out onto a scarlet and gold carpet and swept up into the dim coolness of the temple. She made sacrifice in the sanctuary and went into a small vestibule to take off the robes of office.

The council chamber had already been prepared; her throne stood on a purple-covered dais, a chair beside it for Senenmut. Hatusu took her seat and rested her feet on the golden footstool. Officers and courtiers took their places around her. The priests filed in and, bending down, touched the floor with their foreheads. Hatusu let them stay there that little bit longer.

'My Lord Amerotke,' her voice was just above a whisper, 'you and your companions may now sit.'

They did so quickly and quietly. Hatusu studied them all.

She caught the dislike in the eyes of the high priests but no one held her gaze. Amerotke, she noticed with a spurt of annoyance, wasn't even looking at her but sat, hands on his knees, staring down at the floor.

'We will dispense with ceremony,' Hatusu began harshly, ignoring the small hiss of disapproval from the chamberlains behind her. 'I shall speak and my words will go forth. I sit on Pharaoh's throne and wear the double crown. I carry the flail and the rod. This is the will of the gods!'

'It is! It is!' came the reply.

'I believe that my Lord Amerotke, with the help of the librarian at the Temple of Horus, has brought these matters,' Hatusu chose her words carefully, 'to a rather surprising conclusion.' She now beamed at the chief judge who rose to his feet.

Amerotke gave a succinct description of what had been discovered regarding the Scorpion dynasty, the first Pharaohs of Egypt. When he had finished, Hatusu asked if there was agreement on this. The high priests choroused their assent.

'On the feast of Isis,' Senenmut proclaimed, 'divine Pharaoh will sacrifice in the sanctuary. All the high priests of Thebes will attend and the people will witness their joyful acclamation.' He made a cutting movement with his hand. 'These matters are finished.'

The council sat in silence. Hatusu breathed in through her nose and let out her breath slowly, a sign that she was about to speak. Amerotke could see his companions were tense. He hid his excitement. Hatusu was going to hold court, the murderer was to be unmasked. Amerotke had reached a logical conclusion but proving it was not so easy. He kept his face impassive, carefully avoiding the gaze of his suspect.

'We have other matters.' Hatusu's voice was like a bark. 'The temple doors are sealed. Pharaoh's justice must be done!' Her voice rose. 'Terrible murders have taken place!' She paused for effect.

Amerotke waited. The previous evening he had finished

his reflections and reached a conclusion. The information Shufoy had brought him yesterday had been vital. He had immediately despatched a letter to Lord Senenmut and then, remembering the death of Antef, had issued a decree, under his cartouche, allowing Dalifa to marry and conduct her affairs under the protection of Pharaoh.

'My Lord Amerotke,' said Senenmut.

The chief judge got to his feet.

'I do not wish to go over what everyone here knows,' he began. 'This is the Temple of Horus but red-haired Seth, the god of sudden death, has made his presence felt. Her Imperial Majesty mentioned murder; the roots of these killings lie in treason. Someone, dark of heart with a soul of night, refused to accept the will of the gods. If it could be proved that a woman has the right to become Pharaoh as much as a man, that, indeed, the first Pharaohs of Egypt owed their legitimacy to the female side of the divinity, then all discussion would cease.'

'And such proof now exists!' Lord Hani cried.

'Yes, it does,' Amerotke replied. He noticed that the high priest was trembling, his face ashen. 'Now Neria,' Amerotke continued, 'was a secretive man but a brilliant scholar. He, too, had reached that same conclusion. He had studied the paintings in the vault below the temple. Perhaps he noticed something, then he found the proof in the archives of the temple. Eager to show his brilliance and to receive the plaudits of his old teacher, Neria informed divine Father Prem. He had no time for the wandering scholar Pepy whom he rightly dismissed as a snooper, a searcher-out of scandal. Pepy was hired by Sengi.'

The chief scribe hung his head.

'But Pepy only accepted the task to secure a comfortable bed and good food. Pepy wasn't interested in manuscripts or papyri but in the gossip and chatter of the temple. A man of sharp wit and keen eye, Pepy may have been drawn to Neria by the latter's love of seclusion.' Amerotke paused.

'Pepy must have suspected that Neria had found something and began to watch him closely so as to discover what it was. Instead, he stumbled on something else. Neria was having an affair with someone here in the temple. Pepy may even have found them in the act.' He glanced at Hatusu, who sat watching like a cat before a mousehole.

'He drew an obscene graffiti in his chamber. When I first looked at it, I thought the drawing was of two men engaged in the act of love.' Amerotke walked along the line of chairs and stopped. He grasped Vechlis's hand. It was as cold as ice. He stared down into her dark eyes. 'But of course it was you and Neria.'

Hani let out a moan. Amerotke knew in one glance that Hani had half suspected something was amiss with his marriage.

Amerotke held his gaze. 'I don't know how long this liaison had lasted. Months, perhaps even years. The gardens of Horus are spacious; its temple has nooks and crannies deep in shadows.' He glanced at Amun. 'Is that not right, my lord? I saw you in one of those shadows with a temple girl.'

Amun dropped his heavy-lidded gaze. Amerotke looked back at Vechlis. She remained unchanged, eyes round, face smooth. He wondered idly if she was mocking him with that patronising stare.

'Won't you say anything?' Hani shouted.

Vechlis dismissed her husband with one glance. Amerotke let her hand fall.

'Neria told you what he had found, didn't he? You saw the tattoo of the Scorpion God on his thigh, a rather pretentious act to curry favour with the court. A perpetual boast of his own scholarship. Neria must have known that when his discovery became public, he would receive the divine approbation of Pharaoh and her court.'

The council chamber was absolutely silent. Hatusu had forgotten all protocol and sat, lips slightly parted, though a look of fury blazed in her eyes. Senenmut was leaning forward, as if he couldn't believe what he was hearing. Amerotke had informed him that he would unmask the murderer but had not given a name.

'You killed Neria, didn't you?'

Vechlis didn't answer. Amerotke wondered if she was in shock. She sat chewing the corner of her mouth, her hands resting in her lap. Even now her beautiful fingernails, painted a deep purple, drew his glance.

'You knew when Neria was going down to the vault, a deserted, lonely place in the temple. Everybody else was away, either feasting or recovering from its effects, after the visit of divine Pharaoh. Neria came up the steps. You flung the door open; taken by surprise, he stood there. In a few seconds he was drenched in oil and a flame was thrown in. Neria, his ridiculous tattoo and whatever he was carrying, were turned into a blazing torch. You closed the door, got rid of the oil container and hurried up to his room to conduct a hasty search. After all, you'd know all his hiding places. Anything incriminating, all the fruits of his research, were quickly and quietly removed.'

'Woman, will you just sit there and accept this?' barked Lord Senenmut.

'I listen.' Vechlis's reply was almost a drawl. 'And then I will reply, stonemason!'

Senenmut flinched at the insulting reference to his humble beginnings.

'Do continue, my Lord Amerotke,' Vechlis said graciously. 'Do you remember when you were a boy? I used to love listening to your tales.'

'Aye, my lady, and listen you will. Neria was removed but divine Father Prem also had to be silenced. Neria had shared his knowledge with his confessor. For all you knew, divine Father Prem may also have learnt about Neria's relationship with you. You go across to see him. You plan it well. Prem was a recluse, a hermit. Sato, his servant, his eyes and ears, his fetcher and carrier, was wandering the city eyeing the girls.

249

He was well known for it. He was a joke. Did you engage that prostitute to while away his time? To feed him ale? Whatever, you go up to see divine Father Prem in the garden tower. You take a small rope ladder and place it outside the old priest's room. You go in and talk. Prem is garrulous. You reach a decision, something he says or something he shows you provokes suspicion. You kill him with the old Hyksos war club and search his chamber. But Sato returns. You hide Prem's corpse beneath the bed and you hurry to the top of the tower. You sling the rope ladder over the turrets. You take the old priest's shawl and hat and pretend to be him.'

'Now how could I do that?' she broke in.

'My lady, it was dark. You remove your wig, put on the straw hat and Prem's shawl about your shoulders. You are clothed in the darkness, probably kneeling with your back to the tower door. Sato sees what he expects and lumbers down the steps. Then you come down. To distract him you take off a ring and let it bounce down the steps. While Sato goes after it you enter Prem's chamber. Again it's dark, you are still wearing the hat and shawl and you have your back to the door. Sato puts the ring on the table. You close, bar and bolt the door behind him.' Amerotke shrugged. 'I suppose one scream sounds much like any other. Sato tries the door but it is useless. He goes for help. You move Prem's corpse onto the bed, take the club, leave through the window and climb the rope ladder back over the turrets at the top of the tower.'

'Me climb a rope ladder?'

'Vechlis, you are probably more able than many of Pharaoh's soldiers. A consummate swimmer, you could do it easily. Once you are on top of the tower, you throw the rope ladder and club away, to be collected later from the rose bushes below. You then join the rest when the door to Prem's room is broken open.'

'Yes, you were there,' Isis spoke up, his lips forming into a pout. 'And, on reflection, it seemed you appeared out of nowhere.'

250

'What do you know about me?' Vechlis sneered. 'Keep a civil tongue in your head, old woman!' Vechlis seemed to have lost all fear of Hatusu and her surroundings.

'Pepy was the next victim,' Amerotke continued. 'On reflection, I don't think he blackmailed you. Perhaps he just let slip what he knew about you and Neria. Pepy wanted silver in his pocket, a belly full of wine and his hands round some young whore's buttocks. Purses were left in his chamber as a bribe and Pepy was off to the fleshpots of the city. Of course, blackmailers return, don't they? You had to destroy both him and whatever evidence he might have – notes of what he had seen, for example. His routine was that of any lecher, drinking in the afternoon and hiring whores from the pleasure house.'

'Are you saying that I'd go down to the quayside, me, a high priestess?'

'You are frightened of nothing, Vechlis, certainly not a man! With a gazelle-skin of oil bought in the market place, you could shuffle along under a cloak pretending to be an old woman, wait for Pepy to return home and then strike. Who in the Temple of Horus has any control over the high and mighty Vechlis?'

'You have proof of all this?' Senenmut asked.

'I have proof, my lord.'

Only then did Vechlis's eyes grow more watchful, her body tense.

'The next victim Hathor was chosen at random, to cause chaos and heighten the tension. The tables were laid out in the banqueting chamber.' Amerotke walked over to Hani and looked down at him. 'You were our host, my Lord Hani, but who would decide which person would sit where? Who would supervise the seating arrangements?'

Hani's face had aged, ashen with fear. His eyes cringed, he opened his mouth to reply.

'Vechlis did, didn't she?' Amerotke asked quietly. 'And, before the banqueting began, with servants and musicians coming in and out, it would be so easy to pass along the table and, place poison powder in a beer cup. Who would suspect? Hathor dies.' Amerotke walked back to Vechlis. 'Sato also had to be sent into the night. The murder of Prem was probably your clumsiest. You never really could be sure that poor drunken Sato had not seen something untoward, and he had a tongue like a loose shutter, he'd chatter and gossip. On the day he died Sato wanted to see me.' Amerotke crouched down in front of Vechlis. 'He was quickly marked down for death. Sato could never refuse a flask of wine. It would be like asking a thirsty cat not to drink milk. He dies, you go up to his chamber, wipe up the wine and replace the poisoned flask with an untainted one.' Amerotke got to his feet. 'Sato was not an intelligent man but I think he knew he was being poisoned. He dipped his hands into the wine and made those imprints on the wall. I wonder what he was trying to tell us?' Amerotke lightly tapped the back of Vechlis's hand. 'Did Sato begin to wonder about that figure he'd glimpsed as he put the ring back on the night his master died? Did he see your fingers? The colouring of your fingernails is so distinctive. Sato was trying to say something about the assassin's hand. We'll never know whether it was the assassin's fingernails, the texture of the skin or the ring Sato picked up.'

'And, I suppose, you blame me for the attack on yourself?' Vechlis murmured.

'Yes, I do. It would be easy for the high priest's wife to go down at night to the Sanctuary of Boats, to steal on board with a waterskin full of blood from the slaughterhouse. You emptied the water from some of the jars, filled them with blood, loosened their stoppers and the slats which secured them in the hold.'

'Divine Pharaoh.' Vechlis now sat up straight in her chair, looking directly at Hatusu. 'I have listened patiently to this tissue of lies. Where is the proof – apart from a drunken servant staining the wall with purple grape?'

'How do you know the wine was red?' Amerotke asked.

'My . . . my husband, Lord Hani, told me,' she stammered.

'No, I did not!' The reply was spat out. Hani glared at his wife. 'Before Pharaoh herself I swear I never told you that!'

Vechlis dismissed him with a contemptuous glance.

'You asked for proof,' said Amerotke. He turned and bowed to Hatusu. 'It shall come in two parts, Your Majesty. I went down to the vault on my first day here. I wished to examine a wall painting. An assassin followed me down, loosed arrows then disappeared.' Amerotke paused.

'But why should Vechlis want you dead?' Amun asked.

'My death was supposed to have the same effect as Hathor's, to cause disruption, to publicise the failure of the council meeting of the high priests. They had been asked for their opinion and the occasion had been drenched in blood, a most unsuitable augury for a new Pharaoh's reign.'

'Continue,' Hatusu ordered. 'You were in the vault, my lord?'

'Yes. The attack failed but the archer must have been one of the council members, only they knew I intended to go to the vault. Now, at first I thought it was impossible to trace where everyone was but by mere chance the information was given to me. Amun was busy with a temple girl. Hathor, Isis, Osiris, Anubis and Sengi had actually left the temple grounds, while High Priest Hani went into the sanctuary for sacrifice. You, my Lady Vechlis, are different. Remember that morning? You came into the library with a servant girl. You said you were going swimming in one of the holy lakes. At the time I thought nothing of it. On reflection I began to wonder. Did you come to tell me your intention to bathe so that suspicion would not fall on you? I sent Shufoy to seek out your servant. He took her out of the temple to a house where she is now secure and safe. She remembered that morning well. You were going to bathe but then changed

253

your mind. Of course, as you planned, she was dismissed. You collected a bow, a quiver of arrows then tried to kill me in the vault.'

'If you bring the bitch back here,' Vechlis spat out, 'I'd jog her memory.' She lowered her voice. 'Is that, my lord judge, the only evidence you can produce?'

'No, no, it isn't.' Amerotke turned to Senenmut. He fought to hide his excitement. 'My lord, outside is a woman named Dalifa. I would like her brought in.'

Senenmut rapped out the order. Guards hurried out. Dalifa came in. She looked cowed and frightened as she stood just within the doorway. Amerotke had met her earlier that day and told her exactly what to do.

'Who is she?' Vechlis snapped.

'My conclusive proof. Look at her closely, Vechlis. What do you see?'

'A young woman, no more than a child.'

'Study her features carefully.'

Vechlis did. 'Am I supposed to recognise her?'

'Perhaps, or someone you once knew. May I introduce Neria's illegitimate daughter.'

'Impossible!' Vechlis retorted. 'He told me—' She stopped abruptly.

'He told you what?' Amerotke asked. 'Why should this librarian, known for his secrecy, his love of privacy, share secrets with the high priest's wife? You are Neria's beloved child, aren't you, Dalifa?'

The woman nodded.

'Kept in the shadows,' Amerotke continued, 'well out of view. Nevertheless, Neria used to visit her. He told her everything: about his relationship with you, my Lady Vechlis, and divine Father Prem. What else, Dalifa?'

'What he found in the library,' the young woman replied. 'How excited he was about the tattoo he had on his thigh. He showed it to me. He really did love you.' Dalifa raised her head.

Vechlis sat back in her chair. 'This is not true,' she whispered as if to herself. 'Neria would have told me. He told me everything! We'd known each other for years!'

'What have you to say, Lady Vechlis?' Senenmut asked. 'Grave charges have been levelled against you.'

'Shut up, stonemason!' Vechlis leaned forward, a smile on her face. 'I come from the finest blood of Egypt. I do not answer to stonemasons.'

'Then you'll answer to me.' Hatusu's voice was flat and cool.

Vechlis's smile widened. She looked Hatusu up and down contemptuously. 'If I don't speak to the stonemason,' she sneered, 'why should I speak to the stonemason's whore!' Vechlis sat back and enjoyed the cries of disapproval. 'Little Hatusu,' she mocked. 'I used to dangle you on my knee and wipe your bottom. A pretty little thing at your father's court. How dare you?' she hissed. 'How dare you even think of ascending the royal throne! To make us all nose the ground before you!'

'You'll die!' Hatusu declared.

'Oh, we all die, stonemason's whore!'

Hatusu fought to control her temper. Senenmut's hand went out but then he remembered himself.

Vechlis eased herself up and glanced along the row of priests. 'Look at you!' she snarled. 'I'm the finest man among you, a gaggle of old women! You no more support the stonemason and his whore than I do!'

'Pharaoh is of divine blood,' Amerotke broke in.

'Oh, spare me the speeches, judge!' Vechlis wetted her lips. 'It wasn't because . . . No, no.' She shook her head as if rehearsing her words. 'It wasn't because a woman sat on Pharaoh's throne. It was because it was Hatusu. Little Hatusu, playing with her toys, scampering around. She marries her half-brother and stays in the shadows with her doll-like face. But then the stonemason arrives and everything changes.'

'She is Pharoah,' Amerotke said.

'And what about her little half-brother?' Vechlis retorted.

'So, you confess,' Senenmut intervened, eager to end the tirade.

'I confess and I rejoice, stonemason. This gaggle of old women gathered here, I thought they would sit back and enjoy it all.'

'But you were ardent in divine Hatusu's support,' protested Amerotke.

'Oh, Amerotke.' Vechlis smiled condescendingly. 'That's your problem, judge. You don't wear a mask so you think everyone else doesn't. Yes, I loved Neria. Well, in my own way. I thought this gaggle of old women would discover nothing new until Neria began his chatter about paintings in the vault and what he'd found in the library. The stupid man had a scorpion tattooed on his thigh. He saw this as his great opportunity to catch the eye of the stonemason and his whore.'

Senenmut was about to object but Hatusu lifted her hand.

'Let her speak. Soon she'll speak no longer!'

'That's no threat,' Vechlis taunted. 'I prefer to go to the Far Horizon than grovel before you and your stonemason!'

'It is the manner of your going you might regret,' Hatusu replied.

Vechlis shrugged. 'What does it matter? The wine is spilt and the cup is broken. I was furious with Neria. I wanted to destroy him, destroy him completely! It happened so fast. I don't think he even saw my face. Pepy was no better. A real snake.' She moved her hand, gliding like a serpent. 'He saw me and Neria in the far gardens. He never confronted me but you know what he was like with his sly eyes and sneering lips. I left three purses of silver in his chamber. He left, as you say, Amerotke, to enjoy the fleshpots. I knew he'd be back. He'd found a new source of wealth. So I dressed in an old cloak. It was easy to buy oil. I placed some inside his chamber, more in a darkened recess. He was so drunk, so engrossed with that whore.'

'And divine Father Prem?' Amerotke asked.

'It's as you say. Neria had confessed to him. The old man lived in that garden tower with Sato hovering about him like a fly above ox dung. So I seized my moment. I placed rope ladders at the top of the tower. I intended to leave that way, not be seen anywhere near his chamber. Sato arrived a little earlier than I'd thought. It wasn't too dangerous.' Vechlis shrugged. 'What does it matter? I did as you say. But I always wondered afterwards whether Sato had noticed anything. He died and so did Hathor.'

'You killed and you killed again' Amerotke accused. 'You attacked me in the vault. You put our lives in danger on the barge crossing the Nile. Everybody on that barge would have died a horrific death and for what? Because you could not accept the divine Hatusu as Pharaoh?'

'Go to our libraries,' Vechlis taunted. 'You will find accounts of rebellion where thousands have died. If I was a man, if I was a soldier, I'd have risen in revolt.' Her hand shot out to point at Hatusu. 'How many has she killed to sit where she does?'

'I have heard enough!' Hatusu declared. She glanced quickly at Hani who was sitting, head down, shoulders shaking. 'This council meeting is at an end. The gods have proclaimed the truth and I am their mouthpiece!'

Senenmut rose and went to the door. He came back with a group of royal bodyguards.

'Take her!' Hatusu ordered. 'She is to be detained in the dungeons beneath the Temple of Ma'at. Before dusk she is to be taken out to the Red Lands and buried alive. Later,' Hatusu's eyes blazed with fury as she glared at Vechlis, 'her corpse is to be exhumed and displayed on the walls of Thebes.' She rose, kicking away the footstool.

Everyone, except Vechlis, prostrated themselves. When Amerotke glanced up, Hatusu had swept from the hall. Hani had crumpled into a heap, sobbing like a child, Vechlis's hands had already been bound by the soldiers who pushed

257

her roughly out of a side door. Amerotke got to his feet. He ignored the priests and went and thanked Dalifa.

'What was all this about?' the young woman asked. 'I just did what you told me.'

'It was necessary.' Amerotke took her hand and squeezed it. 'Sometimes, in the cause of truth, deception is needed and no more so than in this case. I had very little evidence, more suspicion, but no conclusive proof. If this had been the Hall of Two Truths, Lady Vechlis may not have been found guilty, I would have had to dismiss the case as not proven. However, I knew that who ever perpetrated these murders had a deep, abiding hatred at the thought of Hatusu wearing Pharaoh's crown. The evidence collected pointed to Vechlis: if she could be provoked by Hatusu's presence, she might rise to the bait.'

He smiled thinly. 'Hatred, like love, always manifests itself. Vechlis gambled and she lost. In losing, she gave vent to her own frustration and trapped herself. So, the truth was known and justice done.'

Coffin texts: Egyptian spells for the afterlife.

CHAPTER 16

Dalifa tried to remove her hand but Amerotke held it firm. Her eyes rounded in panic.

'What is it, my lord? When you visited me, you told me what to say. I have said it. I thank you, I also thank your servant: Antef died the death he deserved.'

Amerotke let go of her hand.

'Did you hear what I said?' he asked quietly. 'How it is necessary for the truth to be known?'

Grasping her by the hand, he led Dalifa across into a small side chamber and sat her down on a ledge. He pulled up a stool and sat opposite. The young woman was now trembling, gnawing at her lip. She could not meet Amerotke's gaze but looked beyond him, as if fascinated by a picture on the far wall of souls travelling through the underworld.

'I had a visitor,' Amerotke began. 'General Omendap. He came to thank me for something, although there was really no need. He'd also visited the Necropolis with some of his officers. Antef's corpse had been taken there.' Amerotke smiled thinly. 'Whatever people say about General Omendap, he's a stickler for the rules and regulations. Antef was a member of a regiment and he had been slain, albeit in self-defence, the least Omendap could do was arrange for monies to be paid from the House of Silver for Antef's embalming and funeral. The commander of the Anubis regiment also went

261

with him. Antef's corpse was already on the table and the embalmers were at work. A mortuary priest had been hired to sing a hymn. The regimental commander was making his own obsequies when he brought matters to an abrupt close.'

'What do you mean?' Dalifa's lovely eyes blinked.

'The commander made a startling statement: the corpse on the table was not Antef's.'

'But it must have been? Perhaps the wrong corpse was taken?' she stammered.

'Oh no. My servant was called and identified the man he had killed as the man who had appeared in my court. The commander explained how, years earlier, Antef had been in a boat attacked by a hippotamus. Antef was one of the few survivors. In his escape,' Amerotke drew a line across the top of his thigh, 'he suffered a terrible scar here. Whether this was inflicted by a crocodile or some other beast, the commander couldn't recall but he did remember the scar because he visited Antef in the field hospital. Now, tell me Dalifa,' Amertoke paused, 'well, you know what I am going to ask.'

She'd turned, pale-faced and shaking.

'Yes, yes.' She swallowed hard. 'My husband had such a scar.'

'But the corpse did not. The commander was truly perplexed. The dead man certainly looked like the Antef he knew: his height, build, features, but what had happened to that scar? He also pointed to other irregularities. Antef had received a knife wound in his upper arm. Again that scar couldn't be traced.'

Dalifa now bowed her head.

'You can imagine the surprise of my servant Shufoy? After all, he had been told by a river wanderer how Antef had deserted from the army and travelled the Nile till he arrived in Memphis where he settled down and married but, because of his dishonesty, Antef was chased from the city.' Amerotke paused. 'Now, the circumstances of Antef's desertion were known only to Shufoy. In the excitement of the last few days who'd care about a deserter, a coward who'd received his just deserts? Even I, not a soldier, should have realised something was wrong. The commander of the Anubis regiment certainly did: he explained how Antef was a member of a crack corps, the Nakhtu-aa. Antef had his faults, cowardice and thievery weren't two of them.' Amerotke narrowed his eyes. 'Can you help me with this mystery?'

Dalifa just stared back.

'General Omendap was also intrigued because he had learned how Antef had some connection with the Hall of the Underworld and the recent disappearance of two young noblemen. The labyrinth has now been taken to pieces, its pits probed. A ghastly experience: the corpses of men, women, even a few children, not to mention animals were discovered. Some dated back to the time of the Hyksos, others were more recent casualties. You do know the Hall of the Underworld?'

Dalifa nodded.

'You were married to Antef when his rapscallion brother took up the challenge to go through it. According to the accepted story, Antef's brother disappeared like so many others have. I don't think that happened and neither do you. What I suspect, is that Antef allowed his brother to escape. What was his name?'

'Kyembu.'

'Well, Kyembu had to disappear. Antef and you were only too glad to see the back of him. Kyembu went into hiding until the recent Mitanni war when all of Thebes was thrown into disarray. Antef and the rest of the army marched north and Kyembu reappeared. You and he met. You made a bargain. Kyembu joined the camp followers – that horde of pick-pockets, rogues, vagabonds, assassins and murderers, whores and hucksters which trail behind every army. He changed his appearance. Nobody would recognise him so no questions were asked—'

'But he was a coward!' Dalifa broke in.

'Yes, he was. Kyembu didn't want a fight but he had little choice, didn't he? The Mitanni attacked the Pharaoh's army camp. Kyembu and the rest of that horde of wanderers were drawn into the fray. Of course, when Divine Hatusu emerged victorious, they were the first to go hunting for rich pickings.'

'That must have been what happened,' Dalifa spoke up. 'Kyembu must have found his brother's corpse, stolen his personal insignia, shaved, washed and pretended to be his brother. They were identical in almost every aspect. Perhaps he inflicted more wounds on Antef's face. Then he travelled up and down the Nile before returning to Thebes with his hard luck story.'

'I would like to think that.' Amerotke replied. 'It's certainly logical and makes sense. This imposter returned to Thebes. He kept well away from Antef's regiment. Even so, if anyone did notice anything untoward, Kyembu could blame it on the campaigns, his wounds or long absence. But you were Antef's wife. He couldn't fool you, yet he did? The other intriguing aspect is your relationship with the young temple scribe. Your courtship was quick, you married—'

'But that was only when I thought Antef was dead.'

Amerotke paused, listening to the sounds from outside.

'I don't believe you,' he replied. 'Dalifa, you are lying. This is what happened. Antef marched off to war. His twin brother promptly re-appeared to find the lovely Dalifa all alone and very unhappy.'

'I was happy enough.'

'No you weren't! Antef was a rough soldier, quick with his fists. Kyembu was no better. One thing which does surprise me is that Kyembu should go anywhere near the army. I suspect you put your heads together and plotted Antef's death. Kyembu was promised payment. Perhaps he desired you and your wealth? So he followed the army only to find himself in the middle of a battle. I was there, Dalifa. The killing took place for miles around an oasis. Did Kyembu find his brother alone and murder him?' Amerotke paused. 'Or perhaps Kyembu insinuated himself into his brother's affection? Antef had protected him before, why not again? You can imagine the scene, Dalifa? Kyembu skulking behind his braver twin? Only Ma'at knows what really happened.

'It wasn't a coincidence that Kyembu found his brother, more the result of his own secret plotting. Amid all that violence, during the bloodshed and the killing, Kyembu either murdered his brother or finished him off. He removed Antef's personal insignia, damaged his face beyond recognition but left enough evidence to suggest Antef was killed. Then he disappeared.

'Now, Kyembu was a swaggerer, a charlatan. For a while he acted the brave soldier. He managed to entice a merchant's daughter and, without a thought for tomorrow, settled down to enjoy some of the spoils of his trickery.'

'Why didn't he return immediately to Thebes?'

'Oh, he would have done, sooner or later, to collect his reward, be it your silver or your charms. However, a rogue is a rogue. The leopard never changes its spots. Kyembu was a thief born and bred. His dishonesty discovered, he was expelled from Memphis, so he sat and plotted. He couldn't continue the masquerade of the brave, wounded soldier who lost his memory for ever. So, it was time to collect his reward or to indulge in a little blackmail.

'Kyembu returned to Thebes but the situation had changed. The lovely Dalifa is married and, more importantly, she is a woman of substance. Kyembu wanted you. He certainly wanted your wealth. The only way forward was to gamble. He continued to claim to be Antef but stayed well away from his old regiment, hoping that any any significant changes could be explained away.'

'I could say he fooled me.' Dalifa blurted out.

'But you are not going to, are you? No one really would accept that you were so easily duped. Kyembu probably approached you first. He could threaten your new husband, ask to be bought off but Paneb would ask questions, wouldn't he? His new wife giving away money? Kyembu, the gambler, decided to play for the highest stakes. He enjoyed a great deal of support: a veteran soldier with a record of bravery, wounded fighting for his Pharaoh, only to return home to find his pretty, young wife in the arms of another.'

'But you didn't believe him?'

'No I didn't. I don't know why. Something about the way both of you knelt in front of me in court. The proof was due to mere accident rather than logic or deduction.' Amerotke smiled. 'Well, in a way, Kyembu brought about his own downfall. He must have expected an easy victory. When I delayed, like the vicious bullly he was, Kyembu struck at me. He'd heard about Nehemu's threats and decided on revenge, till Shufoy intervened.'

'What are you going to do?' Dalifa whispered. 'I could be accused of murder.'

'Tell me your story,' Amerotke insisted. 'Speak the truth.'

'My mother died when I was young. I loved my father, he was a hard-working man.' Dalifa relaxed and, eyes half-closed, leaned back against the wall. 'My father spoiled me. One day I was with the other young women in the market before the Temple of Amun-Ra. I met Antef the swaggering, brave, young soldier. You know the way of youth? I fell deeply in love. My father objected but I insisted that we marry.'

'Did you know about Antef's twin brother?'

Dalifa laughed sourly. 'Shall I tell you how I met Kyembu? During the early days of my marriage I would notice Antef was different, particularly in matters of the bed.' The tears started in her eyes. 'I then discovered his cruel trick. Antef had a twin brother. They both looked so alike, only time taught you how to tell them apart. They thought it was so amusing. They had played the same game on other women.'

Dalifa wiped away the tears. 'For weeks afterwards I felt sick, a deep revulsion. I dare not tell my father. I think that's why my womb closed. I never conceived a child.'

'Did you refuse?' Amerotke asked.

'How could I? It took time to tell one from the other. They made a mockery of me. However, time passed and I noticed more telling differences. Antef was a bully. He drank a lot, was free with his fists but he had some sense of honour. Kyembu,' the word came out in a snarl, 'he was lower than a dog's turd – a gambler, vicious and mean. Antef himself became troubled. Kyembu was always gambling. One night he accepted a wager and lost. He had to pay the price, to go through the Hall of the Underworld. Once he was in our house, he dropped the mask. He became a gibbering coward. Antef said he would act as his guarantor, after all, he was an officer in the Nakhtu-aa. Antef gave him a three-fold offer. Kyembu could take his chances in the Hall of the Underworld, Antef could kill him quite quickly and quietly, or he would arrange for Kyembu to escape, on the condition that he never came near us or Thebes again.'

'And Kyembu accepted the latter?'

'Yes he did, though he was furious with Antef. He accused his twin brother of trapping him, of wanting him away from Thebes. Antef just scoffed. He took Kyembu out into the Red Lands, gave him a little money, some food and came back to Thebes saying our troubles were over. In fact, by then, our marriage was finished but what could I do? Antef was sometimes away on duty. To be truthful, that's how I met Paneb.' She stretched out her hand. 'But our relationship was honourable. Sometimes I suspected Kyembu had slipped back into Thebes in disguise and was spying on us. Then, last year, the Mitanni launched their surprise attack across Sinai and Antef rejoined his regiment. I kissed him tearfully, wished him goodbye and quietly prayed he would never come back.'

'But Kyembu did?'

'Antef was barely gone before Kyembu made an appearance. He was in an ugly mood. He accused me and his brother of trying to get him out of the way. He tried to rape me. I had to do something. Kyembu was swearing murder, demanding vengeance. He was living with villains and rogues outside the city. He said he would join the camp followers and kill his brother. I was terrified. I promised him anything, just to get rid of him. I wanted him away. To be honest, I prayed that both of them would die.' She plucked at the hem of her robe. 'The news came back to Thebes. In the months since Antef left, despite my father's death, I knew real happiness. Now it would last: Antef had been killed. I didn't really care if it was Kyembu or the Mitanni who did it.'

'But you knew that Kyembu must have been alive?'

'I didn't really care. Antef was a soldier. Kyembu was just a rat, scurrying in the corners. I was now a wealthy widow, deeply in love with Paneb and he with me. I took my case to the priests in the Temple of Osiris. They decreed that I was a widow, free to marry Paneb. I did so. Are you married, Lord Amerotke?'

'Yes and happily so.'

'So am I. For the first time in my life I was free of Antef and his hideous brother had disappeared. However,' she sighed, 'one day I was down in the market near the Nile. Kyembu stepped out of the shadows. I thought I was seeing a ghost.' She blinked. 'Had Antef come from the Far Horizon to haunt me? Kyembu was dressed the same, walked the same as his brother.' She laughed sharply. 'Of course, he'd had months to practise, hadn't he? He wanted to live with me. I replied I'd rather die. Then he found out about the wealth. I tried to satisfy him with a little but he wanted it all. He threatened to expose me.'

'But he couldn't do that?'

'No, he couldn't. He might portray me as a murderer but he would have been guilty as well.' She shrugged her pretty shoulders. 'What could I do? Would Paneb believe me? If I told the truth in court I could be accused of murder. I had to just pray and hope all would be well.'

'What did Kyembu really want?' Amerotke asked. 'All your wealth?'

'I think so. I certainly made matters worse. When he first accosted me I lost my temper. I mocked him as a coward, terrified of his brother's shadow. I told him I could always tell the difference in bed.'

Amerotke held a hand up.

'Kyembu wanted you, your wealth and revenge?'

Dalifa nodded.

'If you had ruled that I was Paneb's wife, Kyembu, pretending to be Antef, could have appealed.'

'And if I ruled that you were the so-called Antef's wife?'

'Then you would have condemned me to death,' she retorted. 'Kyembu would have enjoyed me, he would have beaten me and he would have dissipated my wealth. One day I would have suffered an accident, perhaps a fall, or been attacked by brigands.' She rubbed her face in her hands. 'I prayed and prayed then it happened. Kyembu was slain in self-defence by your servant. I thought it was the end of the matter.' She glanced directly at Amerotke. 'So, what will happen to me now?'

Amerotke stared back. Dalifa was comely, pretty-faced but was she an actress? Had she and Kyembu plotted Antef's murder and then Kyembu came wandering back to claim his reward? But, what proof did he have? And, even if she was guilty, hadn't those two men abused, degraded and mocked her? Amerotke stared round the chamber.

'Make an offering,' he replied. 'To the Goddess of Truth.' He got to his feet. 'I will be honest. You may have been party to murder. You may only share some of the guilt or you may be totally innocent.' He touched the pectoral round his neck. 'Only the Goddess knows that. I think you have suffered and the gods themselves put a limit on human pain. As far as I am concerned, Antef and Kyembu are dead. They must answer to the Truth for their sins.' He smiled. 'You are Paneb's wife. May you have long life, health and happiness.'

He walked to the door.

'My Lord Amerotke?'

He turned.

'You have done great justice.'

Amerotke just shrugged and left.

On the evening of the following day, Amerotke, garbed in his insignia of office, sat in the condemned cell beneath the Temple of Ma'at. On the opposite side of the table Vechlis cradled a cup. She swirled its contents round, smiling to herself. Torches fixed on the walls sent the shadows of the jackal-masked guards and executioners dancing, making the cell look like some ante-chamber of the underworld.

'I suppose I have to thank you for this.' Vechlis raised her head. 'It was good of you, Amerotke. It's more than I deserve. I am not sorry for the rest.' Her eyes glittered with hatred. 'Neria betrayed me. He was the cause of it all. Ready to prostitute himself for the royal whore. I loved him, you know? Perhaps that was the canker in the rose. It was bad enough to see all of Thebes nose the ground before Hatusu but Neria, the scholar, the man I loved!'

'But it wasn't only that, was it?'

Vechlis shook her head. 'When Hatusu swept to the throne, my husband Hani was one of the few high priests to support her. I had no choice but to follow. Secretly, however, I corresponded with those who opposed her, led by the old Vizier Rahimere.' She put the cup down. 'But the royal bitch won so I joined in the hymns of praise. Then she was stupid enough to ask for the advice of the priests. That's Hatusu's great weakness, isn't it? She wants to be loved and adored by everyone. I thought the council meeting would prove nothing. The months would pass and I would do my best to fan the flames of gossip. How the divine Hatusu might be this or might be that, but she did not have the full support of the priests of Thebes. Neria spoilt it all! Happy as a boy with a new toy, he was. I clapped my hands and pretended to agree. Oh, he was full of it.'

'Did Hani suspect?' Amerotke asked.

'We stopped being husband and wife years ago,' Vechlis replied. 'He had his, how can I put it, little compensations? My girlhood friendship with Neria flourished. Well,' she pulled a face, 'the past always catches up, doesn't it, my Lord Amerotke? The days of childhood stretch out over the years and drag you back.' She smiled. 'I thought I was safe, especially when Neria died. You know about the water clock?'

'Ah yes,' Amerotke nodded. 'You interfered with it, removed some of the water so it looked as if you were with Hani around the ninth hour when Neria died. You were so certain about where you were, at a specific hour on a certain day. Few people are ever so sure.'

'Ah well.' Vechlis looked round the cell.

'I'm sorry about the attack on you but it was necessary. Let us forget that. Do you remember, Amerotke, when you were a young boy in the palace? I used to come and take you for walks in the garden. I'd show you the different birds and plants, then you'd watch me swim.' She looked at him, head slightly back, eyelids half-closed. 'You are the son I always wanted.' She sighed and picked up the cup. 'Now it comes to this. A cup of poisoned wine but it's better than being buried out in the hot sands, to have your life slowly choked out of you, to have your corpse plucked by the kites and scavengers while the mob looks on.'

Amerotke blinked away his tears. 'Hani is dead,' he murmured.

'I know, I know.' Vechlis stared into the cup. 'He went to bathe in the Pool of Purification. Gossip is that he had a stroke, a failure of the heart. I know different. Hani wanted to wade in the sacred water to purify himself both inside and out. He drowned himself. The priests will look after his corpse.' She leaned across the table. 'And you will have the prayers said for me, Amerotke? You will ensure my body is embalmed, taken across to the City of the Dead?'

Amerotke agreed.

'What did you have to do to soften the royal whore's heart?'

'The divine Hatusu asked what reward I would like.'

'Ah, I see.' Vechlis raised the cup. 'To life, to death!'

'Drink it fast!' Amerotke urged.

'Of course.' She smiled.

Tilting her head back, Vechlis took the poisoned wine in one gulp. She rose, walked to the simple reed bed in the far corner and lay down, pulling her arms across her chest. Amerotke closed his eyes. He heard a moan, her body twitched, and, when he looked, she lay still, head to one side, mouth and eyes open.

Amerotke said the prayer but he was distracted. He was a young boy again, walking hand in hand with a tall, elegant woman through the gardens of Pharaoh.

AUTHOR'S NOTE

This novel reflects the political scene of 1479–78 BC after
Hatusu swept to power. Her husband died in mysterious
circumstances and she only emerged as ruler after a bitter power struggle. In this she was assisted by the wily
Senenmut who had come from nothing to share power with
her. His tomb is still extant, now known as Number 353,
and it even contains a sketch portrait of Hatusu's favourite
minister. There is no doubt that Hatusu and Senenmut were
lovers. Indeed, we have ancient graffiti which describes, in a
very graphic way, their intimate personal relationship.

Hatusu was a strong ruler. She is often depicted in wall
paintings as a warrior and we know from inscriptions that
she led troops into battle.

Ancient Egyptian history produced a number of resolute
and astute female rulers, Nefertiti and Cleopatra to name
but two. Hatusu can be reckoned as the first. Her reign was
long and glorious but, on her death, her successor, with the
connivance of the priests, had both her name and cartouche
obliterated from many of the religious monuments of Egypt.
The power of the priestly caste, particularly in Thebes, was a
potent force. Hatusu must have faced opposition and yet, in
the end, won them over. Decades later one of her successors,
Akhenaton, attempted a religious revolution. When he failed
to win the support of the priests, he built a new city and

moved his entire court and administration to it. The priests of Thebes never forgot this; they played a crucial role in Akhenaton's downfall and the eradication of his religious revolution.

In most matters I have tried to be faithful to this exciting, brilliant and intriguing civilisation. The fascination of ancient Egypt is understandable; it is exotic and mysterious. This civilisation existed over three and a half thousand years ago, yet there are times, as you read their letters and poems, when you feel a deep kinship with them as they speak to you across the centuries.

Paul Doherty